T0246720

The

KINGDOM
LAND

Bart Tuma

2nd Edition

Double Edge Press

Scenery Hill, Pennsylvania

Double Edge Press

ISBN: 9781938002137

The Kingdom Land – 2ⁿᵈ Edition
Copyright © 2011 Bart Tuma

Cover Artwork: Original artwork design by Double Edge
Press/Rebecca Melvin. Elements contained within the original
design include the following images in its composition:

Glacier Farmland – photograph by Bart Tuma. Used with
permission.

Cornfield with Rainbow – photograph by Martha Dough-
erty, website http://marthadouheritage.weebly.com. Used
with permission.

Acknowledgments

Novels aren't created by a pen on paper, but by capturing the sparks of life.

My life would not be complete without the love and support of my beautiful wife Cindy, the joy of my three children Courtney, Shannon and Erik, and the realization that the Lord holds us in the palm of His grace.

I would also like to give special thanks to Double Edge Press for opening a window so others could see this work. And to my mother, my prayer is that her life be full today and forever.

The

KINGDOM
LAND

Bart Tuma

2nd Edition

v

Chapter One

The last trace of black diesel hadn't cleared the stack before Erik jumped from the John Deere tractor landing deep into the lifeless dirt. His day was done. His only concern was if the old pickup he'd brought to the fields that morning would start this afternoon. Each stride become faster and longer the further he was from the tractor and the closer he was to the pickup that had suddenly become his best friend. "Chevy, you're a piece of junk, but you better start 'cause I'm outta here." His stride didn't slow as he struggled to pull off his shirt, flapping it in the wind in an useless attempt to leave the dust of the day behind.

The strides stopped at the driver's door of the '54 Chevy pickup. Years earlier he'd bought the old junk pickup to fix it up and show it off, but it was never fixed and remained the same. In Erik's eyes nothing on the farm would ever change.

Just to open the Chevy's door he had to lift it and pull at the same time. Reaching inside he grabbed a second water jug he'd forgotten that morning. The water was soured by the prairie heat, but it worked well to sooth his parched lips and rid himself of the taste of the day. When he spit the water to the ground the dust swallowed it without leaving a trace.

The jug was thrown back into the cab hard enough to bounce it off the opposite door. He slowly slid into the pickup to avoid burning himself on the hot vinyl seat. He even let a smile crossed his face as the key coaxed the motor to the rattle of life. That sounds of grinding gears and running motor meant freedom, at least for a time.

The road back to the farm house snaked through the fields that should be filled with the green of growth, but now were only dust and wheat so shriveled it didn't even look like grain. Erik didn't care. It was his day off. It wasn't his farm. His uncle owned the farm and lived and died with the wheat. His uncle saw these fields as his life. Erik didn't.

It was August, the hottest month in the northern Montana plains, and the year was 1976, the third year in a row with no clouds breaking free from the Rockies to bring rain to the plains.

The dirt road turned to gravel and finally ended in front of the farmhouse. Erik didn't even bother to let the pickup stop before throwing open the door, but let it lurch a few feet further as the gear bound motor died. He only hit every other step going up the back door stairs which lead to a hallway with a double sink .The smell of roast beef filled the room, and he vaguely heard his Aunt's greeting. He was too hungry to care what Aunt Mary had to say. What she said wasn't important and she'd say it again anyway.

"Erik, hurry up and get washed. Dinner's going to get cold

if you don't hustle," Aunt Mary again said, this time loud enough for Erik to hear. "Your uncle hasn't got back from town. He's still having problems getting the baler working. They better give him the right part this time. He's already made two trips 'cause the kid at the parts counter was too lazy to check the manual. I haven't seen your uncle that frustrated in ages."

Erik was still in the entry buttoning up his shirt he had just donned again after stripping it off in the field. The entryway sink was as polished and organized as any hospital room. His hard strokes loosened the dirt with the pumice soap, but it also cut the flesh from his hand. The dirty suds partly covered his arms but mostly splattered the suds to remain on the floor and counter top. Erik made no effort to clean it up. *Maybe someday she'll get the hint and leave this sink alone. Not everything needs to be perfect. If she wants me to scrub up before eating, she should know the sink's going to get dirty in the process.*

Cleaning himself was an exaggeration. The process Erik undertook was shifting the dirt to where people couldn't see it. He rolled down his long sleeves to hide any spots he might have missed, and left the remaining dirt on a white hand towel that Mary would immediately clean after dinner. He would get to the serious washing later on.

"Anything worth eating tonight, Aunt Mary?" Erik saw his aunt cock her head wondering if Erik was serious or joking.

"What are you talking about? We're having roast beef, and

you'd better just eat it without any comments,"

His aunt wasn't eating, but she joined Erik as he pulled the platters of food closer. She bowed her head to pray. Erik knew what she was doing but kept filling his plate. He wasn't part of that God stuff and he wanted to eat and get out of there. He loved his aunt, and it was nice to have some company, but he knew that her company would also bring her questions so he started eating when he had the chance.

"Pass the potatoes?" Erik asked even before Mary raised her head.

"You could say 'please'," Mary said as she passed the large bowl. Erik had heard her corrections for years, but heeded few. "I see you got all the strips west of the house done."

"Yeah, it doesn't take much when there aren't weeds to kill anyway. I'm mostly just turning dust. It seems like a waste of good diesel to me. I should be done by next week sometime. Before I forget, I had a visitor today." Erik added with his mouth half full of chewy beef.

"A visitor?" Why would you have a visitor?" Mary's surprise echoed his own earlier in the day.

"It was that McCormack guy, the county agent. I was surprised a county employee would work on Saturday, but there he was in that bright yellow Glacier County truck. He came by just after noon. I don't know why you pay taxes to hire someone like him. He's an idiot." Erik's focus remained on his food.

"Why did he go to the fields rather than coming to the

house?"

"I don't know why he does anything except collect a pay-check. He said he was looking for Henry," Erik sneered as he balanced a fork full of peas and corn. "But I think he was lying, or he would have looked for him here at the shop. I imagine he's afraid to come to the house after all his lies. He's been telling people for three years that it's going to rain and it never does. The thing that amazes me is that people still--"

Mary interrupted Erik before he could finish. He was used to it.

"He gets his reports from the weather man, so blame the weather man if you need to blame someone. He's just doing his job."

She always talked. You's think she could listen to him once in a while. "Aunt Mary, anyone who believes that guy or the weather man is crazy. Just look at the fields. They're pathetic. It's August and the grain doesn't even come up to my knees. It's not even going to be worth pulling a combine into the fields. The diesel will cost more than what Uncle Henry will get for the crop. It's even useless for me to run the tractor. The weeds aren't even growing. All I'm doing is raising more dust.'' Erik's voice grew harsher the longer he talked.

"Erik, you know it's not useless. We've got to keep the ground loose so when the rains come, the ground can take it in. We're been through droughts before. They come and go. We just have to wait them out, and have faith that next year will be better. When the rains come no one will remember the drought."

"*When* the rains come. That's a big 'when'. I'd bet against it if I were a gambler. Sure the rain will come back some day, but how many farmers will go broke before that?"

"Just be quiet. It's hard enough without talk like that. You sound like an old man that doesn't have anything better to do than complain. What did the agent say anyway?"

"I didn't pay much attention. If he wanted to do something worthwhile he should have brought something cold to drink. All he did was babble. He said something about the county has been declared a disaster area, as if that wasn't obvious enough. I'm supposed to tell Uncle Henry that the state will help him out until next year. He says he knows it's going to rain next year. I say he's crazy. All that's going to happen is the two of you are going to go further in debt; the government never gives out anything for free. You'll go further in debt and all you'll get for it is being disappointed again."

"I said to be quiet about what you don't know," Mary again interrupted. "Your Uncle knows when it's best to run the plow and when to harvest. Not you." Mary's glare made it obvious to Erik that he had crossed the line. "You aren't helping with your comments. All you're doing is bringing your bitterness to the kitchen table. Leave it at the door with your work boots and gloves. And I better not hear you talk that way to your uncle. You know how important this farm is to him. He's put his whole life into the farm, and if you want this farm you better do the same."

"Thanks, but no thanks," Erik said. "I'm more than happy to help you out for a time because of everything, but never confuse that with me wanting to be a farmer. I'm not the farmer type. You know I could never be a farmer. Either that or you haven't been listening. Just like Uncle Henry keeps telling me: *a farmer, to be a farmer, has to be part of the land. He has to work the soil until the soil gives back the harvest, no matter how long that takes.* I just can't do that.

"Uncle Henry is like that, I'm not. He's so much a part of the farm it's almost scary. When the crops fail, like now, he looks like a broken man. You can see it in the way he walks. His shoulders droop lower just like the wheat. That's not me. I don't want t be that close to anything--let alone dirt.

"You know the saying: *Farmers are the only people who don't have to fear death. They live for the touch of the soil all their lives, but thcy can only enter it once they die.* That's too depressing for me. Way too depressing."

"Erik, you're bound and determined to start a fight tonight, but don't think you'll get a reaction out of me. It's Saturday; can't we talk about anything else? At least your Uncle isn't here. He's a proud man, and you could learn something from him. He's committed to God and he's committed to making this farm something to be proud of. I'm proud of him and I'm proud of this farm. If you can't understand that, keep your comments to yourself. I don't want to hear any more." Mary went to Frigidaire to get a plate of butter that Erik didn't need. Erik watched her hesitate in front of the open fridge and take a deep breath. Mary rarely got that that upset. *The drought has got to her, too.*

Erik was always amazed that Mary could keep her house and herself so perfectly finished when everything outside the farmhouse was dust and brown and dying. For as long as Erik could remember, Mary always had, and still did, carry her small frame with dignity and composure. She put her long, thick dark hair in a bun. She said she did it for convenience, but Erik always thought that it gave her the appearance of royalty. As a young boy Erik loved to sit on a stool and watch her get ready to meet the day. She would pull her hair together with a firm grasp, twist it into the bun and fasten it with one bobby pin. She would never know how much he respected her for being such a rock in this dismal land.

When she returned, her voice had regained her usual soft tone, "What are you going to do tonight? You haven't got together with the Hanson boy in a long time. Why don't you see what he's doing tonight?" Mary asked with a plea in her voice.

Erik knew what his answer would be before Mary even finished. Aaron Hanson was a nice kid, but just too starchy for Erik. For years he knew Aunt Mary's hope was that Aaron's Christianity would change Erik, but the more she suggested the harder he said no. Aaron had never said anything wrong, but

Erik knew exactly where he was coming from and Erik wasn't there.

"As you say, I don't want to hear any more of that talk. Aaron Hanson is boring and we have nothing in common," Erik replied.

"He's boring! And you're the one to talk--Mr. Sociable himself. Why don't you go out with someone else then, anyone, so you don't have to spend another night alone in that bunkhouse? You haven't had a date in ages. It isn't good for you to be alone so much." His aunt's voice was both tired and frustrated.

"Don't worry about me," Erik advised. "I'll take care of myself. I always have. Why don't you get some ketchup so I can put it on this pot roast?" he said the last with every intention of garnering a reaction and changing the subject.

"That's not pot roast. It's the best roast beef in the county and if you want to put ketchup on roast beef and drown out the taste, you get your own ketchup. That roast was in the oven for three hours and I had to work next to that hot oven all day. You feel sorry for yourself working on the tractor, but working next to a hot oven so you can have a nice Saturday meal isn't much better. Your uncle is late because he still isn't done, and all you can do is complain. I don't know why I even try. You get your own ketchup!" Mary slammed her cup on the table and left the room.

It had been years since Erik's aunt had lost her temper with him. *The drought's getting to her, too,* he thought.

Erik turned back to his plate. He'd gotten the quiet he wanted, but not in the way he had wanted.

He finished the meal alone. Erik was good at being alone. He actually felt most comfortable alone, and as Mary walked away it reminded him that he had been left alone before. He lived with his aunt and uncle for a reason. Erik's mother had left the family when he was three and his dad died when he was eleven.

Chapter Two

Erik walked to the refrigerator, grabbed a cold pop and left the kitchen without saying goodbye to his aunt. He walked straight to the bunkhouse with the last piece of bread and the pop, dragging his feet on the dirt path. Although there was an extra bedroom in the main house Erik lived in the old bunkhouse. It was his choice as it was his choice to use the entryway sink. The bunkhouse was close to the tool sheds and grain silos, but far from the farmhouse. It was where he wanted to live. In the bunkhouse there was no one to bother him and he could escape that farm in his dreams. Being alone in the bunkhouse was different from being alone in the farmhouse kitchen. The solitude in the bunkhouse was something he created.

The bunkhouse hadn't been painted or repaired in decades. It was a place no one would want to live, but it was Erik's refuge. He had the bunkhouse all to himself. The bunkhouse was the ideal place for him to dream. This was *his* place whereas everywhere else was *their* place.

Erik went straight to a small room to the left that was separate from the main dorm. It had both a bed and a tin shower stall. It took his eyes a second to get used to the dimness of the windowless room as he stripped and visited the cold-water shower. He gasped as the cold well water hit his chest, but the water had the desired effect. He finally felt different and alive. He finally could forget the farm.

Reaching into the second drawer of a four-drawer dresser, he retrieved a dress shirt that was seldom worn. A chipped runner made the drawer difficult to open, but he had never bothered to fix it. The starched shirt felt awkward, but his donning it signaled a special occasion he so desperately needed.

He plopped himself down hard on the bed. "This is better." He could feel the slope of the bed which was propped up by bricks in one of it's corners to solve a broken leg. It was still better than anything else he had felt that week.

Erik had time to kill before his trip. All week he had dreamed exactly how this evening would go, so it was time to take a nap. He felt himself drifting off while he rehashed the dinner conversation with his aunt. That conversation hadn't been the start to his evening in any of his dreams. He knew his aunt was wrong. *I wasn't trying to start a fight. She needs to listen to me sometimes, and the conversation wouldn't have happened if that stupid county agent had went to the house like he should have. Besides, she doesn't have the right in getting mad at me and trying to tell me what to do with my life. She's a great lady, but she has her own problems.*

When he was completely asleep, an all too common nightmare returned. His dreams took him to another kitchen and a time years earlier. His dad was still alive and Erik was nine. That kitchen was in the old house where he used to live with his dad. His dad had just returned to the table from a phone call that had interrupted dinner. His picked up his fork to eat, but slammed it down hard holding his head rather than his fork. He glared at Erik. It wasn't a mean glare, but a glare of disbelief. Erik didn't know if it he was in trouble, but someone seemed to be. When his dad left the table, Erik instinctively followed. They got into the old pickup and Erik didn't even have to asked where they were going. He just knew

They pulled in front of his Aunt and Uncle's house. His dad got out of the truck and went into the house as if Erik wasn't even there. His dad always walked ahead, but this time his steps looked as if they were in quicksand and darkness covered the cement steps.There were men in the house that Erik didn't know, but they were obviously policemen, maybe even State cops. Erik was told to sit at the kitchen table while the adults went into the dining room; his dad, the police, Aunt Mary and Uncle Henry. Erik could hear their voices, but not their words.

Finally Erik was called into the dining room with its linen covered table. Erik never sat there, when he and his dad shared a meal with his aunt and uncle, they ate in the kitchen, but he sat in the dining room that evening. Aunt Mary tried to look calm with a gentle smile on her face that Erik didn't believe.

"Erik, I have something to read to you. It's a letter your mom wrote when she had to leave. We, your dad, wanted to wait until you were old enough to understand before we read the letter to you. Now we think it is time for you to hear it. These two gentlemen," and she smiled brightly at the police, "just spoke with your mom and she is doing fine, so it's probably time for you to know why she hasn't been here."

Erik still didn't know why policemen would be reporting on someone if there weren't a problem, but their eyes never left Erik, as if he was the one they were looking for.

"Erik, like we told you in the past, your mom got sick and had to go away to get better. She'd be fine, but she had to go, and she wrote this letter. We, uh, we didn't share it with you before 'cause we thought she'd get better right quick and be back in no time... But, well, now seems like we better share her letter with you."

Aunt Mary adjusted her reading glasses without looking at him. Her voice shook and cracked as she began to read from the paper she held in front of her.

"*Erik,*

I love you very much, but I have been sick and I need to go away. I will come back when I am feeling better, no matter how long that takes. I know every day apart from you will hurt me, but I want you to know I will think of you every minute.

I love you, and it's best for both of us that I get well.

I love you, and you are always in my thoughts,

Your mom,

Maggie."

Aunt Mary lowered the paper. Her face and neck was flushed scarlet. She forced herself, nearly defiantly, to meet Erik's eyes, and Erik knew she had just told the biggest whopping lie of her life. There was a soft exhalation of relief from the men in the room. For his aunt's sake, for his dad and uncle's sake, and even for the two strange policemen's sake, he swallowed once, twice, and then nodded.

He wasn't sure if they had just protected him from something, or made it worse.

The dream shifted, morphed, melded into a time ten years later. Erik was in the Cooper's house alone and found himself in front of his Aunt's open jewelry box. He opened the bottom hand carved drawer and found a poorly fashioned fake bottom holding an old note yellowed with age He had found a secret and suddenly became thrilled at his find, until he read the words. It was very short, but instinctively Erik knew *this* was the note from his mother.

I'll leave this so you don't call the cops. I've had enough. I'm leaving the state. Don't try to find me. I won't come back no matter what you say. I can't stand Fairfield and this farm is even worse. I tried. I'm done trying.

The note wasn't signed, but Aunt Mary had noted in the

margin: *December 12, 1957, Maggie.*

Erik wondered why Mary would want to memorialize that day. It would make more sense to burn the note; not burn the date into everyone's mind. Then Erik remembered it was his aunt's insane need to keep everything in place and filed away. At that moment he hated his aunt. It was all her fault. He wanted to go mess up his hallway sink.

Erik quickly noticed he wasn't mentioned in the note. There was no way he could confront Mary since he was the intruder. He simply had to wait and wonder and come to his own conclusions

He found the truth from complete strangers. He was sixteen. Erik was waiting at the Fairfield Five and Dime for his aunt to give him a ride home after football practice. The store had a fountain counter and on this day there were two ladies sitting two stools to his right.

It was obvious they knew Erik. They kept looking at him as if they had discovered someone on a wanted poster. At first they spoke in low whispers, but as their excitement grew so did their voices. This was prime gossip, and the fact Erik was there only added to the thrill. One lady kept staring at Erik while the other spun the story with increasing gusto. At first Erik couldn't hear her exact words, but that quickly changed.

The fervor of her voice grew until Erik's ears throbbed with the sting of her words. *That poor boy. I don't know how he can even go on! How can he handle it?* Her voice feigned sympathy, but her eagerness to share her gossip couldn't be disguised. Erik's ears began to burn. He turned his head away, trying to block the words from his mind, but it seemed as if the harder he tried to not hear, the sharper his hearing became.

His mom abandoned that boy and his dad. She had moved to Fairfield because her dad got a job transfer from Denver with the railroad. She hated Fairfield and everything about it. It wasn't long before she started to get into trouble and everyone knew... well, they knew she really wasn't a lady, but a real fluzie. She was doing whatever she needed to do to get a husband and get out of Fairfield, and she did it with every young boy in town. Finally she found a naïve farm boy who spent so much time on the farm he hadn't heard about the other guys. She got her hands on Jimmie Cooper, that boy's father, and wouldn't let go. The word is she told Jimmie she was pregnant, but she wasn't because she didn't have that boy for a time. She married Jimmie because he was strong and funny and she thought he would take her away from Fairfield.

Little did she realize the place he was taking her to was a farmhouse twenty-two miles north, even more in the middle of nowhere! She could look out the kitchen window and see the hills of Canada, it was so close to the border, but there was little else to see. It was two miles from the closest neighbor, and the neighbors, the Jorgensen, were strange enough to laugh at, but no respectable person would associate with them. Three years later after that she left them without a word or even a note.

Erik fought the urge to jump up and yell at this busy-body with nothing better to do. She was wrong. His Mom wasn't like that and his dad was no dummy. There was a note to prove it. But his voice didn't work and his body was frozen no matter how hard he tried to move. He had to move. He had to scream at those ladies and call them fools. But the harder he tried the more his limbs froze to his side, His only refuge was to turn his head away from the ladies so he wouldn't see their faces. But the face he saw was his Aunt's. She had come to pick him up and she had a grin on her face. The two ladies saw her too and quickly left. Erik became sick.

He awoke in a paralysis, his mouth an open grimace of mute screaming. He saw the walls of the bunkhouse. His nicely starched dress shirt was now soaked in sweat and his arms hurt with exhaustion. He cursed himself for allowing himself to nap since the nightmare was sure to follow. He got out of bed and put only his head in the shower, drenching the dream away. He used the still wet bath towel he had just used to wipe himself down again. Then he left the bunkhouse and walked until he had calmed himself down again. The nightmare was so common it didn't have the depth of horror it once had. He returned to the bunkhouse and the bed.

Erik forced himself to dream. Dreams were the only thing that made him feel real and wanted and they took away the pictures of the nightmare. He dreamt of a woman, different in every way than the bleak land of his life. He dreamt of Laura.Laura was the name of the girl he was going to see that evening. Laura was not just another dream, but a person with features he could see and smells he could remember, and although he hadn't admitted it to his aunt, he had planned all week to visit her after his work was done.

Erik thought of the few times he had seen Laura, a waitress at the Mint Bar in Sweet Grass and Sweet Grass would be his destination that evening. He didn't particularly like Sweet Grass. It was a border town with the Customs stop its only reason for existence. It was only eleven miles east of the Cooper's farm, but in a direction Erik seldom took. In Sweet Grass, Erik was still a stranger.

The town was so small Erik didn't know why they gave it a name except to find it on a map. There was nothing in the town that would remind anyone of sweet grass. It had a few houses for those who worked for the Customs Service and a rodeo grounds used once a year. There were three grain elevators, a Farmer's Union Co-op to get some gas, a church that straddled the US-Canadian border, and the Mint Bar. It wasn't a place you would go for excitement, but rather than Fairfield, Erik would go there to see Laura. He would go there that evening.

Erik remembered seeing her for the first time. He wanted to get away from the farm, but he didn't want to face another night by himself in Fairfield. He went east instead and found himself in the Mint and there she was. She was beautiful, like someone who would be in a big city. She carried herself like someone who hadn't been worn down by farm life, and her clothes, although simple, were different than Fairfield's clothes. Later, alone in the bunkhouse, he reasoned this was more than a chance meeting. It was meant to be. He had found out she worked every Saturday night and he had designed trips whenever he could manage just to be close to her.

Laura was different from the girls in Fairfield. Even the way she walked spoke of grace and class. The girls in Fairfield were the ones you settled for and married and had kids with. They were not girls you dreamt about.

Laura was tall with long dark brown hair that curled at the ends. Erik liked her a lot. He spent hours on the tractor and bunkhouse bed having conversations with Laura as if she were really there. Those conversations heightened his fondness for her. It was fondness that kept her in his thoughts on the tractor and him quiet in her presence. He almost feared her the more he thought of her. The fear was a combination of the fear of rejection and the fear that she might destroy his image of her. It was a chance he didn't want to take. He needed her in his dreams.

Erik finished his pop and threw it on the concrete floor to join the collection of other empty bottles. *It's time to get on with Saturday,* but as he looked at his watch, it was still too early; he would draw too much attention in the bar. The sound of the tractor still rang in his ears and he needed the fresh air to rid himself of the remnants of the nightmare. He went out to is favorite spot.

It was 9:00 p.m. but the sun had not yet set in this northern open prairie land. Behind the house and the buildings and the last barn on the farm, there was a slight bluff that gave way to a large coulee. The coulee stayed green longer than any place else on the farm. Its grass had never been broken by a plow and its ravine held the spring runoff in reserves. Next to the bluff, an oak tree had grown somehow, very much out of place. Erik sat at the base of the tree and watched the picture unfolding before him.

The heat had begun to give way to the cool of the evening, and twilight was advancing. The sunset started with a slight tint of pink and grew as a spill until it totally engulfed the whole land with scarlet. A stray cloud caught fire on its border, and then burst into flames. The alkali reservoir to the farm's east that before was stale and dead suddenly became a pool of gold, and the foxtail beside it, torches of tar. The willow bushes near the coulee seemed to be touched by a spell to become a king's silver arrows.

For those few minutes the land was silent and even the grasshoppers settled into its spell. Erik no longer saw the dryness of the land, but a painting of some lost kingdom. This was a king's land now. The stripes of wheat were roads to the royal palace. The rough field road was a stream rushing over pebbles. The coulee was a valley where the fruit was held ripe to the vine. The land had become the sky, and held the majesty of the heavens themselves.

There was nothing hard in the land of those moments. It was a land Erik would have chosen to be part of. The image imprinted itself into Erik's mind. This was the real land. This was the land as God intended it. Not the dry, the barren, the dead. Erik felt an answering glimmer within him, as though something just as majestic lay within him, waiting to be revealed; God's purpose for him.

The sunset made the land into a dream world, but it wasn't a dream Erik had imagined in the bunkhouse. This was not a fantasy of a distant time or love. This scene was not only created by the sun touching the horizon; in Erik's eyes he could see that the Creator had created this scene.

He didn't have to question whether this was the land or only a mirage. He knew that this was the real land, and not the land of the drought. This was the way God meant it to be. As he thought, he even allowed the words, "God's land," to creep over his tongue, and he smiled to himself.

At this time there was no denying it. He knew God abided here. It was not an Aunt Mary's prayer or Aaron Hanson's conversation. He knew, maybe best of all after seeing the dismalness of the land, that there was the reality of the Creator. The sunset made the land into His kingdom, and for that moment He seemed very close.

Chapter Three

The road to Sweet Grass curved gently to the right and then to the left for no obvious reason. There were no hills or gullies to make the road builders divert their course. It looked as if they had done it to break up the boredom of the country and a road that didn't bend for unnumbered miles.

Erik had driven this road so many times that the curves didn't even break into his consciousness. He had finished cleaning up, and had put on some clothes that were good enough for a trip to town. On most days he would drive this road to get spare parts or take the tractor to the other section of the Cooper's farm. Tonight was different. Tonight he was going to see Laura and hear her voice. It was time to leave everything else behind.

Even if Sweet Grass wasn't big enough to be called a town, he felt a warmth of excitement as he saw those few lights that marked a town. Any lights meant the farm had been left behind.

As Erik pulled into town he made sure he parked the old pickup on the far side of the Mint Bar were no one would see it. He was ashamed of the old pickup. It was a stupid gesture.

Everyone drove old pickups and, besides, they didn't care what a person drove. But still he didn't want to be viewed as just another local, even though it was quite obvious he was. Everyone in Sweet Grass was either a local or asking directions how to get somewhere else.

As he walked into the Mint he picked his table carefully. He chose a table close enough to another that he wouldn't look conspicuous, but far enough way that he wouldn't have to join in with the talk. Also, he wanted a table where he could freely see Laura make her rounds from the tables to the bar. .

A "Lucky" sign revolved over the solid oak bar. A bear frolicked over a waterfall on a clock that spelled out "Hamm's" and the room was very dark. It was dark enough that Erik had to feel his way to the table before his eyes could adjust to the change. He strained to make out more details, and the people that he had joined. Though he still couldn't see much, he could tell from the sounds that the men at the nearby table had already begun to drink heavily. They had quit the farm early that day, and immediately come to their refuge, the Mint.

"What can I help you with?"

His eyes hadn't adjusted to the darkness, but he knew that voice. It was Laura. He hesitated for a second so she bowed closer to speak over the sound of the loud neighbors.

"What can I bring you?" she repeated.

Erik's eyes quickly focused on her. As Laura leaned over to take his order, he picked up a scent of perfume or lotion that perked his senses. Nothing like this was found on the Cooper's farm except in his dreams in the bunkhouse. Now she was there and the reality almost kept Erik from answering even after the question had been repeated. "Just a long neck Lucky will be fine."

When she left, his eyes followed her. He tried to time it so he could glance for a second without obviously staring, his mind worked quickly to absorb every frame of that picture and to capture her lingering scent to his memory.

He was ready when she returned with his beer. He had laid a twenty on the table so she could take what she needed and leave the change.

"Here you go, let me know when you need another," her voice was inviting to Erik's ears as she left the change.

She smiled at him. He hoped she was smiling at him and not just being a barmaid hoping for a tip. In any case, it was appreciated and he stored it into memory. Erik had visited the Mint several times and he wondered if Laura recognized him from his past trips.

Erik wanted to start a conversation, to keep her there at the table and beside him for a precious few minutes, but he didn't know what to say. Laura solved the dilemma.

"Are you here by yourself tonight?"

"Yeah, it's been a long week and I just wanted to relax. I really can't stay long, but its Saturday and I needed to go someplace." Erik thought that was a stupid thing to say since it made him sound desperate, so he quickly added. "I'm going fishing tomorrow with a couple buddies so I need to get to bed early." That sounded better, even if it was a lie.

"Good luck. Next time you come in, you can tell me some fish stories."

Erik had run out of things to say so he simply nodded as she worked her way to the next table. He followed her with his eyes as long as he could.

He tried not to be too obvious with his stare, but even that was ended when she left the next table and went behind the bar. It was easy for Erik to escape in his mind with the darkness of the bar. He lingered with the thoughts of the smell and voice of Laura, but the more he thought the more he let his mind wonder.

He thought of Aunt Mary, not because he wanted to, but his mind got distracted with other thoughts. The dinner conversation crept into the softness of Laura's image. He could have gone to Fairfield like Mary suggested. He knew some people there, people who could even be called friends. There, he could've gone to one of the local hangouts for people his age. He could have recalled old high school days and football, or indulged in small talk. There would have been laughter and bragging in an attempt to impress each other. There might even have been a chance to become closer to some people who were not friends by title only. In a way, that would have been nice, and it would have pleased Aunt Mary. However, the more he thought, the more he knew the impossibility of that dream. He just wasn't like those people.

Those people were part of Fairfield. Their lives were as much of a fixture of the town as the buildings themselves. If by the age of twenty-five a person hadn't left that town, he never would leave. It was almost like a disease that held them there no matter how much they hated it.

He hated the town. He didn't respect its people for their tenacity, rather he blamed them for why he hadn't left

A loud shout burst Erik's thoughts. "Laura, bring us another pitcher, and then you can come sit on my lap." A stocky fat farmer was sounding off at the table next to Erik. Erik looked at Laura and saw fear in her eyes.

"Hurry up, girl. You don't want to be rude with paying customers. I'm trying to drink more of your boss's beer, and you know there's nothing like a nice warm girl to heat up a man's thirst. Don't look at me like I'm some type of dirt. Come over here." She already had a pitcher for another table, but took it to the farmer first. As she leaned to put the pitcher on the table, the farmer grabbed her ass and yelled with glee.

He didn't know what caused him to move. It might have been the fear in Laura's eyes, or maybe the fact he'd just been pulled from a dream taking him from this hated place. He didn't think he simply reacted. He'd never been in a fight and he certainly would never start one.

Erik didn't have a plan. His first step made him trip on the table's leg and fall forward toward the farmer's table. The big farmer pushed Laura aside, stood and grabbed Erik to keep him from knocking over the pitcher of beer. His actions put Erik in perfect position and he slammed his fist into the stomach of enormous fat. He felt his knuckles bulge into the fat and then hit a solid layer of muscle. 'What the...!" was the farmer's only reaction. He stepped back to get his bearings. Erik took the further opportunity to land a blow to the farmer's face that brought the sound of gritting teeth.

Erik knew that would be his last easy shot. Tthe farmer who had now dropped his beer jumped behind Erik, and he felt a fist hard against his kidney. The pain was so deep that it drove his knee to the ground. Erik felt someone else pull him to his feet, first by a firm grip on Erik's short hair, then by a twisted arm. Erik knew he didn't have a hope. The fat farmer coming towards him was snarling with his need for revenge. His punches came hard and fast with Erik's only hope of passing out to void the pain.

Finally another member of the table pulled the farmer back. "You better stop before you kill the kid. He ain't worth the trouble." Erik fell limp to the floor.

Erik was in a haze but still saw Laura pick up the $18..00 left on his table and shout, "Yeah, guys, the kid's sorry and he wants to buy you a round of beer."

Erik tried to stand, but couldn't. The bar owner and a farmer each took a leg and pulled him face down toward the door. Erik felt the wetness of the broken beer bottles and a few slivers of glass cut into his face. Someone stopped them just short of the door.

He only saw her canvas shoes, but knew it was Laura's voice, "I don't know what you're doing or who you think you are, but I don't need anyone's help, and I sure won't ask it from a loser like you even if I did." She picked up his head by his hair and looked straight into his eyes. "You're a loser. You understand? You're a loser, and I hope I never see you again."

Erik was thrown face first down the steps, hitting three then rolling down the last one.

He crawled around the side of the building until darkness covered him and unconsciousness seized him.

When he came to, he was lying on the ground. He recognized the rough wood siding of the tavern and ascertained that he was on the dark alley side of the bar, hidden in the shadows; left there like a heap of garbage. He coughed up the dust from which he had been lying face first in. Mud from the mixture of dust and blood covered his tongue and the side of his face. As he got up from the ground his back screamed in protest, but he pulled himself to the pickup, afraid that the border police might find him and cause him deeper trouble. He was glad he had parked his pickup away from any bright lights.

When he reached the pickup, Erik drove straight to the rodeo grounds where he knew there would be an unlocked restroom. His headlights shone on the "Whoop-Up Days" sign
painted on the side of the building. In the concrete restroom,
the water smarted as he attempted to clean a long cut across his
cheekbone and pulled out the reminder of what looked to be
glass from a broken bottle. The cut wasn't deep, but that was
no consolation right now. The pain was almost welcomed as
atonement for his stupidity. He could endure the cold water for
only a short time. Its effect and his bruised kidney combined to
make him feel faint again. A grab to the side of the chipped
sink turned his knuckles white but kept him upright. He looked
at himself in the polished tin mirror and saw his stupidity.

Afterward, he drove. He drove away from the town and
into the country, making no attempt to miss the chuckholes.
Several times the thick gravel caught his tires and attempted to
drag him to the ditch. He drove recklessly, not because of the
effect of the fight, but out of indifference. His head no longer
had dreams or even thoughts. He wasn't mad or sad or feeling
pain or feeling anything. He was as blank as the fields he
worked every day.

Reality was all that was before his headlights. There were
no dreams or illusions. He had lived off dreams for years, and
now he knew there was nothing, only his foolishness. All week
his only hope to fight the boredom of the farm was Laura. He
had put all his hopes in a girl he had never even spoken with

before tonight.

What an idiot. If my only hope was a barmaid that I haven't even the courage to ask for a date, I really am pathetic. He had lived in a bunkhouse and thought his daydreams were enough. They were nothing. He had nothing. No parents, no girlfriend, no plans on how to get out of Fairfield. He was a dreamer and a bad one at that. The land around him was reality, not his dreams. The fact that Laura was a disappointment was no surprise.

"I should have known this was coming. What's new? It's happened before and it'll happen again."

Without a purpose in mind, Erik turned off the gravel road to an even less traveled dirt road. The road went left into the pastureland. This was land that was not fertile enough to be tilled for crops, but instead it was left for a few head of cattle to feed upon. At this point his mind wasn't registering landmarks or location, he simply drove the pickup to nowhere. This road, probably only used to move farm equipment and for land owners to survey their fences, became even smaller. Soon it was not a road at all, but mere traces of ruts that were not maintained by anyone but the occasional passing vehicle.

The big sky of this land was without a moon or star that evening. Erik kept driving. He had no idea where he was, but he kept going. Finally the ruts turned into merely prairie grass and Erik cut the motor of the pickup without disengaging the gears. The pickup jerked forward with a few last gasps of the motor and came to a halt. As he turned off the headlights there was no hint of light or sound in the land. Erik was alone. This was not a new feeling for him. At times it was a place he sought, but not this evening. This evening the loneliness was not a feeling, but an entity. It was something Erik could physically feel in the pit of his stomach. He ached not from the blows of the fight, but the presence of loneliness.

In the past he would have escaped into his dreams. There were no dreams this night. There was Erik, in a pickup in the middle of nowhere, not knowing where he was going and not knowing how he let himself get to this place.

Since he couldn't dream, he thought of what was. He remembered the conversation with Aunt Mary and her hopes for him. He thought of that sunset and how it had made the land so different. It was the same land he had worked each day, but the sunset had changed the view to beauty. He thought of Aaron Hanson and the talks he had with Erik. Aaron had talked about turning to God and committing your life to Him. They were all conversations that Erik took as religious pat answers. "Turn your life to God and commit yourself to Him and He will give you new life," had always seemed too easy to Erik. Before, it seemed like just another way to escape from what was real. Erik had his dreams. He didn't need another escape. He didn't need another illusion, he needed answers. There was no person to direct his question or provide the answers. There was only him. This evening he had no one to turn to, no dreams to escape to. He didn't bow his head as others did when they prayed, but rather looked up through the dusty windshield at the night's sky.

"God, people tell me I need to commit my life to you. I can't really say I know what that means, but I know I haven't done it. I know You're real, but I haven't ever really acknowledged You're real in my life. I want You. Maybe I should say I need You. I realize I've been living a lie. I can't get along by myself. Please forgive me for ignoring You for so long. I do need You. I need to meet You here and to be held by You. I need to be held by someone who loves me. I haven't done much with my life but mess it up and turn my back on people who cared about me. I don't want to turn my back on You anymore. Please, Lord, hold me and touch me and help me get my life together.

"God, I know You exist. I don't know if You know I exist, but if You do… I need Your help. I don't have any right to ask anything from You, and I know I've probably been running from You. I don't know. I know I haven't wanted to face You. I don't want to be left alone again. Please don't turn your back on me. I know I've turned my back on You, but, Lord, don't do the same to me. At this point I don't know anything, but I know I need You. Please, please, please, touch me with Your life. I have been told You care about every person. That You care about us so much that You sent Your Son Jesus to save us. I need You. I have nowhere else to go. I don't know what to do. I need You, please hear me and touch me with Your arms.

"I can't expect You to hear me. I haven't done anything to make You want to hear me, but if You are as big and as loving as they say, please touch me. It has been so long since I have felt anyone hold me. I don't know if anyone ever has. Please, please, hold me. I don't want to live in another dream, but if You're really here, hold me. Send Your Son to me. I want to know Jesus."

Erik was silent. His eyes searched the silent sky for a moment. Then he looked down. "Whom am I talking to?" Erik asked himself, "*You'd think I'd learned about empty hopes.*" He suddenly burst into tears. There had been times in the past that a single tear had come to Erik's eyes, but this was not a single tear. Streams of tears flowed down his cheeks and through the cuts of the previous beating. They were tears that would not stop. His sobs became so heavy his whole body shook as if it were chilled by a Montana winter's night.

And it continued. He cried and cried and sobbed, but as he did it seemed as if his tears were cleansing him. That pain within his stomach was gone. The entity of loneliness was not present. He felt warm, comforted. Something had happened. Something was different. He had been touched. He didn't know how, but he knew he was different. He had seen that promise of what he could be, was intended to be, within him. He had been touched not by a dream, but by something much more real. He knew at that moment he had been touched. God had touched him. He also knew this was not an undefined entity. This was Christ who had died on the cross and still lives.

Finally, he let go of the steering wheel and lay on the seat. He quickly fell asleep after the long evening of the bar fight and the fight within himself. His sleep carried no dreams.

Chapter Four

As he woke, the pain in his back from the cramped seat and previous fight jolted throughout his body. He struggled to sit up in amidst the tools and junk that covered the seat. The sun was just beginning to envelop the land, but its heat couldn't yet be felt. His face felt tight as he gingerly felt the scabs from the fight begin to form. None of this was the center of his attention. Something else had happened last night, and he was different.

He smiled when he saw the broken clock on the dashboard with the hour hand pointing straight up and the minute hand broken off. *Well, everything's back to normal. Laura was just another in a long string of broken dreams.*

He began to take inventory. He still hurt from the cuts, but he felt there was nothing serious. He was more interested in something beside his body. *Was happened? Am I crazy or desperate? Was I really touched--touched by God?* These thoughts came quickly. The reality hadn't changed in front of him. The prairie land with its short coarse grass still surrounded him. His jaw still throbbed with pain, but something was different.

As Erik sat in that old Chevy pickup he knew things were different. He needed things to be different. Erik knew God had answered. There had been too many times in the past that he thought things were real, like Laura could love him. Erik knew he was a rainbow chaser, and at least to this point had found no pots of gold. This morning seemed different. There was something tangible and different this morning. He should be disgusted and ashamed. He'd just been humiliated and beat up. This morning his emotions had taken a different path than depression about his failures.

He sat on the prairie with the morning sun beginning to warm the land and he thought. He made no attempt to move the pickup or himself.

"*So this is what Aunt Mary and Aaron Hanson were talking about. I've always known that He was real, but He's real, here, now,*" and then Erik spoke out loud, hoping he would be heard in place filled with silence. *"He was really with me last night. He was really with me and it seems like He'd been with me all along. Maybe He has been. It's just as my aunt and Uncle told me. You were here if I would acknowledge You. It's hard to believe how stupid I've been to hear about You and think that You were somewhere far off when You, who I needed so much, were so close."* But Erik's declaration brought up more questions.

The land around him was still barren. The aches from the prior night's fight still stung, but something was different. How could God be in such a place?

He continued to sit in the pickup and he rolled these

thoughts around in his mind as if he was rolling a piece of sweet candy in his mouth. For several hours he simply sat with a sense of calm. The only doubt he had was how God could love someone like him.

But what would he do now? He knew he couldn't talk to his aunt and uncle until he was sure. They had heard too many of his pipe dreams, but the more he sat there and tried to talk to God under his breath, the more he knew he wasn't the same. Most things go away the more you question them, but his sense of His presence grew stronger.

One other reality couldn't be avoided.He was starved. He decided to drive to Fairfield since it was too early and himself too much of a mess to field his aunt's questions. She would be mad and complain that he hadn't let her know where he was. It was rare for Erik to stay away overnight. But he could deal with that later. It seemed like there was much more to deal with and understand besides his aunt's displeasure.

Erik started the pickup's engine, but let it idle much longer than needed. He was in no hurry. He steered the pickup back along the route of the night before, from a place with no road to dirt road, from dirt road to gravel, and finally from gravel to black top pavement. He drove south and then turned west directly towards Fairfield. He knew he needed a meal, but knew nothing else. Things had changed, but he didn't know exactly what had changed, or what it meant.

The morning sun was beginning to heat the land even at

this early morning. He rolled down a window and felt the breeze whip his hair across his face. The cuts on his face still stung, but the sensation made him feel normal. Pain was a feeling he knew more than any other.

***

There was only one restaurant open on Sunday mornings in Fairfield, the Glacier Inn. The front of the restaurant looked the same as the other stores containing hardware or clothing on Main Street. However, the main street was empty on a Sunday morning except for in front of the Glacier.It would be clear even to a passing tourist that this was the place to stop. Erik knew that The Glacier Inn would have every table filled on a Sunday morning and then again about noon when the church services were over. The city folks and farm families had worked hard all week and a Sunday breakfast at the Inn was their chance to forget the work and laugh with neighbors. Erik knew he would have to wait for a table, but didn't care. He did care that most of the people in line knew him, and would see that he had been in a fight. It wouldn't be long before the gossip started. He hoped he could get to Aunt Mary before she heard it. In better times when the crops were good, his aunt an uncle would have stopped here after church, but this year didn't allow for such luxury.

Erik had to park his pickup a block and a half away. From there he could see a group huddled waiting their turn. Some of the men had their arms folded with impatience while the younger kids played tag using their parents as a shield. Erik tried to look down so people might not recognize him. *I'm so messy they'll think I'm a hobo bum.*He worked his way through the group and went straight to the cash register to leave his name. He lowered his head to avoid the stares. There was nothing he could do to change that. The small restaurant didn't have room for a lobby so people were crammed so tight you heard, "excuse me," every few seconds. He was too tired and too confused to care.

"How long is the wait?" Erik asked when he reached the register podium.

"How many?" the older gentlemen replied while ringing another tab.

"Just one." Erik wondered why the question was even necessary with the way he looked.

"You might want to sit at the counter. I have to leave my tables free. If you want a table it'll be an hour, but I can get you to the counter in twenty."

"The counter is fine. I'll be back in the restroom so don't give my place to anyone else." Erik knew the manager, Don, but didn't know if Don knew him this morning. All Erik got was a disgusting look of *look what the cat drug in.* Suddenly Erik felt like one of the bums that worked with him during the harvest season.

Erik worked his way through the line of booths towards the bathrooms. His kept his head bowed. The men's room didn't have a line, but the inside was filled shoulder to shoulder. There was only one sink and Erik waited his turn.

"Go ahead." A man gestured to Erik to cut in front of him.

"Sure? You were here first."

"Its all yours." The man again gestured.

Erik didn't even say thanks as he turned on the warm water. He tried to dab the cut with a paper towel. The paper was so thick and hard it felt like cardboard. Erik grimaced with pain. As he examined his cut in the mirror he saw the man behind him staring. Erik didn't know if the man wanted Erik to hurry, or if he was wondering what fight Erik had found.

"This might work better." The man pulled out a cloth handkerchief from his pocket and handed it to Erik.

Erik felt both grateful and awkward. He took the handkerchief and forgot to even acknowledge the gesture.

As Erik began to clean away the next cut of dried blood, he saw the man still looking at him in the mirror.

"I'm going to be a while. You go ahead. I've taken your spot and your handkerchief." Erik wanted to be polite, but he also wanted the man to quit looking at him. The man quickly washed his hands and was gone.

Once Erik had cleaned as much as he could, he went back to the join the others huddled in front of the cash register. He took a spot at the very back of the entry, but close enough to hear his name called.

The same man who offered Erik his handkerchief was directly in front of him. The man was laughing and talking with a young couple that Erik had seen before at the Fairfield Community Church. The restaurant was loud enough that Erik could only hear parts of their conversation, but what he heard made him inch forward.

"John, you must have faith to be able to laugh when there aren't any carpenter jobs in four counties," a young man standing next to Erik's new acquaintance said.

"I'm not sure if it's my faith, or sheer stupidity," John laughed, "but faith sure doesn't hurt. Faith has been a long journey and has its ups and downs, but in the end, He has never let me down."

Erik cocked his head in an attempt to hear more, but the restaurant manager spoke first.

"John' I've got a seat at the counter for you" the cashier yelled to the same man Erik was trying to listen to. "Folks, move aside so he can get through," At the same time he noticed Erik, "and you behind him, come along also."

The couple from the church looked at Erik, then said, "John, we're next for a table. Why don't' you wait and join us?"

Erik got the hint. He was surprised by the man named John's reply. "No, thanks. I'll take the counter. My coffee cup always stays warm at the counter."

Chapter Five

"My name is John O'Brian." the man offered a handshake as he slid onto the counter stool. "We meet again."

Erik heard the remark but was trying to figure out how to find a comfortable place on the bar-like stool with his back aflame from last night. He turned with embarrassment when he realized John had his hand extended to shake.

"I'm sorry," Erik quickly shook the man's hand. "I'm Erik. I hope you don't mind, but I didn't keep you handkerchief. It looked so bad when I was done I threw it away."

"Don't worry about it. It was so old I would have thrown it away myself." John picked up the sugar jar and tilted a steady flow of sugar into the empty cup.

Erik watched him pour a mound of sugar into the empty cup. "I heard you talking about faith" Erik found himself saying.

John leveled the sugar just enough to stop the flow, and a broad smile followed.

"The usual?" a hurried waitress appeared and waited for John to move the sugar so she could fill him cup. "You're the only man I know who puts in sugar before the coffee, but I don't know if you put coffee in your sugar or sugar in your coffee."

"It saves me time, and yes, the usual. Get my friend here whatever he wants. I'm buying." John pointed to Erik.

"Bacon, two eggs over easy with hash browns, but I'll buy my own." Erik rapidly replied with his eyes never leaving John.

"You two boys can figure out whose paying, just remember to leave a tip" the waitress joked as she wrote and turned to hang the order on the cook's wheel.

John said, "Yes, I know about faith, but all that means is I know about Him."

"Him?"

"Him, Christ, who is the only reason I can have faith or hope or whatever you want to call it. You don't know Him then faith is pretty empty."

"I think I met Him last night." Erik tried to take back the words the moment they were spoken. *What am I doing? I don't even know this guy. He could be some freak or something, and I don't know what I'm talking about.*

"Praise the Lord, young man! How did that come about? Looks like maybe you met more than Christ last night," John had a large grin on his face and laid his hand on Erik's shoulder.

Neither "praise the Lord" nor being addressed as a young man sat well with Erik. He could feel his shoulder tighten under John's hand, and he hesitated to respond.

"You know, John, I don't mean to be rude, and maybe I'm too tired, I've never liked it when people said, "Praise the Lord." It sounds fake, it made me feel like the person thought they were better than me. Every time I hear it I think I'm going to get a sermon.""

Again John chuckled while taking his hand off Erik's shoulder. He took a sip of the hot coffee. "No sermons from me. You asked the question. I gave the answer, and I'll watch the *Praise the Lords*. You'll excuse me if one slips out. It's just something I say to Him, not to make an impression. If you don't mind, and I think you'd tell me if you did, what happened last night?"

"You mean to my face. That's a long story that you wouldn't want to hear."

"Fair enough," John picked up his tablespoon and stirred his coffee for no reason than to give Erik some time to think.

"Well what about meeting with Christ, and I take it that's who you're referring to when you said Him?"

Erik had to answer. He had asked the first question and he had questions that needed answers. "Yeah, I mean Christ," and he stared straight forward. He was trying to figure out if he should go on or not. *Was this a man he should trust?* Everything was new to Erik.

John let him be and continued to stir his coffee.

"I think all that sugar is probably dissolved by now," Erik

broke the silence between them.

"Never can be too sure"

"You must think I'm a nut or something, sitting here all beat up, and then not really answering your question when I'm the one that started this conversation." The silence didn't last long this time.

"It was Christ. I think. I've sat in church every Sunday my aunt and uncle could get me there, but last night was the first time I really spoke with Him. He seemed to be there and be a Him, a person, rather than a sermon."

"What did you two have to talk about?"

"Nothing really, and everything. I got in this dumb fight over some dumb girl that I thought I'd like to get to know. She made it obvious she didn't want anything to do with me. After I got literally thrown out of the bar, I didn't have any place to go. I parked in my old pickup in the middle of a prairie in the middle of no where, and I asked Him for help and to forgive me for avoiding Him for so long."

"Sounds like the right place to start. Do you think Christ heard you?" John asked.

"I know He did. I can't explain it, but I know He did.

"Before last night I thought I knew about God. He was up there in heaven somewhere. I thought I knew about Christians; that they were just dreamers. But now, it's different. I sat there in my pickup and He was there with me. There's a lot I need to rethink, and I don't know where to start. I just know things are different."

Erik had turned straight ahead staring into his coffee as he spoke. "I guess the most amazing fact was I was actually talking to Him. I've known about Him for years, but last night was the first night I actually talked with Him. And then---I don't even know how to explain it, but He answered me. There weren't any actual words, but I know He was there, and His arms seemed to wrap me in His warmth. It's strange, but I know He was there." Erik continued to look down, but he no longer talked.

"I'm sure He was, Erik." He heard John's words, but still didn't look at him. "Anytime anyone admits they need His help and turns to Him, He'll be there. When a person admits they need Him, He answers them just like He did for you. We all need Him, and without Him it's hopeless. We think we can get by okay without Him, but we keep coming to dead ends. Sounds to me like that fight was your dead end."

"The fight made me realize some things. I've lived on empty dreams, and never faced the facts. I used to think Christians were dreamers, but I did the same thing, but my dreams were empty. I had to admit I'm just nobody, and last night that was pretty clear."

"Maybe before you felt like a nobody, but now you're God's child." John quickly corrected Erik.

Erik swiveled his stool back to John. Erik no longer held back, asking question he had asked himself in the middle of no where in the '54 Chevy pickup. The more he talked the easier it became.

"I've been to church before with my aunt and uncle, but I never realized what it was to have God answer me like He did last night.When my aunt and uncle talked about Christ they were talking about someone who lived a long time ago in a place half way across the world. He didn't affect my life. He was for others. But not for me."

"Now that I know that He is near, I don't know where to go from here. It was so simple to just talk to God last night, but now I don't know how to act. I've always thought being Christian just meant rules of things to do and things not to do. It seems like the Christians I've known are caught in a maze trying to find God. They follow all these rules trying to come to the end of the maze and find God, but I never heard one say God was simply there with them. I felt like they knew God was at the end, but they would always have to do more and try harder because they weren't good enough. If they couldn't do it, why should I even try? It was just too hard to work my way through that maze. Now I want to be a Christian and follow God. I feel like I've found God, but there's still that maze. How do I make sure I don't come to a dead end? Do I go back to the entrance of the maze and all the rules or what? Where do I start?"

The waitress laid the two plates before each of them. "I hate to interrupt, but is there anything else you need? Do you want any hot sauce or catsup?" she asked Erik.

"No, that's fine."

With the waitress' interruption, Erik became conscious again that they weren't alone but in a full restaurant and he was saying too much in front of too many. He looked around. No one was listening. It seemed as though the groups were more concerned with their breakfast than listening to what Erik had to say.

John picked up the pepper and put a heavy dose on every item on his plate, including the catsup.

"Erik, as simple as it was last night, it needs to be that simple for the rest of your life. Never forget that He came to you, and all you had to do is ask. There were no magic words or a secret handshake. There was His love for you. The simple fact is He had been waiting for you to ask for help. When you asked for help and recognized Him, He reached out and held you. You didn't need to search for Christ and Christ didn't have to search for you in a maze. He had never been far away. He is the one who was calling out to you and you finally answered His call. He's not hiding for only a few to find. He is going after you. Your fight last night didn't shock God. Do you think I'm sitting next to you by accident? You need to know I'm here because He cares about you, and is looking out after you," John explained.

"I can see that," Erik interrupted John in his eagerness to ask his next question. "But why are there so many rules in the church. I know all about the Ten Commandments, but it seems like there's ten thousand other things Christian can and can't do. Don't smoke. Give you money to the church. Don't look at a girl in the wrong way. You name it, there seems to be a rule about it."

"It's not as complex as it seems. Jesus said in the book of Mark, 'To love him with all your heart, and with all your understanding and with all your strength, and to love one's neighbor as yourself is more important than all burnt offerings and sacrifices.' That's not complex. That's just living with God and the people around you and putting them first rather than yourself. If you make it too complex, you're right, you're caught in a maze and you'll never be able to find your way out amidst all your questions. Don't put your focus on the maze. Put you focus on Him. See how He came to you and simply remember how He embraced you when you called."

"But I still don't know. How can it be that simple? How can one night with God make Jesus want me? I'm not really that much of a likable guy, and I haven't done anything for Jesus to want to accept me." Erik wasn't about to quit until he had some grasp of the situation.

The man to Erik's left reached across him to the creamer that sat directly in front of Erik. "Excuse me," he said, "but I can't drink my coffee straight."

"No problem." Erik pushed the creamer closer to the man and almost appreciated the interruption.

"How's your bacon and eggs?" John briefly changed the subject.

"Fine, but I was so hungry, cardboard would taste good right now." The two concentrated on their breakfast in silence for a time before John continued.

"Erik, you said you weren't that much of a likable guy. No one, no matter how likable or unlikable they are, is good enough to be on the same level as God. He didn't come to us because we had earned His presence, but because He loved us. It's His love that allows us to be with God, not what we've done. That maze you talk about is something men create in their own minds. It's not God's maze. It's an important thing to know He paid the price by His coming to this world and dying on the cross. There's no more maze. There's only free access to God for those who love Him. If anyone wants to try to find God in a maze, they won't. He's here to be found if only you accept His lordship and His love. You can't earn Christ's love…"

"Yeah, I know. I've never been good at earning someone's love." Erik interrupted John in mid-sentence. "My dad died when I was young. I always wanted to prove myself to him, but it never happened and now it never can. I couldn't do anything right in his eyes, and I guess I thought God was the same way. I wanted to prove to both of them I was good enough."

"Erik, you did what almost everyone tries to do. They want to get by without God and do things themselves."

"But if God loves me that much," Erik said, "I'm afraid I will still disappoint Him, and it will be worse now that I know Him. I also know now that he knows all about me so He'll know it when I fail. I mean, there seems to be so many "do's and don'ts" in Christianity. What happens if I blow it after I know He's real?"

"You're right. He knows you and everything about you. He knows you aren't perfect. That is why the price He paid on the cross allows grace to cover our mistakes. You're His kid; He looks at you with love and forgives your mistakes if you ask Him. His love for you is constant.

"But let me talk about those "do's and don'ts." Remember, they all come down to loving God with your whole heart and soul and loving your neighbor as yourself. Now that you know Christ, you'll still make mistakes, but now you'll have a chance to walk away from those mistakes and not do them. These do's and don'ts you're talking about weren't written to take away all your fun, nor were they made to continually show you how bad you are when you fail.

"You live on a farm," John continued. "You work with machines. Each machine has an operating manual. In that manual, it instructs you to change the oil every so many miles, grease the parts after so many hours, etc., etc., etc. Why does the manual say these things? It doesn't give the directions to waste the farmer's time and burden him with meaningless tasks. Simply, the machine works much better if you follow the manual that shows how the machine should operate.

"In a way, the Bible is God's operating manual for man. God states how man should live not to cramp his style, but so that man might live to the fullest. Man has free will and can do whatever he or she wants. Unfortunately, bad decisions can kill you inside and out. Just as the motor will seize up if not greased and oiled, a person will seize up inside if they ignore God and go their own way."

"But this manual is so big and so complicated," Erik said. "I've tried reading the Bible before and there's some weird stuff in it. People killing people and having affairs and all sorts of stuff that just doesn't make sense."

"You've read the Bible before. You read it as a book. Now read it as your guide," John encouraged. "Start with the words of Jesus in Matthew, Mark, Luke and John. The Bible is God's word and the words of Jesus and his disciples. Read those words and see how simple Christ's message really is. Don't dwell on any one verse, but read the Gospel and see how God's plan is to save and protect his children.

At the same time, don't quit asking questions of people you can trust. You'll need to rely on His Word and His servants. See, there is a true living God, but there is also a true enemy who would like to fill your mind with doubts and lead you away from the faith if he could. So find the Bible and people who know Christ when you get confused."

"But, there is one thought I can't seem to get past," Erik

steeled himself to ask his most painful question. "How can the God that created the universe, who made the stars and the oceans, care enough to come to me? I'm a nobody. My parents didn't even want me. Why would Jesus? I haven't done anything to earn His love."

John's answer was firm. "First, I'm not sure about your parents, but I do know about Jesus. Jesus does love you. It shows how much he loves you by calling to you even if you don't deserve it. It says in the Bible that He called you by name. He doesn't just love all mankind. He loves you and who you are. His love is not determined by what you've done, but by the depth of His love for you. He created you and has one hope for you. He hopes that you'll be His child. He wants to love and be with you and help you as you turn to His arms. That is the greatness of our God and the depth of His love for you."

They both sat in silence. The sound of a crowded restaurant continued around them; a waitress scolded the cook for forgetting to put hash browns with the eggs, a lady's high pitch laugh told everyone the joke was great, and John and Erik listened.

John said, "What about your parents? It's none of my business, but you said you couldn't measure up to your dad, and I don't understand what you meant, that your parents didn't want you."

"My mom left when I was three and my dad died in a car crash when I was eleven."

Once again the sound of the restaurant became obvious and neither Erik nor John spoke. Erik surprised himself by bluntly stating the facts. Suddenly the conversation had gone from the love of God to the reality of Erik's life. It took time for either of them to speak. Erik knew John wanted him to continue, but Erik couldn't find the right words.

"I'm sorry. I was too busy giving my sermon that I forgot about you," were the only words John could muster.

"Not much to ask about. As I said, I live with my aunt and uncle, Henry and Mary Cooper. Not much excitement there. They've gone to Fairfield Community for years. You probably know them if you go to church." Erik saw John nod in acknowledgement.

"Yes, I know them. They're great people. I don't go to Fairfield Community, but to New Life Center, but that's not important. What is important is you."

"My mom left dad and me before I could remember. I was about three. It took me years to find out what happened. People don't seem to want to trust me with the truth. My good Christian Aunt Mary even lied to me. That happens a lot. I guess people think they're doing me a favor by not telling me the whole story. I don't know why they do it, but they're lying.

My Aunt told me my mom had to go away 'cause she was sick. The only thing my mom was sick of was me. She left me and my dad and I guess she didn't like the farm. I don't know where she went or where she's at now. I quit wondering about her years ago. If she didn't care about me, why should I care about her?

"It's not just my aunt who's lied to me. I can't really think of anyone who hasn't lied. My mom did by leaving. My dad never told me the truth, and the list goes on. It's like they think I'm a basket case or something, and think they should hide everything. There're no secrets in Fairfield; we all know that, but they try to keep things from me anyway. "

"Why didn't your dad tell you about your mom?" John asked.

"I don't know. He was never much of a talker. Just like me, but you won't know that by the way I'm going on today. I think dad was probably embarrassed. Probably felt guilty that he wasn't a good enough husband to keep a wife. He never said much of anything to me. I loved—love him a lot, but he took it hard when mom left, and he never had much to say to me." Erik's mind went back thirteen years, and as he sat at that counter, it seemed as if his dad was still there with him.

In the midst of the Glacier Inn that carried the smell of frying bacon and large quantities of strong, brewing coffee, Erik could almost smell the distinct smell of his dad. When he smelled that mixture of shaving lotion and hard work, or anything else that replicated it, it seemed as if his dad was with him again. At that moment his dad seemed so close Erik forgot about the restaurant and even John. There was nothing in that café that would have generated that smell, but Erik sensed it anyway as he spoke of his memories.

"Mom didn't leave dad 'cause he was a bad man or wasn't good to her. From what the gossips in Fairfield tell me, he was very good to her. Dad wasn't a bad man. You know what a man is like when they've lived too long in Fairfield. I can only hope I don't become like that.

"My uncle is the same way. A man goes through enough droughts and enough blizzards, they become like everyone else. They work hard, get dragged down by the work, drink hard, and try to forget. Dad tried to be a good father to me, but with trying to run a farm and trying to forget a wife who left him, he didn't have much time for me."

Erik remembered back to the two of them living in a farm-house that carried the signs of two bachelors. The house was rarely clean, and his dad made sure they never got visitors, he didn't want them to see the mess. The door to his parent's room was always locked. One day when Erik was left alone he found an old key in the medicine chest. He tried it in the door, and it worked, and he walked into the room for the first time he could remember.

The room still carried the touch of a woman; a small, empty jewelry box, some small figurines that she probably didn't have room to pack, and even three simple dresses in the closest. It was obvious to Erik that his dad had locked the room the day his mom left and had never opened it again.

To Erik the room carried a sense of emptiness, almost a

haunted feeling. There was little talk between Erik and his dad. Erik didn't blame his dad. He knew all too well that to survive on a farm, the farmer had to put in 16-hour days, especially during seeding and harvest. There was no room for frivolity or play. It was work. It was hard work, and the end of the day meant only escaping to a coma-like state in a recliner in front of the TV to make it to the next day. There was no time or energy to relate to a young boy. This wasn't Jimmie's fault. It was his lot. To some degree Erik might have realized that fact, but still he needed some touch of some type. Being twenty-two miles from town and other people, Erik's dad was his only human touch, but there was little response.

John interrupted Erik's silent withdrawal. "You said you loved your dad. There must have been some good times on the farm,"

I'm not sure that I would exactly say "good times." I tried. As early as six I started to do chores on the farm. Dad told me to do them, but it gave me a chance to be with him so it was fun, at first. He had me feed the chickens and gather the few eggs they produced. I made sure the water tank was full for the few cows and I held the light when dad worked on the farm equipment late into the night. When Dad told me to do something, I didn't walk. I ran. If dad needed a socket wrench that was in the shop 300 yards from the barn, I'd run to the shop. I knew dad would yell at me if I didn't run, even at the age of six. But I also ran to please dad. Sometimes, not often, it worked.

"Some of my best memories were of doing something right for my dad. It made me feel like I was part of his life and just like him. I would do anything to just see him nod his head in approval. A "thank you" or "good job" wasn't necessary and wouldn't be coming. But a nod: a nod was enough.

"But I made mistakes. I remember when dad wanted me to gather the eggs. I was lost in my own little world and didn't look in all the usual places around the farmyard where the chickens laid their eggs. I was too busy hiding in my own dream world to think of the chores. When I came back to the house the basket was half full.

"'That basket isn't very full. Did you look everywhere?' my dad asked.

"'Yeah, I guess the chickens just aren't lying. Maybe a coyote made them nervous.' I lied. Just like other people lie to me, I lied; I panicked and lied to my dad to hide my mistake.

"'Did you check the feed stalls and the straw pile by the barn?' Dad knew I was lying. He probably could see it in my face. I'm a terrible liar.

"'Yeah, I checked. Just no eggs today,' I found it easier to lie the second time.

"'Well, I'll go check myself.' Dad called my bluff.

"The only thing I could think to do was to circle around and check those places before my dad got there. Sure enough, there were eggs in the horse stall, and I quickly scooped straw over them to hide my error.

"Unfortunately, dad walked in right when I was covering the eggs. He saw what I'd done and lost control. I felt the sting of his words and of a horse bridle that hung nearby which was used as a whip. I know I deserved it, but it hurt. The only thing I could do was try to make it up to dad, and try hard, try to please him. It was only the two of us, so when he was mad, it followed me."

John said gently, "There must have been some good times. What about them?"

"I remember going to the Blackfoot Indian reservation and fishing at the beaver dams. Have you ever been up there?'

"No, I hate to admit it, but I'm not much of a fisherman. I'm too busy with everything else to learn." John replied.

The beaver dams Erik talked about were at the foot of the Rockies. The Cooper's farm, although carrying none of the life of the Rockies, was only fifty miles from their ridges. Unfortunately, these ridges also robbed the clouds of all their moisture before they reached the Cooper's farm. The Rockies were in sharp contrast to the dreariness of the Plains. The Rockies held color and coolness and the smell of life. The pines swayed to the breezes and the sound of their rustling limbs brought a smile to Erik, as they had to his dad.

"The beaver dams are great. By getting away from the dirt, dad and I could even talk next to the bend in the stream where the biggest brook trout lay. The talk was never about anything important, but it was great."

"'Hey, first fish of the day doesn't have to clean the rest,' dad would cry out to me. We wouldn't fish next to each other, but close enough to still communicate.

"'Fine, the most fish doesn't have to clean the stove when we're done.' I'd yell back.

"The rules were always the same, but we always said them. It was kinda like a secret club's password. Dad would even take the time to teach me the finer points of bait fishing.

"'Put it right at the top of the bend and let it float down until it stops in the still water next to that branch. The trout will be lying right next to that log. They use it as protection and to hide from the insects they are going after,' he'd tell me.

"I knew how to fish, but it was great to have dad teach me. It seemed like he knew I was there. On the farm I was just another hired hand, if he even knew I was there."

Erik quickly added, "He wasn't a bad man. That is just you way men become when they live around here."

John's lived here. He knows what its like. I'm not sure why I keep making excuses for dad, Erik reasoned to himself.

"So it sounds to me like he was a pretty good dad in a bad situation; trying to raise you by himself and trying to make his farm work." John said.

"No, he wasn't bad. He wasn't in an easy place. We were only leasing the land so he was stuck with the seed and equipment bills in the bad years, and in the good years a good part of the profit went to pay the lease.

"He did have one problem. Same problem a lot of people have around here. He was a drunk. Not a constant drunk. It didn't happen every day, but when it did, it was bad. I was told he only started drinking when mom left, but that wasn't the only cause. Dad's only escape was at the B&M Bar, and the only way he would be comfortable with the other men was to drink a beer. Actually, it was after several beers.

"His biggest problem was me. What do you do with a kid too young to work, but old enough to get into trouble? Sometimes he'd take me into town if he had to pick up parts or something. It was an easy ride as I never had to worry about talking since dad never had anything to say and it was nice to go to town. The only bad part was when it got later in the day. I'd watch every clock I could see since I knew after three Dad would have to stop at the B&M bar 'cause he'd need his beer.

"'I have to talk to George about buying some more laying hens,' or some other excuse he'd make up. 'I'"ll just be a second so just hand tight.'

"I knew he didn't need any chickens and I'd have a long wait until he came back. In the summer it was boring, but in the winter it was torture. Dad would take the keys and my legs were too short to push the clutch and gas anyway. So I sat in the cold that was so bad I couldn't feel my feet after a while.

"Twice I went into the bar to get Dad, but I quickly learned it didn't do any good. First time he was sitting by himself on a bar stool at the big oak bar that was taller than me. All he did was yell at me and call me names and everyone looked at me like a stray dog. The second time the cold got to me so bad I didn't think I had a choice. Dad was leaning on the bar almost falling off his stool. I tapped him on the shoulder, but he wouldn't even turn and look. The bartender told him I was there but all Dad said was, 'I don't have any kid.' I never went back in after that. I'd curl up in a ball as best as I could and wait.

"The drinking finally caught up with him. One day when I was eleven I came home from school on the bus. There was a note on the table along with the dirty dishes saying he had to run some errands in town. He wasn't home when I went to bed, which wasn't unusual, but it was unusual when uncle Henry showed up later next to my bed, tapping my shoulder.

"I remember a lot of things about dad, but I can't remember the words my uncle told me. I knew what he was saying, but I can never remember the exact words. Dad had driven home late at night. His Buick had hit the ditch and flipped straight into a telephone pole. He had died immediately, they said. They didn't say anything about him being drunk, but everyone knew."

Erik lifted his eyes from looking straight into the coffee cup to looking straight into John's eyes, wishing he had some answers.

"I should have never asked about your parents," were

John's first words. "You should be excited about your new life with Christ, and I've changed the subject to what people can do wrong. I shouldn't have done that.

"The reason I asked is, what happens in our life is important. We aren't just looking up at heaven and not affected by what's happening here.But I'm sorry. I'm sorry for what you've faced and I'm sorry for asking about something that was none of my business."

"That's fine. I would rather tell you the story than have someone tell it wrong, and make up more lies. I know there're plenty of lies out there about what happened. You may as well hear the truth."

"But this isn't the time," John's voice rose with conviction, "to be pulled back to the past. The greatest day in you life just happened, and that's all that's important. I can't fathom how much hurt you must have lived with. But a new life has opened its door within you. Your heavenly Father isn't too busy or too pre-occupied to simply sit with you and hear all you want to say.

"He loves you Erik. He loves you more than you know. I don't know about your parents. Sometimes people get distracted and forget what's important, but Christ; Christ wants to be with you. The Bible says God is our Abba Father. That means He is the most intimate Father possible."

"I thought I came here to get breakfast, and I had a lot of questions in my head. I didn't even ask the question that matters; yet, you just answered it. You said to keep it simple. What you said about God being my Father is simply what I needed to know. Is this how God works? Does He bring you to a place where you went to by accident, and then He answers you?"

"Yeah, Erik, I think you're right. God has a way in leading us so He can show He's watching after us."

Erik suddenly realized the restaurant wasn't as busy as it had been.

"John, I probably made you late for church."

"I can go to church any Sunday. I don't as often have a chance to meet a new friend and be excited with him."

Erik thought of his own responsibilities. "The first thing I need to do is check in with my aunt before she sends out the search teams. After that I need to get cleaned up. Hey, this is my day off. I was going to relax and now look at me." Erik picked up his check, and was ready to leave.

"Sorry, I've got that." John pulled the check out of Erik's hand. "Don't make me a liar, too. I said I'd buy you breakfast. I have something else for you, too."

John pulled a small leather bound book from his back pocket. He handed it to Erik. It was a Bible.

"You might want this to answer a lot more questions," John said. "It's just the New Testament and Psalms, but it's small so you can always have it close by."

"I can't take this. It looks like you've had it a long time, and it has all your notes in it." Erik added as he thumbed through it. He made to return it.

"I have had it a long time. It's time for me to get a new one, and it's time for you to have one close by. Just do me one favor, Erik? I'll meet you next Sunday at 10 o'clock at New Life Center. Until that time, read my gift to you, which is actually His gift to all of us."

"Thanks, I'll see about meeting you next Sunday." Erik still felt reluctant to commit to anything. When he had opened the Bible, he saw John had marks and note on almost every page. Erik felt like he had a cheat sheet for his high school exams. He knew he needed every answer he could get.

Erik left John in the cashier's line. Small as the town was, Erik had never met John, but many people in line clearly knew John. It was obvious they had just come from church. *Those are his type of people...and I guess now I am, too."*

Chapter Six

John quickly moved to the now considerably shorter line to pay his bill. Through the diner windows he saw Erik get into his pickup and John worried. *How much can one kid take? He'll need someone to help him so he doesn't get lost in his problems again. Christ will surely help, and that help also needs to be from a mature Christian.*

John knew how hard it would be because he had been the same as Erik not that long ago. He remembered the exact day he met Christ.

On that day John walked into a church not to pray, but to get a handout. He, too, had looked like a harvest bum, but at the time John *was* a bum, a hobo. He had just arrived in Fairfield early in the day in 1969. He hadn't picked Fairfield as a destination; no one would. John rode the freights, not as a paying customer, but as one who had found an open door on an empty boxcar and jumped aboard. John was hungry when the freight stopped in Fairfield, so he slid off the car and looked for the nearest church for a handout.

It wasn't unusual for such visitors at the New Life Center. Fairfield was located on the Great Northern train tracks that were the main route from Minneapolis to the Port of Seattle. The train traffic brought its travelers, not from Pullman cars but from empty freight cars. These men were the rejects of society; the ones who couldn't make it within the main stream. John was one of them, but God still beckoned.

His life, and that of the other hobos, was the life of the big freights with four locomotives that could take twenty minutes with their seemingly endless line of boxcars to pass through Fairfield. As the trains slowed to pass through town, it was easy to see those open cars with men's legs dangling out the side as they sat staring at nothing. To the kids of Fairfield, watching by the siding, these men were exciting. These men were foreign travelers who were free to come and go as they pleased and the kids would fantasize of the exciting trips they would encounter.

The reality of John's life wasn't a fantasy. It was the life of a person who had to search for every meal in trashcans behind restaurants or at soup kitchens. It wasn't a life anyone would fantasize about or choose to live. It was a life reserved for those who had left their lives and their hopes behind. No one knew or cared about these men.

When John had hopped the freight days before in Seattle, God knew his name and cared to follow him. All of the bums had a story; most were fiction. John's was true and known by God. John's story began in the Vietnam War. Most of the people of Fairfield would never hear the stories of what John saw.

John was so determined to leave that hell behind that he would not repeat its misery. Later, a few people came to know John had served two tours of duty in Vietnam.

He arrived in Vietnam early when many in the States weren't even aware there was a place called Vietnam, let alone a war. He stayed through some of the fiercest battles. But he never would tell how it felt or how it looked to be part of such chaos. Only those who fought by his side could relate. At first, John didn't talk about the war because he couldn't. After meeting Christ, he didn't talk about it because he felt the Lord had done such a miracle of saving and healing him from that hell that it would be an injustice to take anyone there in stories.

John was neither a wino nor a dropout. The war had left him beat up, much like Erik, so he hit the trains as a bum with nowhere to go. By the time he got to Fairfield, he knew the fine skill of panhandling and the rituals of soup kitchens. Usually, if the church had such a ministry, they would have food, but the food would come with a price. The price was not dollars the vagrants would not have, but a lecture on the greatness of God and the need for salvation. John knew the ritual well and would bide his time to get the food.

At New Life Center it was different. They invited him in, set real dishes, not paper plates, before him and let him eat in peace. They had noticed a tear in his shirt and asked him if he would like a different one from a collection the congregation had contributed. It almost seemed to John the people felt it would be an honor if he would take one of their shirts. It wasn't like they were doing him a favor. It was his favor to them. Somehow this attitude confused John about the reason he was there. He was there to get some food and be gone. Suddenly, he felt he was part of their lives.

When John asked the pastor when the sermon would be given, the pastor looked surprised. "I'm sorry. I don't have a sermon prepared. I'm not sure I know what you mean." What John meant was that his experience with the church had always come with strings attached. "We'll do this for you, but you have to do this and be this way and listen to that." Here, there was simply giving as if it had already been given to them.

They had even offered to let John wash up in the restrooms and use a new toothbrush and comb they put by the sink. After he was done, John didn't leave. He stayed to hear their lives and then to hear the story of their Savior's life. He had gotten off a freight train because of hunger, but he didn't realize the food he would receive during those days would make him never hunger in emptiness and loneliness again.

The pastor of the church, Pastor Hodgson, had been in Fairfield long enough to know its people. He knew they would quickly brand John as a hobo, and that distinction would never be lost. He was a man who wasn't concerned about where a man had come from, but where he was going. He made sure the people of Fairfield would only know that John had come from the West Coast and that the railroad had brought him. John had worked for the engineering corps in the Army building bridges and temporary camps. It was natural for him to become a carpenter. It was only a matter of days before John looked just like a native Montanan.

Fairfield was a town that knew everything about what every person did in town. They didn't know or care about what happened in the world outside of Fairfield. Fairfield was its own universe and life outside of it really didn't matter. So it was an easy place to start a new life. They would never know the other life of John that had ended when he hopped off the freight.

John quickly became part of the community. He was strong and knew how to work, and that was what people respected. The Lord had found a place for him long before he knew the town and His touch healed John of many of the scars he had received during the war. The greatest miracle in his life was that the Lord could take a man completely demolished by the misery of war and heal him so that his hard heart was a soft cushion for others and his faith a strength to many.

John could talk to Erik about the simplicity of Christ because the simple touch of His hand had touched John. Those people who knew him now would never guess the hell and mess his life had passed through, and that was fine with him.

It was because John knew his own past that he said a prayer for Erik as he drove away. John's healing had come quickly and his transition to the life of Fairfield short. He didn't know if the same would be true of Erik since Fairfield had already formed their opinion of him. Besides, John had the wounds of several years at war. Erik's wounds were a lifetime of abandonment. It might not be as easy for Erik. A hardened heart is harder to heal than a mind damaged by the images of war. War is terrible, but a heart is life.

Chapter Seven

The drive from Fairfield to the Cooper's farm took twenty-five minutes. The drive always seemed too long and tedious to Erik. At the same time he had driven the route so many times that his mind responded to every chuckhole and dip in the road without any conscious awareness. It was a good time to continue his thoughts. There were still many questions, but they seemed to all come from the last statements John had made: "Christ loves you. He loves you more than you know." He thought of the past when he drove this road with his dad.

He remembered the usual times of quietness. Although they were both in the car there would be no conversation. There was a certain comfort in knowing his dad was there, but he also wished they could actually talk. The topic of conversation wouldn't be important. Just to be recognized would be nice. As the fields of grain and occasional farmhouse passed the windows, Erik never knew how to take the silence. Was his dad just not a talker? Were his thoughts of his work all too consuming? Was Erik just a kid who didn't warrant comments or concern?

Typically, Erik had avoided these thoughts whenever they

crept into his mind. Today, as were many things, was different. The thoughts of his dad still stung. His questions were still many, but now there was another reality. Now he knew that there was Someone who cared. God cared for him, and as he spoke with John, John also seemed to care. What John said made sense. Maybe his dad hadn't ignored him out of indifference. Maybe his dad was so caught in his own despair and sense of abandonment that it was impossible to reach out to a kid.

He also thought of his mom. This hurt was deeper than that which he felt towards his dad. He remembered her abandonment. He had never found an answer to how anyone could be so cold hearted as to simply leave her child. Even after the talk with John, the feeling of brokenness toward her existed. The only reason he knew there was a difference today was that he continued to think of her instead of quickly wiping any thought of her away.

John had mentioned the love and forgiveness of Christ was meant to be extended to others through his followers. John had explained that since Christ had forgiven him, Erik would have to forgive others. John said that people could and would hurt you, but that you needed to depend on Christ for His healing power. Regarding his mom, this wouldn't be easy.

It wouldn't be easy, but Erik began to see it as a necessity. It was a necessity, not because John had talked about forgiveness, but because his mother was his only tie to a real family.

He could talk about forgiving his dad and carry out that process, but that would all happen to an empty stage. His mother was alive. She was someone he could stand in front of and begin to show how Christ had changed him. She was alive and real and, to make his move to Christ tangible, it only made sense that this would be the starting point. He didn't know how successful his attempt would be after so many years. As the pickup left the blacktop and entered the gravel road for the last six miles to the Coopers, Erik formulated a plan to start that process.

But then his mind switched to the Coopers. He had always known they cared. They had always tried to show how much they cared. At the same time it was hard to accept their efforts. First of all there was the matter of the land and farmhouse that he lived in with his dad. Uncle Henry got it when his dad died. His dad's farm was always too small to be profitable. He tried leasing land, but the lease was too costly and drove him deeper into debt.

When he died the bills were more than the land was worth. Henry agreed with the bank to pay the bills and take the land. His plan was to one day give that land and all of his land to Erik. Henry never told Erik his plans. He wanted to wait until Erik had learned to love the farm as he did. Later Erik found out Henry struggled for years to pay those bills, but he got more land, and land was king to a farmer.

And the farmhouse he and his dad lived in. The house was a wreck and never kept up once his mother left. The sheds around the house were even worse, but they sat on five acres of futile farm land. They sat empty for seven years falling apart even further and doing no one any good. No one told Erik. No one asked Erik, it was just one of many things hidden from Erik. One day Uncle Henry hired workers to tear down the house and sheds. The workers got the lumber from the house and Henry plowed the land into crops. No one would even have known there was a house there after the crops took over. Erik dreams were the only place that house would be found.

It was only by chance years later that Erik drove by the place and found out what happened. That was the day he moved out to the bunkhouse.

Erik knew they hadn't taken him in for the land. Erik rationalized they had little choice but to take him. Land or no land Erik had no place else to go, and his aunt and uncle had to take him.

Erik thought back to the early years with his aunt and uncle. He had felt as if he were a stranger in their house, no matter what they did to make him feel included. He remembered as a kid he would sneak away as if he were a runaway. It's hard to be a runaway when you were twenty-five miles from town and too young to drive. He would go down to an old tin culvert on the road to Fairfield. The culvert was big enough for him to sit in and escape. The culvert was only yards away from the farmhouse, but in its closed space Erik felt far away.

It was in this culvert that he began his dream life. The feel of cold tin against his back took him far away from the farm. In the culvert he couldn't see the land except the hole of light at both ends. The ribbed metal looked as if it were a different world of an exotic vehicle. The different world of this place allowed him to dream.

Erik would dream for hours. He would fall into self-pity as he thought of how unfair the world was to him. When the self-pity turned to a cloud of depression, he turned to his dreams. The dreams were of his dad and his love for Erik. In the culvert he could almost feel the cool breezes by the mountain beaver dams. His dreams never contained the amount of fish he caught or the big one that he landed. The only figure he could see was his dad. In the culvert his dad hadn't left him, and he was almost close enough to touch.

His dreams took him to another world, a much better land.

He was surprised when he came back to the farmhouse after his attempts of "running away". The Coopers seemed as if they had never even realized he had left. Erik never knew how long he stayed in the culvert. A watch was not necessary for a kid on the farm. To him, his dreams were so enveloping he imaged himself gone for days. He didn't know if he should feel hurt that they didn't miss him or hurt that his world was so different from theirs.

It was these dreams that he would carry into his teens and

then early twenties. That culvert was his escape, and he remembered those times as he drove to the farm now. It was time
to move beyond a hollow dream in a hollow tube. It was time
for him to talk to the Coopers as if they were his family. They
were the only family he had and he knew he had hurt them too
long. It was time for a change, more than just a night in a
pickup or a talk in a church. John said the simple task of the
Christian was to love God and his neighbor. It was time he
made that a rule to the Coopers and thanked them for their
love.

The rest of the trip home was short, with only the sounds of
meshing gears and roaring motor. Just the idea that Erik
thought of this trip as going "home" made him realize that he
really had changed. Now that his decision was made, the
sooner it was carried out the better. The pickup sped up even
when the road went from blacktop pavement to gravel, and as
he turned into the Cooper's farm he was going so fast the tools
on the seat slammed hard on the opposite door and Erik could
feel his rear tires sliding in a fishtail on the loose gravel.

He drove to the main house rather than stopping by the
bunkhouse to clean himself of last night's fight. As he walked
towards the house he pulled hard on his shirt in an attempt to
straighten any wrinkles.

Both his aunt and uncle met him at the door. Their concern
was evident on their faces. "Erik what are you doing, you just
about took off the front gate. Did you forget where you lived or

something? Slow down." Henry spoke first.

Mary spoke nearly simultaneously. "Erik, what's going on? We didn't know what to think. We didn't know if we should call the police or just get mad at you. Why didn't you call? And what's happened to you," she continued without even a breath. "Your face is all swollen and cut and bruised."

"Fightin', is my guess," Uncle Henry answered before Erik could begin.

Erik stopped the volley of questions "Please, just let me talk. It's been a long night, but I want to explain."

They moved aside and followed him a little bewilderedly into the kitchen.

Erik sat at the table and stared at his hands gripped together, and wondered how to put words to something so personal. How could he explain what happened without them judging him, and thinking this was just another one if his dreams? He still didn't know exactly what had happened, and he didn't know if they would understand or not. They were godly people, but did they know his God or just a church?

"I know I look terrible, but don't look at me," he began. "Last night, something happened. I talked to God last night."

"What did you talk about? Uncle Henry asked.

Erik looked back to his hands when he heard this question. He suddenly felt uncertain.

"I told Him that I needed Him and that I know I had turned my back on Him for too many years, but I didn't expect Him to care about me 'cause I'd never cared about Him."

"And did God talk to you?" His uncle asked.

"No, He didn't, but, yes, He did. I mean, I didn't hear a booming voice or anything, but I could almost feel Him hold me like to say *its okay.*"

Uncle Henry reached across the table and placed his hand on Erik's. The unforgiving farm work had twisted Henry's fingers, but Erik only felt its warmth. It reminded him of the warmth of God's touch last night. "Erik, thank you for telling us. It's good to hear," Uncle Henry said.

Erik recounted the events of late Saturday night and Sunday morning to his aunt and uncle. They had hoped for this day ever since they had taken Erik into their home. Their goal for Erik had always been for him to learn the reality of Christ's love. They had almost given up hope as Erik had gotten older and more hardened in his isolation. They listened carefully as Erik erupted with an outpouring of words for one of the first times they could remember.

Erik went through every event carefully, making sure he didn't miss a detail. He explained his conversation with John, a man the Coopers were familiar with and trusted. Only when he came to the part of forgiving his mother did darkness seem to come over their faces.

"I realize now that I need to forgive," Erik explained. "John said that God can't heal something if we keep tearing it apart.

Like picking at an old scab. That makes sense. He also said that Jesus would help me as I tried to forgive them. I want to try. I've thought about it on the way home, and I know I need to try. It might be good if I went to Dad's grave and talked to him there. I don't know.

"I might have to think about this, but I think I need to find her, my mother, Maggie." This was the first time Erik had used her name in years. "I though about it coming home. At first I doubted if I should see her, but the more I thought about it, the more I got excited. I guess the reason it's so important to me is I can't talk to Dad. I can go to his grave, but I can't talk with him. But, my mother… It seems important that if I really have changed that I should be able to share that with my parents, and my only parent is Mother."

"I sure agree with John," said Uncle Henry. "It'll be important to forgive, but don't rush on how you will carry out that forgiveness. Forgive them in your heart and the other outward statements of forgiveness can come with time. A lot has happened and a long time has passed, so nothing needs to happen in a day. I'd be glad to go with you this week to your father's grave," he offered.

"Yeah, I know a lot has happened, but I have blown it for so long. I need to make things right. I've never known her, but maybe I need to know her now. Maybe that's part of showing that a difference really did happen in my life. Maybe I could even start over again and be a son to her, but I need to see her first."

"Erik, let's talk about this later," Henry replied. "First, let's get you cleaned up and you can get a good night's rest. You must be exhausted. You can make those decisions when you're rested."

"No, Uncle Henry. I need to know about her now. The more I thought about it, the more excited I got. I need to do it now. I need to finish what started last night." Erik took a steadying breath. The lack of sleep was catching up with him, making him on edge. Added in was the feeling that his uncle, although sincere in his joy that Erik had come to Christ, seemed strangely uncooperative in regards to Erik's mother. His uncle's attitude made Erik all the more resolute. He tried to explain, "I made a big step this morning, but I don't think it will be a complete step until I've talked to my mother face to face. If I'm going to change, I want to change completely."

"Good, Erik, but let's talk about this after you get some rest."

"No," Erik set his jaw and tone with firmness. "What's the matter? Is there something you don't want me to know? I'm not leaving you folks. I just need to talk to my mother."

"Henry, maybe it would be good if we talked with Erik today," suggested Aunt Mary. "He needs to know, and tomorrow won't be any different from today. I don't think he is going to give up, and he's ready."

Erik didn't know what to be ready for, but many thoughts

quickly ran through his mind. Henry hesitated, but finally gave a slow nod.

"Okay, we'll talk, but before I do, I want you to remember things can be different now. Things *are* different now. There is a God, Jesus Christ, that loves you. It's not a hopeless world, and you're not caught in a hopeless situation. No matter what other people do, God will never change. When things don't make sense, don't just shut people off, turn to Him."

Erik clasped his hands again and looked away from his uncle. *I don't need a lecture I just want to know about my mother.*

Uncle Henry began, "After your mom left we found out she went to San Francisco. We only found that out by chance when a bill collector called on a loan we had co-signed with her. We didn't directly hear anything from her for years. We tracked her down when your dad died since they were officially still married. We talked on the phone for maybe ten minutes at the most, but she just hung up on us, saying that your dad had been forgotten. That her marriage to him was long ago and a mistake. She gave her address in case your dad had left her anything in his estate, which of course there wasn't. We sent her several letters so she could know how you were doing. After the first one they were just returned to us unopened and marked, 'return to sender'.

"Then when you were a Sophomore in high school we got a letter from the state of California with a death certificate asking if we wanted to be responsible for burial costs. Erik, your mom can't be found, she's--she's dead. At the time, you were going through so much we were afraid that it would only drive you further away if we told you."

Erik sat stunned. He was silent for many moments, only aware of the two faces looking at him, concern and distress etched into the work worn crevices of their features. "How did she die?" Erik's finally spoke.

"That's not important. She's gone, and we're your family," Henry firmly but gently stated.

"How did she die?"

"Erik…" It was obvious Henry was again reluctant to go further.

"Don't' try to hide anything else from me. I want the truth. How did she die?" Erik's voice wasn't tired. It was angry. It was no longer just about his mother. It was about respect.

Henry looked down. "She died of a heroin overdose. Things hadn't worked out for her. She was never able to find a place of happiness. It's a shame, but some people just can't cope with life. Now that you've found His life, it's time to move on." Henry didn't know how else to state the facts.

Erik didn't know what to think. More emotions were thrown on top of all that he already felt. There had been so much elation and relief and now reality. That mother that he had only referred to as "her" had truly abandoned him. She had been given a second chance to take him when his dad died. She may as well said, "What kid, I don't want any kid." His mother was nothing better than a dope-head who didn't care about anyone, even herself. His dad was a drunk and his mom a doper, and he came from them. He carried their genes, which said a lot about his worth.

Why would he expect anything else? He was a fool and only had empty dreams. A day ago he thought a barmaid would be his future. What a joke. Today he had dreamt of finding his mom 'cause she'd love him. *Why do I even bother? When am I going to realize that No One wants me.* Suddenly the arms of God seemed far away.

He now knew why Henry had lectured him before he started. He had been right, but Erik didn't want someone to be right. Tears began to well up. He redirected his energy in an effort to fight the tears.

"No wonder you lied to me all these years. What else haven't you told me? You think I'm such a basket case you can't even tell me the truth. You needed to tell me. This is the second time you lied to me. You told me when I was a kid that she left to get well and she really loved me. She never loved me. She never even cared about me. What else have you lied about? How am I supposed to believe anything you say?"

As soon as he said the words he knew he was wrong, but he also knew he had been wronged. He was too tired to know what else to do. "Now I'm supposed to forgive people who I can't even talk to. What's next?"

His aunt and uncle had no reply. They could have suggested that he spend some of his newfound faith on forgiving *them* for the honest mistakes they had made, but they felt so profoundly guilty in the face of his bitterness that they could not even speak.

Chapter Eight

There was little sleep that evening, neither in the main farmhouse nor the bunkhouse. Mary and Henry didn't get up from the table once Erik left. There was no discussion. They both simply sat and prayed in silence and thought in earnest.

"What a great day!" they thought, but following on the heels of that thought was the irony that instead of bringing them healing, it seemed as though Erik's going to Christ had caused a greater rift between Erik and themselves. They felt helpless to know what to do, how to make things right between them. They could only rely on God.

They knew the Lord had answered Erik's call. In actuality, Erik had answered God, who had called to him for years. They had seen so many times that Erik had a tender heart, but it was also a heart that he kept closely locked so that it couldn't be hurt again. Now their fear was that he would once again feel betrayed by God and close his heart forever.

Erik was so hard to read. Even as that eleven-year-old boy at his father's funeral, it was hard to tell how he would react. He was so quiet and if confronted he would shrink back into even greater silence. He would talk about things, but he would talk at his own time of choosing. Months would pass after a big event in Erik's life and only then would he explain how he felt and how much it meant to him. That is why they were so excited to see him so open about Christ and his excitement about serving Him. Now neither of them knew how Erik would react, but they both knew they couldn't force an answer from him.

Finally, Mary got up and did needless chores around the kitchen. She cleaned and organized the lazy susan, which was already clean and organized. She cleaned the cabinet tops. She scrubbed with the dishrag so hard it looked as if she was trying to remove the top layer of laminate. Mary worked to clear her mind of despair. Maybe it was all her fault. Maybe she could have changed everything. She was the big sister to Erik's dad. She should have done more when she had the chance. She thought of her time with Jimmie.

As a kid Jimmie was mischievous and fun loving. He loved a practical joke and loved to tease his sister. Mary also thought she took great care to look after her younger, but now she wondered if she could've done more. He took he took great delight in watching her eyes as he did daredevil tricks out of her reach. He knew, once she was assured that he wasn't hurt, that she would shake her head and say, "You'll be the death of me yet, if you don't kill yourself first."

There was a seven-year gap between the two, but somehow the gap seemed like twenty-seven years, at times. Mary was serious and focused. Jimmie was fun loving and cared only about the next weekend.

As he got older he began to change. It seemed like the farm did something to Jimmie as he got into his teens. The long summer hours of work seemed to dull his spirit and his practical jokes came less frequently. He became part of the other men's conversation about the farm and the weather and the fear of drought and hailstorms. Many of the men talked this way to pass the time.

Jimmie took these conversations to heart. When an older farmer would talk about a past drought the next man would tell a story worse than the rest. To the men, story telling was a game, a social event. Unfortunately, a teenaged Jimmie believed ever word and thought their reality would be true of his farm. He felt his only chance to survive was to work harder than the rest. Soon he became obsessed with the weather and the health of his crops.

When he met Maggie, Mary was excited to notice that he had once again picked up his zeal for life, and he now played the tricks on his wife rather than Mary. Maggie gave him a chance to think of something besides the farm. His obsession soon turned to her. He did everything he could to keep her happy and be in love with him. The only thing he couldn't give her was a return to Denver. He was a farmer and the land was his life. Soon Maggie realized she was stuck on the farm, and Jimmie's attention only suffocated her more. She wanted her freedom and excitement and Jimmie no longer gave her either.

His new zeal for life ended when Maggie left. He became completely wrapped up in the life of the farm since the land was the one thing he knew would never change. He worked longer than he had to, and when he did take a break, it was to get drunk.

Mary saw the effect on Erik's life. A boy matures faster on a farm, and by the time he was nine he seemed nineteen. Since he had little attention from his dad, Erik became quiet and went out by himself when other people were around. Whenever she went over to visit she would bring a toy or a game or anything possible to give fun to Erik's life and to show that someone cared. It was only after Jimmie died and Erik moved to their house that she realized how much he had become like his dad.

When they were young, both Mary and Jimmie attended the one-room schoolhouse located just a mile over the hill from their farmhouse. Mary was in the eighth grade and Jimmie was in the first. The county didn't have buses so each family was paid transportation money to get the kids to school. In turn, Mary's dad offered them half of the money if they walked themselves over the hill. It was a way for the kids to get an allowance and for the family to use the money saved towards other necessities. The two jumped at the opportunity to get money and walked whenever the weather allowed.

Because of the age difference and because the school was only to the eighth grade, they only walked together one year.

This was the time Mary remembered most about Jimmie.

On those walks Jimmie would open up like he never could at home. He was full of dreams of being a fireman or a soldier like any typical six year old. But he also had stories he had created in his mind that Mary would never have guessed a six year old could hold.

Since the Winters' farmhouse only had two finished bedrooms, Mary got one, the parents the second and Jimmie would sleep in an unfinished room in the basement. On the walks to school, Jimmie would talk about the nightmares he would have in that basement room. He would talk about the dream of being buried alive when the family left him behind while he was sleeping. He didn't know they were gone until he woke to the sound of the basement beams mourning as if to fall. He would try to go upstairs, but his legs wouldn't walk, and when he finally crawled the stairs to the door, the door was locked. He screamed for help, but no one would come. No one had remembered Jimmie. The beams cracked even louder until they crumbled under the weight of some unseen force. Tile and furniture and kitchen appliances came falling down as the beams collapsed. The debris fell and fell, and Erik could only wait for himself to be engulfed.

Only later did she realize these were not nightmares he had in his sleep, but horrors he feared as he lay awake in his basement room waiting for sleep to overtake him. These were not dreams of sleep, but fears Jimmie faced every night.

Mary knew an eighth grader shouldn't have such dreams,

but she didn't know how to help, but she made sure she said goodnight to Erik in his basement room.

After Erik arrived, she would wonder if that was why Erik slept in the bunkhouse, even though he never knew about his father's basement room. Somehow it seemed Erik had inherited more than the same colored hair from his dad. She wondered what nightmares Erik must be having now.

As she waxed the floor for the second time that evening she wondered if she should have done more.

"If only I had given Jimmie more attention. Mom and dad were too busy, but I had the time. Maybe he wouldn't have had those nightmares, and maybe he wouldn't have felt left alone so often. Maybe Jimmie wouldn't have shut himself up and escaped to his work. Maybe Maggie wouldn't have left him and maybe Erik wouldn't be facing what he is today. Maybe I could have stopped all this from happening if only…"

Her guilt was without bases. She had been a girl, but in the '40's the farm demanded as much of her time and attention as anyone else. She still drove a tractor and a truck during harvest. Their family had been poor and only rented most of the land they worked. There was little extra time to look after a younger brother since they couldn't hire extra hands. Mary was the hand that filled in when needed, and she was often needed.

She enjoyed the farm life. It gave her a sense of accomplishment to see the fields she had planted and worked to produce a bumper crop. A farm kid with her responsibilities matured fast and they become single-minded in their lives. Her life was working on the farm to help the family.

Going to a one-room schoolhouse with six kids in eight grades does not allow for a social life. The farm life itself is not designed for companionship. It is designed to work the land. Once a month there was a dance at the Haylake Hall, and this was Mary's chance to socialize. There was no lake in the area, but someone must have thought it made the place sound better so they built a grange hall and invited a couple musicians, someone to call the square dances, and invited everyone for a potluck.

It was a very basic shell of a building with no definable features. However, once Mary opened one of the two large entry doors and heard the music and the people, her heart would jump with excitement. To the right were long rows of tables with fried chicken and black beans and garden grown squash. To the left was a row of young men looking across the way to a row of young women waiting to be asked to dance. They would wait all night. On the dance floor were only the much older parents and grandparents and an odd combinations of young kids. The kids attempted to follow the directions of the caller but mostly they would bump into each other and anyone else close to them. Some of the kids were short, some awkwardly tall for their age; and all carried big smiles of excitement.

The middle-aged men would gather together and talk about the crops and the price of wheat and what they thought they would plant next year. The man with the largest farm would quiz the others, "Would it be a good year for winter or spring wheat? Would any of them take a gamble and hope for malting barley, knowing if the conditions weren't right that barley would have to be sold as feed barley for a fraction of the price? How about mustard? I hate harvesting mustard with its small seeds; the combine has a terrible time." The men had come to leave the farm behind and enjoy the dance, but they quickly fell back to its talk.

The ladies made sure the food stayed fresh and warmed by the oven in the back room. They would talk about their kids and craft projects and hopes for a vacation and throw in a little gossip. But they would never talk about their husbands. It simply was bad taste to talk about the husbands or the state of one's marriage, good or bad.

Mary would quickly examine the room once she entered. She had a purpose here more than the food or the dance. Mary never did remember if the music was good or the dancing skillful. She just remembered looking for Henry. It was at these dances that she first met Henry. She loved to dance and although she was only fifteen, and much too young to date according to her folks, she wasn't too young to dance with a handsome young man with jet-black hair. They would dance maybe two dances; the others their age staring, and then they would retreat to their place. There was a stage at the front of the hall where the caller and musicians would play. The side curtains provided a barrier for young people to talk.

They did nothing but talk, but when she returned to the farm she would treasure every word that Henry had said. The curtains around them drawn close together creating their own little cubby hole within. Here the rest of the world didn't exist. They would spend part of the evening with their other friends, but they cherished that time alone. Their companionship sheltered them both. It was here that Henry shared his life with Christ and here that Mary responded. It was here that their closeness began to develop. Years later, their life would continue with the same sense of closeness and self-sufficiency, relying on the Lord and each other while still having the ability to not close themselves off from the need of others.

Over the years, it was amazing to see the Cooper's love for each other. It was as solid and unmoving as the land itself. The simple life of the farm made it easy to rely on each other, but at the same time they never allowed the troubles of the farm to enter their marriage.

They were childless, not by design, but by nature. It was to this comfortable nest that Erik was brought that fateful evening. Mary worried at times, and especially this evening as she thought back over the past, that Henry's and her closeness had not allowed Erik room in their lives. They had tried as best they could, but they had been married twenty-one years when Erik moved to their house. Maybe they hadn't realized it and had shut Erik out, no matter how hard they tried. Guilt is a terrible thing, especially when it is unjustified. That evening guilt was tearing at Mary as she remembered the nightmares of Jimmie and worried that maybe she hadn't done enough to prevent Erik's nightmares.

She didn't know. She could only pray and hope she had done enough, and pray some more. But none of this allowed her to sleep that night. Finally, in the morning hours, she gave up and walked to the kitchen and started the coffee pot. As she opened the drawer to pull out a spoon she noticed a worn corner of the metal cabinets. They had installed metal cabinets in the farmhouse because they were told they would last forever. However, the porcelain had flaked off years ago and the cabinet showed its age. Mary also felt her age, but at the same time she remembered how often she had gone through the same morning routine. There were days that started with joy and anticipation. There were days that started after sleepless nights worrying about the crops or some other crisis. Each day brought its own chores to be done, farm tasks to be completed and sometimes tragedies to face.

As she looked at that worn edged she smiled. No matter what the day brought, she still went on. Her life might seem like that worn edge from day to day, but there had never been a time that the Lord hadn't been faithful. Even as that old drawer opened each time it was pulled, Christ would open a way, and she needed to remember that. Every time to this date that her life had been filled with fear, He had sheltered them. She knew

He would be true even today. She knew the same could be true for Erik. And she waited for Erik to come to breakfast

When Erik went into the main house at 6:30 a.m., he smelled the coffee that meant Aunt Mary was already up. She urged him to go back and sleep longer. "The fields can wait. Take a couple of days and just relax." Erik made some feeble excuses that the work had to be done and it was his job. His only reaction to the turmoil of the last thirty-six hours was to go back to what was most familiar: the tractor and its endless laps around the stripes of fields. He knew he was going to the fields today not for the work, but the chance to sort things out in his mind.

It was unusual, but he didn't see his uncle at the breakfast table. He didn't know if his uncle was hurt, angry or ashamed. Erik didn't quiz his aunt nor did he add further conversation. He simply ate the pancakes and bacon and headed for the fields. His aunt watched him go, silently praying that his lack of conversation was not a sign that Erik had once again retreated away into his isolation.

Erik went through the regular routine of preparing the John Deere for the day's labor. He filled it with diesel from the large pump tank. He greased the plow and checked the dual tires by bouncing a hammer off their treads, inspecting them to make sure no rocks had become lodged between them. But this routine was done without thinking. He worked as a machine doing its task. It was only when the tractor started and the plow was plunged into the soil that Erik began to think.

In the past he would have taken this opportunity to escape to his dreams. Today he could only think of the reality of the last two days. There was something about the deafening roar of the tractor and the taste of dust in his mouth along with the routine of endless circles in the field that made his mind clearer. As much as he hated the work, it was on the tractor that he could try to make sense out of the last few days.

His uncle had said that the state had asked for money for funeral expenses. He wondered if the Coopers had sent money or if his mom had been buried in a cheap box in a pauper's grave. He thought it was almost a peculiar speculation. Certainly she had never cared nor given anything to anyone else. Why should the Coopers send money? They had supported her child for years, wasn't that enough? Still, it was a question that came to him, and a question he knew he would never ask. This was a woman who had cared for no one, but this woman was still his mother. He hoped she had been buried right.

The questions he asked himself allowed Erik to know that he had changed in a short period of time. In the past, he would not even have acknowledged his mother's existence, let alone worry about how she was buried. He knew something was different. It was ironic that the difference of caring meant a renewed sense of abandonment and betrayal. When he had talked with John in the diner, it all seemed so simple. Love God and your neighbor. God forgave you so you needed to forgive others. That reality seemed so simple and easy as they talked just a day ago. Now he had just gotten hit with the cold reality of how difficult it could be to forgive.

He then thought of his uncle. He found it impossible to be bitter towards him. His uncle hadn't done anything wrong, no matter how hard Erik tried to find fault. His uncle was right. What good would it have done to tell Erik years ago? Erik had never expressed any interest in his mother, had never asked of her. He realized that his uncle could have thought it would drive Erik away even further. He also realized his uncle hadn't caused his mom to be a druggie. He was just the person that got the death certificate. What was he supposed to do?

Erik felt ashamed of himself that he had responded so bitterly towards them last night. He wished his uncle had been at breakfast, but he also knew he needed time. The Coopers had done so much for him and had tried so hard. They had made mistakes, but the mistakes were never out of spite or anger or lack of caring. They had never had kids themselves and Erik knew he wasn't exactly the easiest person to parent.

On the way home from the diner he had known that he had to reach out to the Coopers. Then within hours he had slipped back into his old shell. Again, that which had seemed so clear and so simple was going to be harder to live than he anticipated. Just as he knew there had been a change within him as he thought of his mother, he knew he had to also change from his old habits. His habit wasn't booze, like the winos that worked during the harvest season, or like his dad, for that matter. His habit was cutting himself off from people. He knew now he could no longer be a loner that needed no one. Again the simple reality was that he needed to love God and people. It was the people who had abandoned him so many times in the past that would make that task difficult.

He had told the Coopers that he needed to forgive his parents. He knew he had to first ask the Coopers for their forgiveness. Forgiveness was needed for all the years he had been rude to them, including last night. It had been a shock that he couldn't go to his one remaining parent, but the Coopers were only a couple of hundred feet from his bunkhouse. Maybe it was easier to think of forgiving parents that weren't close. It was harder to look the Coopers in the eyes because of all that had transpired.

His mind thought of the past day and then the long process it would take to really make the changes necessary. He then thought of the farm and the harvest. He hated the first day of the harvest season. It meant for the next three weeks the only thing he would be doing is work and sweat. Each year when they pulled the combine into the first field it seemed as if the harvest would never be done. But unless the harvest was started there would be no hope for its completion. It was only the completion of the harvest that meant all the months of labor had really been worth it. As he looked at his life, he knew a lot had to be done, and it wouldn't be as simple as it seemed when talking with John. He also realized it was only by accepting and relying on Christ that he could begin the harvest of making his life different. Christ had planted the seed and tilled the ground; now Erik was going to have to complete the harvest by determining to get into the fields of change.

Even as he thought through this reality, the pain was still sharp. He still couldn't overlook another example of people leaving him. He couldn't think of an example of any person loving him without having him dropped on them. He wanted to be a son with a family, even more so after his talk with John. He had determined it in his mind to be part of a real family. Somehow, he had expected that he would find his mother and everything would be magically different. All the years of pain and hurt would be gone, swept away by a new beginning. Now he knew that had only been another dream. His only option, he concluded, was to have a family of his own and raise his own son. Certainly in Fairfield there was no woman that would take him. Certainly the thought of his own family was as distant as the changes he needed to make.

About noon he saw a car coming up the dirt road to the fields. On the plains the dust thrown up by a passing vehicle made its approach visible long before the car actually made appearance. When he could finally see the car, it was one that Erik couldn't identify. It was a late model car that wasn't suited for the dirt or ruts of the field road, but it was obvious it was making its way to Erik. There was nowhere else to go in this land. As Erik drove the tractor down the hill after another circle of the field, he saw the car door open and John stepped out. He had something in his hands. Erik was both glad and hesitant to see him.

Erik pushed the throttle to stop the John Deere and opened the side window of the tractor's cab. "John, what are you doing out here? That's an awful fancy car for the fields. A rock will put a hole in your oil pan."

"Your aunt made a casserole and I brought you a dishful. She thought you might like that more than your bologna sandwich. I also have some cold pop."

"That's nice of you, but it's a long ways from Fairfield to be an errand boy," Erik replied, but he knew the food was secondary to John's visit.

"I found myself in the area today. Thought I would stop in and visit. Your aunt and uncle are concerned about you," John leveled with him. "They love you a lot and they asked if I would talk to you. I understand it was a hard night last night."

Erik looked away. "Yeah, it was," he admitted. "There are some things I need to think over."

"Well, why don't you climb off that tractor and get into this food before it's totally cold. It has to be cooler inside my car than inside the tractor."

Erik hesitated. He was reluctant to leave the sanctuary of

his tractor. The tractor was his territory and made any real conversation impossible through a half-opened window. He considered a moment, and then gave in, climbing down the tractor rungs and into the Buick. John handed him a plate after removing the tin foil cover and opened a can of 7-Up.

As Erik took several mouthfuls of casserole without acknowledging him, John broke the silence. "Your Uncle told me what happened," he began. "I'm sorry."

"You better watch saying you're sorry," Erik said around a mouthful of food. "Someone might believe you." He regretted his words as soon as he said them, but today he was going to be much more guarded than he had been yesterday. Still, the remark's rudeness was too obvious. Moments before on the tractor he had determined to trust that the Lord would make a change in his life. Now as soon as he saw John he was rude, insulting even. It seemed as if he was climbing a hill of loose shale rock. As soon as he tried to take two steps forward with change he quickly slid back a step to old habits. He had done the same thing the night before with the Coopers.

John refused to be rebuffed. "I hope you do believe me. Is there anything I can do to help?" he asked.

"I wish you could help. I don't even know how to feel, let alone what to ask for. Do you think you could give me a mom or a dad?"

"I think you know the answer to that, but I do know this is an important point in your life. A lot has happened in a short time. Don't let bitterness drown out the joy I saw in you just yesterday."

"But yesterday things seemed so simple," Erik said. "God loved me and had come to me. Now I know there were lies I didn't even know about. Maybe His love was just a fantasy and He will leave me just like my mom and dad did."

"First of all, Erik, you need to know that people will disappoint you and won't always be there when you need them, but Jesus isn't like that. He is constant. His love is constant. Even before you knew Him, He knew you and loved you and He will love you forever," John said.

"If He knew me and loved me before, how could He let all this happen? How could He have let my parents get so messed up? Why didn't He keep them alive until I had a chance to talk with them and explain how much I needed them?" Erik asked.

"God allows free will, Erik. It was your parents' choice to live like they did. It wasn't God's choice but He won't force anyone to do anything.

"The second thing you need to remember is that *none* of this changes the way He thinks of you. He loved you and chose you and He called you by name. I know you feel your parents abandoned you, and I guess they did. He won't."

"But I thought you said that all I needed to do was love God with my whole heart and people the same way and everything would be okay. Nothing feels okay right now. I've even hurt the Coopers again. They're people who don't deserve what

I gave them last night."

"No, they don't deserve to be hurt," John shook his head, "and neither do you. But they understand you're hurting. That's why they asked me to talk with you when I showed up. They care about you.

"I did say that all you needed to do was love God and your neighbor. I never said that would mean you would never face problems." He gave a low sigh before continuing. "Look at Jesus' life and the life of His family. An angel comes to Mary when she's pregnant and says her child will be the Messiah. What a great moment as she realizes that God is entrusting her and Joseph with the promised King. Then after the birth they have to run to Egypt to escape death and it ends with Mary seeing her son die on the cross. Somehow, I don't think they expected things to go that way. But it was God's route that the prophets had predicted for centuries, and by those events happening, God's plan could be completed.

"Jesus' life wasn't easy and neither was His family's, but it was victorious through all the turmoil. He lived it to experience the same pain we all feel and then He died on the cross to be a sacrifice for us. His Easter shows that anything can be overcome, even death, through Him. The pain you're feeling now doesn't mean God doesn't love you. It means you need to continue to go to Him because without Him you are alone. You're a needy person, as we all are. What we need--who we need, who we *all* need, is Christ"

At first Erik didn't have any response. They both sat in silence. Finally, Erik broke the silence with another question.

"You know, John, I don't even know how to feel or how I should act. I don't know if it's wrong for me to feel hurt. Like maybe I'm saying God isn't good enough for me. I just don't know what I'm supposed to do," Erik said.

John's said, "I can't tell you what to do, but whatever you do, be honest. Be honest with God. You should cry if you have to cry. Yell at God if you have to let Him know how you feel. He can take it. Tell Him you don't think it's fair, but don't turn your back on Him and yourself and go back into your shell. God can handle your complaints 'cause He has felt abandoned just as you have. Just don't turn your back on Him and quit believing He loves you.

"Really, Erik, it's a simple decision we face every day. You can believe that He loves you and has come to help you or you can choose to turn your back and tackle the world by yourself. You can't have it both ways. But no matter how much you hurt, you need Him to lead you out of the hurt.

"Let me read you something," John, said as he reached for a worn Bible wedged between the car seats. "I told you to go to the Bible for answers. This is the prayer that Jesus prayed for us right before He faced the cross:

'My prayer is not that you take them out of the world, but that you protect them form the evil one.'

"See, Jesus didn't pray that we would be taken from the

pain and feeling of the world, but that we would be sheltered from that which can kill us for eternity. There is a difference between being sheltered from the physical world we live in for a short time and being sheltered from the spiritual world that is for eternity. We aren't little robot babies that God programmed to never stub our toes. We're people feeling all that goes along with being people, and that includes pain and that includes joy and that includes love. Erik, all I'm asking you to do is to be honest with the pain you feel, and at the same time not to shut off your hope for the future."

Erik sighed. "John, you make it sound so simple, but it doesn't feel simple when I get alone."

"No, it doesn't always feel simple at all," John, affirmed. "Not when you're hurting. It would be easiest to just give up. But then where would you be? It's hard to know anyone loves you when you're hurting, but give God a chance to prove Himself."

Again there was silence as Erik simply stared straight ahead to the long fields of grain. As John had talked about not giving up, he remembered the culvert he would run away to as a child. Giving up was to return to the culvert. He'd been in that hole already. He didn't want to return to it.

"Thanks, John, I need to go." Erik said abruptly, his words giving John no clue which direction he would go. He opened the car door and started to climb out.

"Your aunt and uncle told me to tell you that you don't

need to work today or tomorrow if you need some time to rest," John added, causing Erik to pause a second. There was nothing in John's voice to suggest whether he thought Erik should do this. Evidently, he felt as though he had said enough, but he did carry the message from the Coopers.

"Yeah, I might do that," and Erik rose from the car and shut the door behind him. He climbed back on the tractor, but didn't start the diesel. He waited until John's Buick had left the fields and then Erik climbed back off the tractor and went instead to the 54 Ford pickup.

Erik did not go back to the bunkhouse to lie on the bed and dream as he normally would have in the past. Today he headed the pickup west into the Rockies. Although the Cooper's farm was in the barren plains, it was still only fifty miles east of the Rocky Mountains. The continental divide made a sharp contrast to the terrain. Only miles west of the harshness of the plains lay the grandeur of the mountains. The mountains were Erik's favorite place, as they always seemed to put a different perspective on everything. He needed a different perspective far from the depression of the bunkhouse, so he turned the pickup west. He saw the peaks of the Rockies covered with snow on the horizon. It was so different from the farm he was leaving. Maybe there was hope.

To get to the Rockies from the Cooper's farm he first had

to drive back through Fairfield. As he entered the town he remembered the thoughts he had just the day before. He remembered the excitement that he felt when he thought of his future. Now, a day later, it seemed as if nothing had changed. Yes, there was no question Christ had come to him, and, yes, he still knew that reality. At the same time everything around him was the same.

It was a silly thought, but as he drove this road that he had driven hundreds of times, he had expected somehow for things to have changed, not just him. He didn't know if there should be more flowers or less heat, but things should be differen.What he saw were the same lifeless plains. It was a stupid to expect such a dramatic change, but somehow, because of his new hope, he thought everything would be different. He quickly realized that these thoughts were in common with the fantasies of his dreams. Christ was real and Erik had experienced Him in the real world, not illusionary dreams. His dreams were fantasy, as were some of his expectations of Christ, but the truth of Christ was total reality. The reality just didn't fit what he had expected.

After passing through Fairfield the road turned west, straight towards the Rockies. Each mile brought a new change to the terrain and took Erik closer to the beauty of the mountains. After ten miles the flat plains became hilled pastures. The soil was rich here, rich enough to grow wheat. Here the sod would not be broken by a plow as it was was used instead to feed the large herds of cattle on the Blackfoot Indian Reservation.

After another ten miles, pine trees started to appear. Erik wondered how these lone trees east of the Rockies survived. They seemed to have broken loose from the rest of the forest that lined the mountains. Maybe a bird had carried a pinecone and dropped it far from its origin, but those solitary pines showed a change was coming as Erik drove west. Erik didn't know if those pines were weaker in their isolation from the others or stronger than the others to survive far from the established community of fellow trees.

Finally he came to the thick underbrush that hid the beaver dams. Erik remembered the fishing trips with his dad. Even after his father died he would come to these same beaver dams to catch the brook trout. He hadn't wanted to forget those memories of his dad that brought comfort to him like a warm parka on a winter's walk. Today he glanced at the dams, but he didn't slow the pickup. Today, Erik was not looking to the past. He was somehow trying to make sense out of the present and his future.

It was only a few more miles until he became completely engulfed by the mountains and all the change they brought. The transfer from the plains to the mountains happened gradually, but it was the change he had hoped to see when traveling the road to Fairfield. Things were different here. There were more flowers. There was less heat. It gave Erik a chance to think differently.

Chapter Nine

The mountains were beautiful to Erik. They contained green colors that never touched the plains below. They smelled of a mixture of pine and wild flowers. Even though it was August, there were still fresh blossoming flowers in the high meadows. Some of the plants were buried with snow except for this brief time when the summer sun set them free. They would only see the sun for one month and they literally sprang up from the ground overnight when the snow left. They came so quickly that one day there would be snow, and the next, mountain irises. On the prairie the summer sun brought drought, but here it brought life. The bushes that had been laid to the ground with the weight of the snow now flexed their branches to the air.

At this altitude even the small streams ran swiftly with new water. Erik found one, following its babbling, and sat by the stream mesmerized by the water that bubbled with freshness and energy. It too had been freed from its winter's sleep. After a time he ascended even higher up the slopes.

It was this beauty and the freshness that had led Erik to undertake the six-mile hike to the face of Chief Mountain. He had never taken this hike with his dad. This was a route he had discovered years after his dad died. That is why he chose this trail. He wanted to be alone, alone even from his past. He knew the sharp ascent and unimproved trail would take him beyond any wandering tourists. He needed to be away from the farm and he needed to be clear in his mind without interruption.

Erik sat on a cliff whose ridges overlooked Hidden Lake. Hidden Lake was at the base of a grass filled meadow. It looked to Erik as if God had taken a giant ice cream scoop and removed the surrounding granite to form a lush meadow that was hidden from the casual observer. The water of Hidden Lake carried a deep blue tint that was only possible with the effects of the glacier runoff. The blue carried the impression that it also hid secrets in its deep trenched waters. A high mountain stream fed its color as it emptied into the lake hardly wider than a pond, but certainly as deep as the sea. Erik could even see an occasional trout jump to feed on the afternoon hatch. The sides of the mountain were sheer rock and void of growth. In the bowls made by the intersecting peaks the glaciers had deposited rich layers of runoff soil. In these bowls the lakes and meadows formed the soft side of the hard cliffs. In these bowls was the greenery of meadows. It was a beautiful sight of postcard perfection but with a vibrancy that no photograph could ever capture and do justice.

The eastern edge of Chief Mountain was filled with sheer cliffs chiseled by glaciers centuries earlier. From the plains you could easily distinguish Chief Mountain from the rest of the mountain range; it rose almost as a pillar with its rock ridges, and it was set further east from the rest of the peaks. Erik guessed that it was called Chief because it was separate and more distinct than any of the other mountains. The other mountains seemed to be melded together into a unit, but Chief Mountain was its own entity. Chief Mountain was his favorite.

To his left were mountain sheep carelessly playing, unafraid of Erik, knowing his awkward human limbs could not carry him to their playground. However, as he found a solid rock perch to rest, it wasn't the sheep or the lake or the meadows that held Erik's attention.

He looked east toward the plains. From his vantage point he saw beyond the green foothills to the plains, to the prairie that housed the Cascade County farms. From this distance he couldn't pick out a specific town, or for that matter, even the brownness of the land. The air above the plains was too thick with dust from the drought to see that distance. But as he looked to the east he fell deep into thought and, with a telescopic effect, began to see things his eyes could not literally reach.

He saw Fairfield, and he pictured the diner in which he had the conversation with John. He saw an unmarked spot on the prairie where he had driven in despair and felt life and hope for the first time, and he savored the innocence of that moment with God. He saw the Coopers farm with the John Deere tractor waiting for his return to work, and the bunkhouse with its staleness and bare walls.

He thought about the Coopers and how hard they had tried to show their love to him. Erik's thoughts were not romantic dreams or negative laments as he had held so often in his bunkhouse. He looked at his surroundings and he communed with God.

"Lord, so many times I have dreamed about the future, but I knew the dreams would never be true. It seemed as if I didn't have a future. Nothing to plan for or aspire to; I just wanted to get out. Get out of the farm and get away from Fairfield. But now, Lord, if You do have a plan for my life, if You have called me by name like John said, there must be a purpose for me. For the first time it seems as if a future, not just a repeat of today, but a future, is possible. Lord make me a future. Show me Your purpose. I want to do something and be someone. Lord, show me what I can do for You."

Just the evening before Erik marveled that God would answer him, and now his heart was excited that God might not only touch him, but also have a purpose for him.

As he thought and prayed he still looked to the east, to the plains. It seemed odd to Erik to look towards the deserted plains when he was in midst of such beauty, but it was the plains that pulled him. It was on the Plains that the work needed to be done mixed with a purpose directed by God. The work that needed done would not be done with a John Deere tractor, but in his partnership with Christ. It was the Plains that held his attention. It wasn't a conscious decision to look east. Erik's eyes were pulled there as if he had left something behind that could only be found by looking back.

For the first time Erik began to realize that he was part of that land and a farmer. As he knew before, a farmer wasn't an occupation, but an identity. A farmer was as much a part of the land as the wheat fields planted in it. Erik had never wanted to admit to being a farmer. That barren land was Erik's identity. He never wanted to admit it and he never wanted to be part of it, but the land had formed him into a farmer. No matter what happened in the future or where life would take him, his identity would still be that of a farmer. He would always be a farmer.

That reality didn't bring joy or freedom to Erik. If God has designed him to be a farmer, He must also have a plan for Erik within the land; a land that, although short in distance, was still far from the beauty of the mountain meadows.

John had said that Jesus had not prayed to His father to take the believers from the world. Erik knew that his world was not the beauty of the mountains, but his world was the survival of the plains. He might have prayed that Jesus would take him away from the farm, but he knew that time had not yet come. He was a young man who had to make something of his life. No matter what he thought of the farm, it was his life and he could not leave it until whatever purpose God had for him there was done. Maybe his parents had run away, one to drugs, one to alcohol, but he needed to finish something in that land. He didn't even know what that something was, but he knew it would only be found in the fields of the barren plains.

He prayed again. *"God, if you really want me to go back to that place, please generate within me a love for the land. Maybe, I shouldn't say, land, 'cause I don't think I can ever love dirt. Give me a love for my purpose within the land. I have no family. You knew my parents were dead long before me. Lord, give me a new family with new love and new hope. My past had nothing, please, Lord, make me a future that includes love. Bring new life to my hardened heart."*

He smiled as he realized that in the last few minutes he had prayed more than he had his entire life previously. He smiled that instead of praying for escape, he had prayed to find strength and purpose to remain.

"It took me twenty-two years to mess up me life, I wonder with Him how long it will take to make a new one." Erik spoke aloud to no one but the mountains goats, but it seemed as if he had just signed a contract for the rest of his life.

The plains stretched before him below his mountain perch. He would go back to the Coopers and to John and to God. That land was his, given to Him by God, and he was part of that land and the lives that inhabited it. If God was powerful and loving, He would not only send Erik to the plains, but would meet Erik on those plains.

Finally, it was time to leave the mountains. He no longer had the luxury to merely think and dream. He had already wasted the bulk of his life wondering and dreaming. It was time to act, not dream. Erik brushed his jeans of the meadow grass and he started towards the plains.

As he worked his way down the mountain trail the sun began to set behind him. It was August in the Big Sky country so the sunset was late, but the mountain peaks began to hide its warmth. He quickened his pace so he wouldn't be stranded in the darkness. The sound of a large stream to his left mimicked a large gust of wind through the pines. As long as he kept the sound to his left, he knew he would reach the main trailhead. Occasionally, he would stumble on a rock hidden by the twilight shadows, but he never lessened his pace. The shadows gave way to grayish tones as the mountains reached into evening. It almost seemed as if the beauty of the forest had entrapped him by having Erik linger too long. Now the mountains held him in an ever-increasing darkness. That which had been so beautiful was now a blackened maze. Erik wasn't afraid, but he was aware the cliffs of Chief Mountain would not allow for any stray step. Erik mused how something so beautiful could be changed into danger so quickly. The plains held no such beauty but also no such danger. When he finally noticed the trail moving from a sharp descent into the gradual slope of the meadows, he felt more comfortable. He would make this trip again, but he would not let its beauty hide from him the reality of its cliffs.

His thoughts still raced as he made his way along the easy last two miles. He remembered the fight two nights before. It was obvious that the barmaid, Laura, was another one of his fantasies, and he wondered if there would ever be someone who would fill the need of companionship for him. She had filled a purpose, but not the need. He still needed a family and that would only be obtained by finding a real girl who would make for a real relationship.

Erik didn't know if he could have a long term relationship with anyone. People had always left him in the past. Could he really be that close and that trusting of anyone? If he hadn't been able to accept the Coopers love, would he be able to accept a girl's arms either? The more he thought, the more he realized he was once again thinking too much. As John had told him, he needed to keep it simple. He needed to go back to the farm and simply believe that things were different and God would help. Other than that, he knew nothing about what the future would bring. It was not a decision to leave the mountains so much as it was his destiny.

Chapter Ten

The last pair of foothills gave way to the level plains and the lights of Fairfield.It was a long drive after a long day and Erik hadn't eaten since the quick lunch in John's car. The hike to Chief Mountain had left him weak with hunger. He'd need to get something to eat in Fairfield. He didn't want another stop, but he was too hungry and afraid he might fall asleep at the wheel if he didn't.

Since leaving Chief Mountain, Erik's eyes and mind had only focused on the headlights that pierced the darkness. The last days had carried more thoughts and emotions than he could handle. Now he was only left with a sleep deprived stare, and the need to eat and get to his bunkhouse bed. He could visualize the lopsided bed and the smell of the room. Some days he felt disgust at their condition, but tonight even the bunkhouse bed would feel good.

It was approaching 11:00 and the only thing open would be the Point drive-in. The Point was at the fork of Highway 2 west and roads that headed north. Every car, truck or occasional tractor had to pass the mammoth, neon Point sign, which was the only thing that distinguished Fairfield from the eighteen other towns on Highway 2. The restaurant at the Point was a square cinder block building with large pane windows slanted outward to give the illusion it was bigger than the seventeen seats within. A corrugated tin canopy kept the sun from a single row of intercom spaces without. The intercoms hadn't worked in years, but people didn't park for convenience but the opportunity to eat without having to talk. Inside, in addition to the seats, was a U shaped counter which ended at the waitress station. The grill was in full view of everyone, and its open vent carried an irritating hum.

When Erik pulled into the Point, there was only one other vehicle, an older Datsun mini-pickup, so he didn't even bother to tuck in his shirt or straighten his hair with fingers used as a comb. Erik's only concern was how fast he could get something to eat and hopefully feel more awake. He had to grab the pickup fender before his legs became legs again. He arched his back walking the few steps to the door. There was one other person at the counter, and the cook, a guy, partially blocked his view of who it was. *Must be a girl,* Erik thought. *That cook never pays attention to anyone unless it's a pretty girl.*

The ding of the bell on the closing door alerted the two to Erik's presence. He saw the girl lean back away from the cook's conversation, which she must not have found too exhilarating if her eagerness for distraction were any indication. It took Erik's tired mind a moment to registered who she was. Erik had never seen Laura outside of the Mint, and certainly didn't expect to see her here. He didn't know how to react once he recognized her. His first instinct was to turn around and leave.

He didn't have a chance for retreat. She had already seen him, and her words showed that she recognized him much more easily than he had her.

"I know you. You're the idiot that decided he could fight a guy three times his size." She gave his face a critical look. "You look just terrible. I'm surprised you aren't in the hospital the way you got dragged you across the floor. You better pick your fights better next time."

"Great that's the third time you've called me an idiot. You made it clear what you think of me. I wasn't trying to start a fight, but you're right, I was an idiot to try to protect you from that drunk. The only thanks I got was you yelling at me while your boss drug me across the floor."

Erik was mad at Laura, but was reminded again of her beauty. She really was everything he had dreamt of. He didn't want anything to do with her, but was stilled awed by her presense.

Laura shifted back on her seat and now used the cook as a barrier. Unfortunately for her the cook had enough of this game and went back to the grill. Laura looked away and then back to Erik

"I'm sorry. I didn't mean a word of it. I had to put on a show so my boss wouldn't fire me. It didn't work. My boss let me go. Let's say he gave me the chance to find new employment. Told me he didn't need me having my 'boyfriend' coming in and causing problems with the regulars," she gave a little mirthless laugh.

"You got fired? I'm not your boyfriend."

"Boy, you're quick aren't you? I told him that you weren't any boyfriend of mine, but it didn't matter. He's been looking for an excuse, anyways, so don't give yourself too much credit. The place has been too slow and he's pretty tight. I knew he couldn't afford to keep me much longer, you just gave him a good excuse so he didn't have to feel bad about it." She shrugged.

The cook interrupted. "I don't care about your two's family reunion. I'm closing the grill in five minutes and the doors in fifteen, so if you want anything you better get it now,"

"Give me a hamburger with hash browns and a cup of coffee" Erik replied. He looked to see if Laura needed anything, but she already had a plate of fries.

"That'll take too long. I'll give you scrambled eggs and put some sausage gravy over toast. Take it or leave it. I still have to clean the grill before I can get outta here."

"I'll take it, but make sure the gravy's hot."

Erik watched Laura pick up her plate and walked to sit directly across from him at the U shaped counter. She only came closer to get a better look at his cuts.

Erik said, "I'm sorry you lost your job, and I'm sorry I

played a part in it."

A small smile formed on Laura's face "Better take some lessons on ducking if you want to fight again. But I told you; it was going to happen anyway. The guy that was my boss is a jerk. Every time I turned around he was staring at me. It was creepy. Besides, he smelled like he'd never taken a shower in his life. It was hard to even walk past him." She hesitated a moment, the smile flickering from her face. Hesitantly she added, "You gotta know I was only calling you a loser because I panicked. I never thought you were a loser. I'm sure you're probably a great guy, but I had to do something cause I saw the look in my boss's eyes when he was pulling you out," she added.

Erik's shoulders relaxed as he found himself smiling. "Forget it. Serves me right for being an idiot." Simultaneously, he became acutely aware that after working in the field and then his hike up the mountain, his clothes probably smelled as bad as her boss had. He was glad she hadn't come any closer. "So what are you going to do now?"

The cook placed a plate of eggs, toast and sausage gravy in front of Erik. He took a bite, noted that the gravy was far from warm. He looked over to complain, but concluded it was a waste of time. Instead, he returned his attention to Laura as she answered his question.

"I'm not staying in Sweet Grass, that's for sure," she said. "I have a few boxes to pack and I'm out of there for good. I did some exploring around Fairfield today. WinRight needs a checker. That'll pay more than I made at the Mint, and the Highline Apartments are half empty, so it'll be cheap housingIf the WinRight job comes through you may have actually done me a favor."

"First you told me it wasn't my fault, and then you tell me I did you a favor. I guess I come out okay in the deal?" Erik had a slight lisp trying to talk with a mouth full of toast and gravy that he'd put in his mouth before Laura sat down again. He felt disgusted at himself. What am I doing? Show some class, he thought. I'm not having lunch on the tractor. I'm sitting next to the prettiest girl I've ever seen.

"Yeah," she said, looking at him. "You came out alright. Except your face..." she shook her head with a little laugh. "They did a number on you, didn't they? Where'd you go after that?"

"I've been home." Erik washed down the remainder of his food with a quick drink of cold coffee. "I've been home and just about everywhere else since then... I've had a lot to think about. Right now all I want to do is clean myself up and sort out some things and I guess let my wounds heal," Erik commented as he put his hand on his still swollen and scabbed jaw. "After I first left the Mint I just drove for a while and ended up sleeping in my pickup."

"Sounds like you had a great Saturday night, just like me." Laura said as she leaned over the counter to get a closer look at

Erik's wound.

"In a strange way it was a great evening. I'll never forget it." To Erik's surprise, he kept talking, "I felt so messed up. I prayed to God. I'd never really prayed that way before, and this time it seemed like God was right there with me. I don't even know how to explain it, but He touched me and He was right there with me." Erik's words flowed easier the more he talked. When Laura had just been a dream, he hadn't been able to think of anything to say to her. Now, when she was a reality, he was saying things he couldn't have fathomed saying to anyone before.

Laura was quiet for an uncomfortable minute. She hadn't expected nor wanted to get into a conversation about her past and Jesus. Finally, she said, "Sounds to me like you gave you life to the Lord."

Erik placed his fork down on the now empty plate. "So, you know the Lord, too?" he asked.

***

It had been along time since Laura had talked to anyone about Christ. Either it was the undertone of excitement she heard in Erik's question or it was the desperation she had felt over the past two days with losing her job and knowing she had to find another and move. Maybe it was a combination of it all, but his question had reminded her of how she had been in the past. She was suddenly acutely aware of where she was, what time it was, the diner, the cook, and Erik. It was the acuteness one feels when they are suddenly totally in the present. When all thoughts in a person's head stop and they are faced with one pressing question; the question Erik had asked. *So, you know the Lord, too?*

She answered slowly. "Yes, I have been a Christian. I met Him about six years ago, although it seems longer than six years. When I met Him, it was the best time of my life, but things change." And so did her voice

"What do you mean by that?" Erik asked.

"Stuff happens." She sighed.

"I don't know what you mean about 'stuff'. What stuff?"

"You don't want to know. It's not important, and it's probably just me. Enjoy your food and your new life with Christ, and forget I said anything. It's just me rambling."

"No, you need to tell me what you're talking about. I'm new at this and I don't know what to expect. I just got done talking to a guy who has been saved for years, and he seems more excited about the Lord than I am. He said to keep it simple, and not let things confuse me."

"Yeah, he's right. Listen to him, not to me. It's been a long night. I just got fired, and I'm tired. Don't pay any attention to me. I'm just a girl who doesn't know what she's talking about. Everyone knows girls just talk and it doesn't mean anything."

Laura didn't want to get into a long conversation about Christ with a guy she didn't even know, and she swiveled her chair towards the outside windows. She thought how nice it was for Erik to be excited about Christ, but she had been there before. She had hoped for so much, but the reality around her didn't carry much hope. She was at a small greasy diner with a cook who had been trying to hit on her, and a stranger with a beat-up face and smelly clothes. This was no longer the good old days.

The cook returned from cleaning up the grill. "Hey, the party is over. I'm locking the doors." He reached under the counter, pulled out a set of keys and moved to the door and impatiently waited for them to follow him.

"We need to talk, we really need to talk" Erik said to her as Laura was forced to turn towards him as she left. "Do you mind talking in my pickup?" Erik asked as he rose to follow her from the diner.

Laura's past meant she would never again be alone in a pickup with a guy. But... She looked at Erik. There was something about him and the way he spoke to her about the Lord. She surprised herself by replying, "Okay, but I need to get home, so it has to be short. I've got an interview tomorrow."

Chapter Eleven

The earlier heat of the day on the northern Great Plains had yielded to the cool night of a cloudless sky. Laura felt the evening breeze on her face and couldn't help but feel relieved to be out of the diner, but her feet still moved slowly. Erik was at the pickup door before her slow steps had left the edge of the Point. Her eyes watched his every movement searching for any hint of danger but she found none, only the comical movements of Erik trying to quickly straighten up the passenger side of the pickup truck which held an array of tools and farming apparatuses.

Erik worked at clearing a spot in the open door of the pickup and wondered if she was even going to get in. His mind raced. He was about to be alone with Laura. It would be great to talk about Christ, but what else would he say? He had never talked to any girl about anything important, and this wasn't any girl.

"Sorry about the mess. I wasn't expecting visitors." It was all Erik could think of to say as she at last arrived by his side and waited patiently as he pushed the junk and tools off the seat, and shoved the big pipe and tire wrench behind the seat.

Laura's concern wasn't the mess. She climbed into the truck but left the passenger door open as he went around and got into the driver side of the pickup. The open door was more symbolic as they would still be very much alone. She felt better leaving one hand on the door handle. Then she waited for Erik to say something.

The silence made Erik's first words even more awkward.

"What should I know about?" he asked after clearing his throat once. He had been fine in the diner, but now it was just the two of them, and he was mortified to find that he was as awkward and nervous as he had been when in her presence at the bar. But he wanted to know, so he forced himself to continue. "Is what I'm feeling now about Christ going to change?"

Laura unclenched her hands as she realized Erik really did want to talk about Christ. Without thinking she closed the door but her hand remained on the handle. "No, no. Don't think that. Erik, don't let me give you the wrong impression about what I said. You tell me about the other night. That's more important than my problems."

Erik didn't know what to say or how to start. This was all new to him. Once again the awkward silence filled the cab as Erik stared straight forward until he realized that her question was easy to answer.

"Okay." Erik turned to look at her. "When I left the fight I didn't know where I was going, but I guess He did. I've known God existed. Maybe I should say I hoped He did, just in case I needed Him, but Saturday night was the first time I asked Him to be my Lord"

Erik fumbled with his words. "I can't exactly tell you what happened. I don't know what happened, but I prayed to God. I know that, and I know He answered me. I can't even tell you how I know, but I know. Before this, God was just something out there that, if He existed, was too far away to make a difference.But after I prayed, He wasn't out there. He was in my pickup with me, somehow, someway. He was there. I needed His touch and it seemed like He held me in His arms. Nothing exactly happened, but I knew He was with me and had heard my prayers." Erik looked at Laura for acknowledgement that he wasn't just dreaming. "Is that strange, or did the same thing happen to you?"

The lights of the Point went dark and soon after the cook came out and left in an old car. It became almost completely dark, and only the outlines of their faces could be seen. The silence drew out until Erik repeated himself.

"Is that strange or did the same thing happen to you?"

And Laurie was forced to reply. "No it's not strange. Hold on to that: knowing how close He is, and don't let it go." She straightened herself in the seat, no longer leaning hard on the door. "I've almost forgotten it, how sweet it is to be close to Him. Don't let that happen to you. I remember the first time I recognized His touch; different circumstances, but same result as what you said." Laura's voice was so soft Erik leaned towards her to hear and then back when he saw her flinch. Again, he had to restart the conversation

"How could you almost forget something like meeting the Lord? What happened?" His question was almost plaintive, as though the thought of it was a tragedy.

"What happened?" Laura replied. "So much has happened. I don't want to give some "poor me" story. Besides, it's too long, and it doesn't make a difference."

"Of course it makes a difference. It happened to you and it might happen to me."

"Let me just tell you the good parts, the part where I met the Lord, like you," Laura said.

"I had just gotten out of high school and things weren't good. I was having a hard time with my parents, and I had no idea what I was going to do with my life and no one to give me answers. On October 6th, I'll never forget that date. I decided to go for a little picnic. There's a big wooded park in Billings and the leaves of the maples had just been touched with the first frost. They were ready to fall, but the bright orange and brown colors seemed to hold them for one more day.

"I didn't have anything else to do so I packed a lunch and went alone to my favorite spot. My parents always mocked Christians so maybe out of spite I started going to church. It bored me, but yet I knew the people were talking about something that was real, and I didn't have it. A couple of weeks before this in that church I simply prayed that I wanted what they had. That certainty. That faith.

""When I got to my place at the park, I laid out my lunch and spread it before me. Playing pretend, like a schoolgirl, I imagined I was having a catered lunch with friends. I didn't notice right away, but two men sat at a picnic table right behind me. I overheard snatches of their conversation and I couldn't help but strain to hear what they were saying once they had my attention. They were both about my age. One wore a tie, and the other one dressed like he had just came off the oil fields. He did little talking but he seemed to be listening really carefully.

"As soon as I focused on their words I knew the Lord had brought me there. The one with the tie was talking about being committed to the Lord. He talked about God's love and the plan He had for each of us. The more he talked, the more I turned to catch every word. I didn't care if they saw me, and soon it was as if I was part of the group without even being introduced.

"The man made it so simple. He explained God wanted to be with us. He pointed to the lunch I had spread on the lawn.

"'It's like the feast that this young lady has set before herself,' he said. 'Christ has invited us to join Him as you would invite a friend home for dinner. Although He is God of the universe, He doesn't sit at some far off heaven's table. He has joined us where we are. Here. He's God and we're just people, but He still has loved us with all our problems and all our faults. He has never told anyone they aren't good enough. He came to bridge the divide between troubled men and women on earth and a perfect God in heaven. And the only way that divide could be bridged was for God's Son to become a man, to feel the experiences, even the pain that man faces, and then He died on the cross. He died taking every sin, everything man could be guilty of, and every problem Satan could lay on men and women, and He took them all upon himself.He sacrificed Himself in our place. Today, all we need to do is to accept how much we need His sacrifice, His forgiveness, and find the shelter of the cross of His forgiveness, His love.

"'In fact, He became a person just like us and felt everything we feel, so there wouldn't need to be any explanation on our part or an separation from Him. He comes to us where we are at, even if it is a sack lunch in a park.

"'All we need to do is accept His invitation and acknowledge we need to be with Him. She knows what I'm talking about, don't you?' the man pointed to me. I said, 'Yes,' so he wouldn't quit talking. No one had ever explained God and Jesus Christ in the way he had, but I knew it was right. It wasn't that it only *seemed* right. I *knew* it was right.

"The man then said, 'Sometimes accepting that invitation is scary because it means we need to trust someone bigger than we are. And that we know His banquet is much better than anything we could do by ourselves. Sometimes, the sheer possibilities of what He is capable of doing in our lives is so intimidating we're afraid to take Him up on it.

"'And at times our pride gets in the way, and we say we don't need what He provides because we can sit at our own table and eat what we want because we don't want anyone telling us what to do. Like we know what to do in the first place. We're getting His love, we're gaining the freedom to try to live the best life we can, to make mistakes, and to still be forgiven no matter how badly we may mess up.

"Then the man asked the working man if he would like to talk to God with him, and simply say, "I need you, Lord, 'cause I know I can't do it by myself, and I give up my demand to do whatever I want. Instead I'll look to You and call you Lord, since I want you to be Lord over my life.'

"The oil worker replied, 'You said to talk with God. I don't even know Him so how can I talk with him?'

"'The answer is the only way to get to know Him is to talk with Him,; the other man said. 'A prayer is simply talking to God, the Lord of the universe.'

"'It seemed strange cause the man talking started to pray. He didn't bow his heads or clasp his hands. He talked to God as if He was right there, and then I realized He was, and I said the same words as he led us in prayer without him even knowing it.

"Even as I think of it again, I'm amazed how God used a man to talk directly to me without him knowing. God was answering my prayer that I had said in church weeks before. He was showing me the way."

Erik realized Laura wasn't talking to him as much as she was remembering her own experience.

"He assumed I was already a Believer. He didn't know that he brought me to Christ right then and there in that park. He invited me to a bible study. I couldn't believe those first days with our Savior. God seemed to answer my every prayer in a way that couldn't be denied. It was like God had put me in a green house to nurture the seed He had planted to full growth. It was a magical time. If only I could be that close to Him again."

A passing car's headlights made Laura's face clear for several seconds. A stream of tears had quietly formed without touching the tone of her voice. She had felt what Erik felt and more.

With the passing car, Laura became conscious of the tears and Erik. She repeatedly, rapidly blinked and reached up to brush her cheeks. Silence filled the pickup's cab.

Erik asked, "Why can't you be close to Him now? I don't understand. What happened?"

"I told you, it's not important." Her tone took on a sharp edge.

"So is that what I should expect? I just had a man talk about how simple it is, and you say it's not? Did God leave you or was that time at a picnic just to give you a brief nice feeling?"

"For the third time…it's not important," she said. *Why does everything have to be about him? I've got my own prob-*

lems and he hasn't helped. "It wasn't God's fault, it was mine. It wasn't just a nice feeling, it was real, but I walked away. It's my life, it's my mistake, and I don't want to talk about it. You got me fired last night by barging into my business, now just drop it."

Even in the dark Laura's voice cut like a knife. Erik flinched as if he had entered a cold shower.

"I have to go. I have an interview tomorrow. It was nice meeting you." Laura said. She started to open the pickup door.

"Stay a little while longer" Erik urged. There's a church in Fairfield. New Life Center. It's just off Main about three blocks east of WinRight. The guy I've been talking to about Christ has asked me to come Sunday. Can I meet you there?"

Erik didn't have the chance to think what to do. He awkwardly moved his arm in the tight confines of the pickup to touch her shoulder. His elbow cracked hard against the back window.

Laura jumped at the sound and turned to see Erik reaching for her. She slammed on the handle and kicked open the door. The dome light came on, and Erik saw someone different. Laura's jaw tightened and her wide eyes became narrow slits. Her icy glare didn't fit Erik's dream images of Laura.

"Don't touch me, don't even think about it!" Then she was out of the truck, turned and was gone.

Erik waited until Laura had reached her pickup, and then he hit his head hard on the closed window, and again, and again.

How in the world can I be such an idiot? How could he continue to botch everything up? When would he learn not to reach out, not to ask for help or try to give it?

He started the pickup before he did something else dumb. As he turned west on Highway 2 he took one last glance towards Laura.Her Datsun hadn't moved, and her silhouette sat motionless.

Chapter Twelve

Laura tapped her key ring on the steering wheel while watching Erik's lights head west on Hwy 2. The taps became harder as her thoughts began sharper. Laura wanted to be mad at someone. She wanted to be mad at Erik. *Who does he think he is? First, he wants to be a hero and fight for me, and then he thinks he can tell me about Christ. He'll learn. He'll learn. It's not his business. I don't need to explain anything to anyone.* But she knew it wasn't Erik's fault

She tried to get mad at God as she no longer tapped but pounded the wheel. *Why can't He just let me forget? Why do I need to be reminded everyday? I know what I did. It's my fault. Call me a sinner, that's obvious. I was the one who failed Him. But why can't He let me just forget it. Why does He have to remind me? He's supposed to forgive, not torment.*

She didn't directly address God. She couldn't even raise her eyes as she pounded her hand on the steering wheel until, out of exhaustion, her head fell limp on the wheel.

As she sat alone the memories of the last year flooded her thoughts, and she seemed caught in time.

The memories never left her. Most days they were a cloud that followed her, but tonight they weren't just memories, they were images that were as real as the "POINT" sign above her. Her tears flowed so thick she knew she couldn't drive. Her hands shook with the sobs that couldn't be stopped. She didn't dare leave the lot. She collapsed to lie on the full length of the seat, pulling her legs tight to her chest. She could only lie curled in a fetal position and see the pictures that her mind could not delete.

She remembered. She remembered that night that changed her life. It all started with a guy and a simple date. She hardly knew him. Earlier that week a church friend introduced the two of them. His name was Marcus.

Later in private the friend told Laura that Marcus had just got into town and had been through some hard times, none of which were his fault. The friends suggested it would be great if the two went on a date. It would be a fresh start for Marcus to have a casual night out, and it would be fun for Laura to meet someone new.

"He's a great guy, and I know he's close to the Lord" the friend said. Laura finally agreed. Marcus called to take her to the movie that Friday.

The date started better than Laura could imagine. They went to a movie she wanted to see, and afterwards got a burger to go and went to a park to eat in the cool evening air. She should have wondered why he went to the back, dark side of the park to find a table. but he was a great guy so it didn't matter.

After eating the last few fries, they climbed back in Marcus's van and Laura playfully punched him in the arm. It was like a game a guy and a girl would play in grade school. It was all in fun, but then Marcus grabbed her arms.

Laura still wasn't concerned. Laura thought it was part of the game to stop her little jabs. But his grips became hard and controlling. She should have fought harder when he pulled her to the back, but she had no idea… She pushed him off her twice or was it three times? It was no longer a game. It was rape.

That night at the Point she thought of everything she should have done, but hadn't. She could have screamed and maybe he would have stopped, but she didn't. She could have said she'd walk home, but she didn't. She didn't listen to the warning signs.

So she blamed herself. *Why would anyone with any sense get into a van and be driven to the back of a dark park.*

Before that evening she had never define the word 'rape'. Later, she was too isolated with guilt to tell anyone what really happened. It happened and that was all that needed to be known.

Within weeks it wasn't just a matter of guilt. It was a matter of life. The picture in Laura's mind eye flashed in the night sky at the same time a car passed by on HWY 2. She saw herself standing in her apartment's bathroom holding a blue positive home pregnancy test while her roommates laughed in the next room. She had been sick for several days and then she missed her period a second time. What Laura feared the most had happened. That test meant a child had formed and was forming more life each day. Her stare at the positive strip was broken by her roommates telling her to hurry. They were late for going out. She told them to go ahead without her. She didn't realize they would never ask her out with them or for anything else again. She made a doctor's appointment as soon as possible and it was confirmed.

In the darkness of an empty Point drive-in space, sweat dampened her shirt. Once again she found herself alone with her tormented cries. *How could He let this happen? You don't get pregnant after being with a man once.* It was not a prayer, but a statement. After the night in the van there had been few prayers

She also remembered going to confront Marcus. Laura knew where Marcus and most oilmen ate dinner. She wore the ugliest clothes she had and went to the restaurant early. She pretended she was watching a pool game, but actually was using a big surrpport beam to hide behind. She didn't want to give Marcus a chance to leave before she told him, and she wanted to be in full control of what would happen.

Laura guessed right although she had to wait. Marcus showed up late, and sat down at a table right next to the beam with an oil-man friend. They studied the menu that hadn't changed in years, but it still held their attention. They both jumped when Laura suddenly came out from her hiding place accompanied by a loud, "Hello." At first she thought Marcus might run, but he couldn't since his friend was there.

"Didn't mean to surprise you." Laura lied, "but we need to talk."

"About what?" Marcus asked.

"I thought you might want to know something. I'm pregnant."

"Why would I want to know that?" Marcus asked.

"It's… it's your baby." Laura hadn't come prepared for a straight denial. She was shocked at how nonchalant he was acting.

"Give me a break. You came on to me and you had a good time, now don't think you're going to hang something like this on me. I can tell you've been around. Talk to all the other guys. You've come to the wrong place if you think you're going to pull me into this. You've blown this one, not me."

Liar! Laura wanted to yell, but chose her stare to carry her disgust. There had been no other man and no other possibility. Another word would be a waste of time and would only invite further insult. She'd done her duty.

Laura's pause let Marcus grab his coat off the seat next to him, and he motioned to his friend that they were leaving. "Sorry to hear about the bad luck," he said to Laura. "I'd take care of that quick if I were you. But I've got a new job and my boss is waiting for me. Wish I could help, but times are tough for everybody." With those few words he was gone, and Laura was alone again.

She hadn't expected anything different, and wouldn't know what to do if he had wanted to be a father to the child. She was alone, and it would stay that way.

From there Laura went straight to the house she shared with three others. She needed someone who'd understand and hug her and cry with her. These weren't just roommates. They were Christian sisters, and they'd understand.

She told them without details what had happened. At the end Laura reached out for a hug, but there was none. All she got was troubled looks, and, "We'll pray for you."

Later, her closest friend, Robin, cornered her in the kitchen, saying she'd received a word from God about how disappointed He was and that only time would prove if Laura had the fruits of repentance to be part of the church again.

After that she was afraid of going to any one else from her church. Her parents had quit welcoming her once she became a Christian. They both had drinking problems and thought Laura looked down on them for their non-belief.

Boy, wouldn't they love it to hear that after all my preaching to them, I'm the real sinner.

Her only companion during those months was the child growing within her womb, and she found herself talking to that child often.

I hope you like Italian food 'cause a feast is coming your way. I read today that protein and calcium will help you grow, so enjoy all you can grab. I've heard that later I will get cravings for strange food, but the only thing I'm craving for now is you to be healthy and strong. Alone with her child she would sing lullabies and a few times hopeful hymns. The hymns weren't to God, but for her child.

That evening at the Point the weather had started to cool, but Laura found sweat soaking her body. Her sobs shook her entire body when she remembered the second doctor's visit at the end of her first trimester.

She didn't have money or insurance, but something wasn't feeling right.

"How's mom today?' the slightly heavy nurse asked as she walked into the room. "My name is Nancy." On the first visit a different nurse had cared for Laura, but Nancy looked just as nice.

"I'm fine. A little nervous. Maybe I should say very nervous. I'm trying to do everything right, but I'm so afraid I'm gong to hurt my child. I feel like I'm carrying a dozen eggs and I'll break one if I turn too fast."

"Well, let's hope you don't have a dozen eggs in there," the nurse patted Laura's stomach. "Most people are very happy to have one egg fertilized and hatched nine months later. Let's see you have," she turned the page on the chart, "six and a half months before that egg becomes a baby in your arms."

"It's a baby already and I can't wait to hold that baby in my arms!"

"Great," the nurse ignored Laura's comments. "I see too many girls your age that don't feel that way. I hope dad feels the same."

"Dad's not around." Laura did her best to keep her voice upbeat, but looked away in case she failed.

It was necessary for the nurse to ask the question. The chart didn't list a father. The nurse had seen this too many times to care one way or the other.

"Well, fine, we'll just have that baby by ourselves won't we? Those men just get in the way anyway." The nurse took her pulse and temperature.

"Well, this visit we do an ultra-sound to see how thing are progressing.

"How much does that cost? I don't have insurance and I don't have a lot of cash."

"The state will cover it, honey. They always do in these situations…" she changed the subject. "This is going t be cold," she said as she squirted a clear lotion from what looked like a mustard bottle onto Laura's belly.

The nurse was good. She was experienced. She could perform the exam and not give the patient a hint that something was wrong. She was also experienced enough that she knew something was wrong. *God I wish this girl hadn't called this embryo a child. It makes it so much harder when this happens.*

Nancy left the room with a smile and warned the doctor about what he would be walking into.

"Good afternoon, Laura. Nice to see you again. Remember me? I'm Dr. Sorenson. I want to do a quick ultrasound exam on you."

"Nancy already did one a few seconds ago. I'm sorry, but I don't have insurance so I would rather pass on another test."

"Don't worry. I 'm sure you aren't happy about being a burden on the state but we only want to do what is best for you, right?"

The doctor took longer and wasn't as good at hiding his expression. Laura could tell something wasn't right.

"Laura, there is a problem with the fetus."

"What is it?" *Am I supposed to guess?* she wondered at the doctor's long pause. To her, it almost seemed like he was trying to be dramatic with the long pause, like a bad actor.

Finally he said, "It looks as if the fetus is no longer developing. It doesn't show the signs of life I would expect." He waited for Laura to respond or react. She did neither, but only stared straight forward. He had been an OBY/Gyn for eighteen years, but he still couldn't predict how a woman would react to this news. He decided to simply continue his explanation.

"I don't think the fetus will develop any further. It looks as if the pregnancy has been terminated."

"Fetus, why do you keep calling my baby a fetus? Why don't you just say my baby is dead? That's what you're trying to say, isn't it?"

"I'm saying fetus because it hasn't yet developed specific organs or features. By definition it remains a fetus, so you have not lost a child. Nature has simply protected you before the fetus becomes more than a simple mass."

"A simple mass! How dare you call my child a 'simple mass'? That child was birthed in my womb."

"I'm sorry. I misspoke. I know there is a segment of the population that has that opinion, and I didn't realize you were one of them."

"I'm not a 'segment of the population' and I don't know what you mean by being 'one of them'. I'm a mother and not a population. I know that child was alive in my womb, not as a mass, but as a creation of God. That child was a part of me, and I gave it new life every day as my baby grew. Don't tell me it wasn't a child. You might be a doctor, but I know better. I'm not talking because I'm part of a group. I WAS THAT BABY'S MOTHER..." Laura remained composed but adamant. She still had a child to protect even if that child would never be held.

So, she's the hysterical type. I need to get out of here before she loses it even more.

"You need to know that 95% of all stillbirths are defective and would be grossly handicapped if they came to full term. I hope you can take some comfort in that. Now I'm very sorry for all your suffering, but I have other patients that need me, and there is nothing else I can do. Nancy will give you follow up instructions."

There was no comfort in knowing statistics or that the evil, terrible man had left. She would have no comfort, and even years later as she sat in the Datsun in the Glacier Point stall, comfort had not yet reached her heart.

Even worse news came as Nancy entered the room. She carried a yellow sheet of paper with writing dim from being the last carbon copy.

"I'm sorry. I only hope one day you will realize that it is for the best. Everything happens for a reason."

"You knew when you first did the exam that my baby was in trouble. Why did you run rather than tell me then?"

"I didn't know for sure. That is the doctor's place to give a diagnosis. It's strictly against policy for me to say anything."

"Well, then someone should make a policy against calling my child a fetus, or for that matter not letting my baby die."

Nancy put the paper in front of Laura so she could read the almost illegible words. It was obvious to Laura that the once warm nurse would not answer her questions.

"Dr. Sorenson has prescribed some codeine so you can be more comfortable and hopefully sleep tonight. Sometime in the next three to four days expect a heavy discharge. When you feel it coming, it will be heavy, so be close to a restroom. If you don't have the discharge within five days, call immediately and we'll have you come back in. If you have continued bleeding after the discharge call this number. If you need additional medication for comfort call this number."

Nancy had finished the written instruction and handed the papers for Laura to sign.

"What about my baby?"

"As Dr. Sorenson explained to you, your pregnancy has been terminated. Your body will naturally expel the fetus."

"Are you telling me that I am supposed to go home with a dead baby in my womb and just wait for my child to be expelled? Expelled is something that happens in high school. It not something that ends my baby's time on earth."

"I wish there was another way, but the safest for you is to just let nature take its course.'

"Nature has already worked its course and nature took my baby." Laura couldn't outright say that God had taken her baby, but that thought went with her and she left that office promising herself she would never come back there regardless of what happened.

That evening in the truck Laura relived every thought of her loss and her sin. She had thought of her child almost daily for the past year. She had told the people at the Mint that she had a baby boy so they wouldn't bother her. She had decided to call the baby a boy because he would be the last male she would allow in her life.

She thought of the child often, but never in such detail as this evening. Usually it was merely a memory sparked for a second, but tonight it was every detailed relived. When she came to the next detail of her horror she turned on the car to simply have the company of the running motor rather than the silence.

After leaving the doctor's officer, the next two days were filled with horror. She couldn't' go to her past friends in the church. They were no longer friends or sisters. She couldn't guess how they might react. They might tell her, as she already felt, that the death was God's punishment for her fornication. She wasn't going to tell Marcus even if she could find him. She didn't want him to feel off the hook. Let him think for the rest of his life that he might get a knock on the door one day and find his child asking questions.

She couldn't feel relieved that the problem was gone. She couldn't now move on with her live as if nothing had happen. She knew her life would never be the same. As she sat in the empty Point parking lot she could still feel herself sitting in a half empty apartment, afraid to leave and unable to even eat, waiting for nature to take its course. Laura sat alone, but death sat with her.

Finally, cramps started and the ordeal ended. She had run to the toilet with the pain of the cramps, but after, the child was terminated by definition, but not from her life. She looked at the toilet for only a second and then closed the door from the outside. She couldn't look at the child. Certainly, she couldn't flush the toilet to dispose of her baby in some city sewer. She didn't know what to do.

Her only answered was to get the apartment manager and tell him the toilet was plugged. It wasn't the best decision, but she couldn't think of anything else. The manager looked perplexed at the request, and even troubled as she left him alone in the apartment, going to her car and leaving.

She would return to the apartment, but only to get her belongings. She owed three weeks rent for not giving notice, but that was a cheap price to leave that place.

The corrugated tin covering of the Point seemed to be a screen that held the pictures of those events, and she couldn't take it any longer. Her tears still flowed, but she pulled out of the drive-in stall and headed towards Sweetgrass. The first portion of the trip, Highway 2 to Shelby, would have very light almost nonexistent traffic. By the time she hit the truck traffic heading north to Alaska on Interstate 15 she hoped to regain her composure. She simply couldn't sit still in the lot anymore. Her thoughts churned her stomach too much to simply sit there.

The traffic was very light to Shelby and her only company on Interstate 15 was the semi heading north to Calgary or Edmonton. She was unable to completely block out the images of the doctor's words or the left behind apartment. She was able to restrain her tears. But she could still tell her cheeks were puffy from their effect.

She pulled into her parking place at the Dew Drop Inn, a converted motel that was now apartments. She noticed the owner's lights were still on. This wasn't unusual, as the owner, Gracie, always complained about insomnia. Then Laura saw that not only was her lights on, but Gracie was pacing in front of her units while taking a puff off of one of her ever present cigarettes every third stride. Laura would have loved to avoid a conversation. She knew that would be impossible.

"Girl, it's too early to be home if you coming from the Mint, and it's too late for a nice girl like you to be out on the town," Gracie said as Laura got out of the truck. "I didn't know who to expect out here when I saw the headlights appear. Oh, my god, what's wrong with you?" Gracie pointed a lit flashlight at Laura and saw her tangled hair and swollen eyes.

"Nothing, Gracie, it's just been a long night. Let's leave it at that."

It was nothing new for Gracie to see Laura's tears, but

these tears weren't tears of a good cry but tears of a fight. Gracie just didn't know Laura was fighting with herself.

"Did someone beat you? Let me know their names." Gracie was a big black lady who would bring fear to anyone who crossed her.

"No one beat me. It's nothing."

"Don't tell me it isn't nothing. Let me get you a warm washcloth. Maybe some ice, and you can tell me all about it."

"No, Gracie, I've done enough talking tonight. I just want to go to bed. I've got a job interview at the WinRight grocery in Fairfield in the morning, so I have to get my sleep."

"Okay, I'll let you get your sleep, but I won't let you get away so easy tomorrow. Before you go to sleep you better put a pretty picture in you mind. There's no use fretting about what happened now."

Not only is Gracie sweet, but she's smarter than a lot of people who call themselves God fearing, Laura thought. She nodded. "I will. Thanks, Gracie."

Chapter Thirteen

The sun slivered through the bottom of the plastic window blinds and left a line on the opposite wall to mark its presence. Laura focused her eyes and saw 8:30 on the face of her watch. She had the habit of sleeping late after the Mint's night shift. She was irritated at having woke early until she remembered there was no more Mint and late work to be done.

The WinRight appointment wasn't until 2:30. That would give her time to get her things together and move out.She hadn't thrown away the boxes from her last move so the chore would be easy. Her worldly possessions were few and would only fill half the bed of the pickup.

She also knew Gracie would be waiting for an explanation. Gracie was always there when Laura needed her. Laura had never met anyone like Gracie before and Laura doubted she would have ever made it through the last year without her. She thought about the day before when they had discussed her getting fired from the Mint, but Laura had managed to keep it short and slipped away to Fairfield before Gracie could ask too many questions.

But this was today and there would no avoiding the inevitable. Laura pulled on the jeans she wore last night and picked up a small toaster oven and a box of worn shoes and headed for the pickup with her first load. It was frivolous to take a box of shoes that she no longer wore and probably would never wear again, but she needed some connection to a time when life was normal and there were no nightmares.

She took a last look at the Dew Drop Inn to imprint the image in her mind. The Inn was better than living in the pickup, which she had done for a time, but not much better. The Dew Drop Inn had been built in the thirties and for years had been a 12-unit motel. Each unit was a separate, albeit small, building with the units arranged in a straight line to draw attention to the passing travelers heading to Canada and needed a stop. Now the only permanent tenets were the mice from the nearby fields. Only Laura and Gracie's units were filled. Gracie had become the "owner' when she was offered a 100 year lease.The landowner would keep the land and Gracie would have the headaches of maintaining the already rundown units.

Laura turned toward the parking lot and the pickup. She wasn't surprised to see Gracie leaning on the side of the truck, putting as much weight as possible on the bed of it.

"Did you take my advice or are you still beating yourself up this morning?" Gracie asked. Laura didn't say anything but put her shoes and oven in the back of the pickup, and turned to go back for a second load.

"Why are you acting like a little kid and pretending that if you don't look at someone they don't exist? God knows, everybody in the county knows I exist." Gracie's head went back as she laughed at the own joke.

Gracie was one of only a few African-Americans in the area, and her huge overweight frame was accentuated by a cherry red smock that could be seen in a white out snowstorm. Laura had never seen Gracie without the smock, but it was always clean and pressed.

"Are you going to keep playing this game or are you ready to talk?"

"I'll talk.Got some good news. I got an interview to be a checker at the WinRight store in Fairfield, so my luck might be changing. I think I found a place to live, so that problem might be covered. It's nothing like your fine apartments, but nothing can be like the Dew Drop." Laura knew better than to think she could get by with that short explanation, but she tried anyway.

"Don't be smart with me" Gracie's black Southern drawl added to her persona." We both know this place is a dump and if I had a chance to leave it I would, just like you. You know that's not what I'm talking about. What about those tears last night? What's up?"

"I told you, it was nothing, Oh, yeah," Laura tried to act as the event was so insignificant she had nearly forgotten it. "I stopped by a drive in that was empty, and in walked the same guy that started the fight at the Mint the other night--"

Gracie didn't wait for Laura to say another word but raised

her weight off the pickup and pushed her short sleeves higher.

"He hit you, didn't he. I thought you might've been hit when I saw you last night."

"No, he didn't hit me. Why on earth would he hit me?"

"Well he must have done something. Some people don't have to do anything. But breathe and trouble follows them. It sounds like this guy is one of those. Keep away from him."

"After the way I left him last night I don't expect he'll want anything to do with me. But it wasn't him. It's me. I'm trouble.'

"Don't give me that foolishness. You're like a broken record, blaming yourself for everything. I know you enough to know you aren't trouble, but you carry your problems around like they were your only friends. You aren't fooling me. These cheap walls are as thin as paper so you don't hide anything. I hear you even when you think I can't hear you. You're going to run out of tears if you don't watch it."

A semi passed on the nearby highway with its horn blowing and a cat whistle from the driver as an obvious gesture to Laura's beauty. Again Gracie stood up from her resting place, shook her fist at the trucker and yelled, although she would never be heard over the loud diesel.

"You keep that truck moving. There's nothing for you here. Find some cheap tramp in Canada. This girl has way too much class for you." She positioned her weight once again, and resumed as if her sentence had not interrupted.

"I don't know what you brought with you when you moved here, but it must have been bad and you're probably packing it up to take it with you. Now, If I carried all my past from North Carolina I would have shot myself years ago. The past is past; you can't do a thing to change it. You're getting away from the Mint, now go start a new a fresh start, and I mean fresh. If you carry your problems to your new place, it's like cleaning your refrigerator to get rid of the smell and putting the rotten food back in again. That fridge is going to smell as long as that food's there. Don't keep your rotten past around."

"I know that, Gracie, but it's not that easy, and every time I try to forget, in the end it all came back to me."

"What's this all about? You've been here four months, and we've talked about everything but what's really bothering you. What'd you do, steal your fiends lunch money in grade school? You remind me of someone who got a rock in his or her shoe and never takes it out. They can still walk, but every step reminds them of that dang rock and not what's in front of them. Stop yourself. Deal with it, and get on with your life. It can't be that serious."

"It is that serious." Laura turned to walk away, but turned back without taking a step.

Gracie shifted her weight on the pickup. "Well, are you going to tell me about it, or feel sorry for your sore foot?"

"I got pregnant and I've never been married." Laura interrupted Gracie

"And?"

"And I got pregnant," Laura carefully formed the words, "and I lost the baby".

Gracie nodded. She didn't look shocked, only pensive. "How long ago was this? And how far along was the baby?"

"I lost the baby two weeks before I moved in here, and the baby was four months old. I could feel the baby move, and that baby was all I had…."

" From what I hear almost all babies that miscarriage have problems that wouldn't make them whole. Maybe it's better."

"Don't tell me it's better. I don't care if my child had to be fed and carried the rest of my life.That was my baby and I needed it."

"So you needed her more than what the baby might have to live through. Being a mom isn't for the mom, it's to protect their children."

"Gracie, that's my point. I didn't protect my child from the very start.It wouldn't have happened if... The baby would have lived if I hadn't abandoned God. There was no love in what I did. It was disgusting and terrible. I walked away from God and God took my baby."

"Girl, how did you ever come with that answer?What type of God do you follow?

Sure, let's say you're bad and all that stuff you Christians feel guilty about. That baby didn't do anything. You're saying God killed an innocent baby cause you did something He didn't like. We're all in big trouble if that's God. If a man did that they would put that person in jail for the rest of their life and he'd be considered the worst of the worst. Now you're telling me God is that disgusting."

"I didn't say God was disgusting and I didn't say God killed the baby"

"Sure you did. You said He took the baby, didn't you?"

"Yes"

"Well, that's using nicer words, but it means the same."

"Gracie, it's not that easy, you aren't listening."

"I'm listening. Now listen to yourself. You've got a good head on your shoulders, but you aren't making any sense. I know it must have been the worst thing in your life, but you can't dwell on something so painful for so long without going crazy. You know you didn't cause God to 'take your child'."

"But He had every right to take it. It was terrible and I wouldn't expect you to understand. How could you? I can't get the image from my mind. I just keep thinking about it over and over.

"I think about my baby. Gracie. let's say you're right and God didn't take my child, but the baby died because of me one way or another. Maybe God didn't do it, but if I hadn't let him rape me this wouldn't have happened."

"Raped. My God"

Gracie couldn't move fast, but fast enough to wrap her arms around Laura before another word could be said.

The night before Laura tears had felt as though they were ripping her apart. That day the tears mended, and they didn't stop.

After uncounted minutes Gracie lowered her arms and looked Laura straight in the eyes while softly brushing her tears away. Without a word she turned and walked into Laura apartment.

As in all days the heat of the land grew to meet the morning air, and the wind stated its presence. A gust whipped Laura's long hair against her face with the reminder it was today and not the terrible past. Laura looked around as if she would find someone, but she knew there was no one. Gracie's touch had held her warm. Gracie was gone, but not her words. *"What type of God do you follow?"* Laura knew her God, Christ, had died so others don't need to die.. She also knew she needed to talk to Him. Laura prayed as she stood, feeling the wind skim across her face.

God, I'm so sorry. Gracie's right, you haven't done terrible things. Terrible things happened, but you didn't cause them and You didn't change from the loving God I always knew.Last night that guy, Erik, reminded me that You still touch people's lives. I guess I have to allow the possibility that You still love me with the same fresh touch as the first day I met you. I heard that hope in Erik's voice.

No, no. Your love is not a possibility; it is the reality. Just because I don't feel the wind one day doesn't mean the wind is gone. Everyone knows the wind will return. Just because I don't feel You one day doesn't change the certainty of Your presence.

All I have to do is feel at the hugs of Gracie or hear the excitement of Erik and I know it's You.

"Girl are just going to stand out there and let me do all the work?' Gracie yelled from the cabin.

"What are you doing? You walked away without saying a word," Laura asked as she followed Gracie to the doorway, but Laura didn't forget her prayer.

Gracie had picked up a light box of socks and intimates off the set of drawers and headed back to put it in the pickup like she was part of the moving crew. "What was I supposed to say? So I went to work rather than talking. There's too much talking done, and not enough doing.In my book, doing is always better than talking anyway. Doing makes a difference, talking can make things worse.

"I wouldn't know what to say anyway. You just told me a horrible, sad event that happen to you, and I could hardly breathe, let alone talk.

"But you can't keep reliving that day. If we kept talking you'd live it again.You've got to move on. So, the only thing I can do is help you pack. Do you want this in the back or front seat with you?"

"The front will be fine." Laura went to opened the pickup door. They both worked until all her belongings were out of the unit and into the pickup and Gracie again took her position leaning on the die of the truck once again. She needed the rest and to say her goodbyes.

"Gracie, you're right."

"You say that like its some rare occasion. I'm always right, and if you don't believe it I'll tell you again, "Gracie said with a laugh.

"It wasn't God's fault, and I really don't know whose fault it was. The problem was I forgot He was the one person I needed to turn to, and I didn't, and I've been so lonely since."

"Thats good to know, but don't break out in Christian talk thinking I'm going to be one. I don't need all the guilt trips.I'm a sinner and I know it, and I know there is a God somewhere, but I don't need a church full of Christians telling me everything I'm doing wrong."

"But it's not about what you've done wrong, but about how much He loves you." Laura said.

"That isn't what you were saying last night, and I heard the same things from Christians for years when I lived in the South. No thanks. Now about your apartment you're leaving: I'll have to go through it with my white glove to know if you're going to get any of your deposit back, and you know you didn't give a proper two weeks notice. I've got people lined up every day for that unit and I've been telling them no."

Once again Gracie changed the subject, and Laura knew there would be no more talking about God.

They both knew there was no deposit and the rooms couldn't show more damage. Notice wasn't necessary for the almost empty motel, and Laura smiled as Gracie reverted to her old role.

"I'll come back and visit one of these days."

"No, you won't, so don't even say you will. You just get that job, and be happy and once in a while remember this cranky lady. If that God of yours really does listen and you're on talking terms again you might send a prayer or two my way."

"I'll guarantee that."

Gracie lifted her weight from the pickup and shuffled back to her room.

Chapter Fourteen

Erik's only problem driving home after his evening with Laura was keeping his eyes open. He didn't think of Laura, or his mother, or anything but making sure the ditch didn't meet his tires.

Once back at the bunkhouse Erik didn't even bother to undress. He remembered no dreams as he slept.

The next morning Erik awoke without feeling the cuts in his face.

I have to fix those blinds. The light came freely through slats that were misaligned by a pull string broken years earlier. Erik could also hear the sound of a grinding stone in the nearby shop. Uncle Henry probably had already been at work for hours, as he never slept past 5:30. Out of total exhaustion, Erik had slept until 8:30.

I have some explaining to do, and I might as well apologize right now. Right now would have to wait until Erik took a shower to attempt to clean off dirt from the last two days. The bunkhouse shower was a simple stall with rust lining its corners. The shower head had most of its holes plugged by the hard water's calcium, but it served its purpose. The water felt refreshing and Erik noticed even his back felt better. No matter how good it felt Erik had other matters to attend to. He exited the shower, toweled off, dressed and headed to the shop and the noise of the grinder.

A steady stream of sparks flying from the grinder's wheel outlined Henry's profile as he held a dulled plow's shovel against the grind stone with more pressure than necessary. The display of sparks was solid and impressive. Erik had seen money spent on fireworks for less of a show, but this was work and not a show.

"Don't grind that too hard or you won't have anything left."

"Erik, sorry I'm being so loud. I hope I didn't wake you."

Erik suspected that just the opposite was true. He wanted to point out that sharp plow shovels wouldn't made any difference in the lifeless soil anyway, but he refrained. Instead, he said, "I'm the one that should be saying I'm sorry."

"For what?" Uncle Henry asked.

"For getting mad at you about my mom and calling you a liar. It's my mom's fault, not yours. You and Aunt Mary have always tried to protect me, and I should have thanked you rather than storming out of the house."

"Apology accepted, if you accept mine for not telling you earlier. You were right. You're an adult and I should have told you years ago. Sometimes we might try to protect you too much.Where did you go after you left us?" There was true curiosity in Henry's voice. There was much he didn't know about Erik. They lived on the same farm for decades, but they still didn't know each other's lives.

"I went to the mountains, Chief Mountain. I thought a lot. I don't know a lot about Christ yet, but I do know He cares about me, and I've got a lot of work to do to get my life straight. I guess I also came to the realization that He would help me if I allowed Him to."

"Sounds to me you know a whole lot. If you know what you said, there's not much else you need." And with that, nothing else was to be said between the two men.

Instead they turned to the one bond they shared, work. Erik filled the big diesel storage tank in the back of the pickup and pumped the grease guns full. He put two of the plow shovels Henry had just sharpened for spares in the bed of the pickup and made sure the crescent wrench was in the truck.

"Erik you know you don't have to go to work today. Why don't you catch up on some rest, but I wouldn't go too close to the house," he added in caution."Mary isn't going to let you get off without a hundred questions. She care's about you and for a woman, I guess that means she'll worry herself sick until she knows everythingMary doesn't want to pry, well maybe she does, but she can't help herself.She wants to, *we* want to make sure that you get to know how great a God you serve."

"Yeah, there's a lot I need to get straight in my own head. I was trying to put into words everything that has happened, but

I don't even know how to explain it.

"As far as taking the day off; I'm fine. If I start getting tired, I'll came back. I promised to get the field done by this weekend, and I want to honor my word."

"Erik, take your time with the field and don't worry about us. If I know you, you'll talk when you get things get sorted out. But, if things get confusing, don't hesitate to come to us. We're here to help, not to run your life." Henry broke into a wide smile and laughed. "We know you're going to do want you want anyway. You always have."

Erik grinned, but didn't laugh. Again enough had been said."I'll never get those fields done if I hang around here all day." The grease gun he threw bounced hard off the box of the pickup, producing a scowl from Uncle Henry.

It wasn't long before Erik was behind the wheel of the giant diesel watching the plow's shovel digging deep and breaking the soil.He twisted sideways in the seat that did not turn and found his familiar spot. In this spot he could watch the plow and at the same time see what lay ahead. In the midst of his hatred of the land, the land gave him purpose. His task was to keep the plow tracking flush to the previous row. It was routine. It was easy, and he glanced to the rest of the farm. The only sign of life was the shadow of the tractor that churned round after round making no obvious difference except to raise more dust to choke the air. The sun was Erik's only companion and that was the way he wanted it that day.

In normal years Erik plowed the land in hope for a bumper crop for that year and the next. This year the crops didn't need plowing, but only rain. The crops had long ago dried brown to match the land. Erik churned the soil anyway because that was what he was sent to do. Almost in defiance to the sun he methodically traced smaller and smaller circles around the field. Erik moved the tractor like a soldier on guard pacing before a destroyed village, not knowing why he was there but doggedly continuing his assigned task.

He had followed the same path and the same routine for the past eleven years. Little had changed for those years, until last weekend. It seemed like more had changed in the past week than in the past eleven years combined. That day he was satisfied to merely plow and let the sound of the tractor drown out his thoughts.

God, I wish I could get a crash course in how you work and what this all means. It seemed so simple when I was talking to John that first day at the Glacier.

When I was talking to John I had a mom. I know she wasn't much of a parent, and I can't remember ever talking with her, but she was a parent. In my mind I still had someone I could call Mom. I felt like I belonged to someone. Now I'm an orphan. An orphan that doesn't belong to anyone.

And Laura meant there was a chance to be with someone. Now, I don't have a clue what to think of Laura. I dreamt

*of her so often in the bunkhouse that it's strange that she is
someone real now. If my meeting her at the Point was part of
Your plan it would be nice to know that for sure. Maybe it was
just an accident, but I'll need a lot of time in the bunkhouse to
sort this out. I hope You don't mind listening.*

Instinctively, or by God's nudge, Erik didn't want to tell
anyone about Laura. It was too complicated for him to even
know what to say. He had never been around women, other
than Aunt Mary, let alone try to figure them out. Erik didn't
know if he was attracted to her or to his old dreams. He didn't
know anything about her, especially after that last outburst. At
the same time he couldn't quit thinking about her.

*What are the chances that Laura would be a Christian?
Then just when I had wondered if I ever could be close to
someone she was the only other person at the place I stopped.
That's pretty strange. Gotta wonder if it is God.*

On the other hand, he didn't understand her last outburst.
"It wasn't God's fault, it was mine. It wasn't just a nice feeling,
it was real, but I walked away. It's my life, it's my mistake,
and I don't want to talk about it." *It sounds like someone that's
got more problems than me.* It was fine to imagine Laura in the
bunkhouse, but Erik didn't know if he wanted to be that close
to someone that fast. *What if I messed up something that God
wanted to be in m life?"*

Erik knew he would have to leave the bunkhouse at some
point, but not now, not until he could make more sense out of

it. He would eat in the house and try to not let Mary and Henry sense anything was going on. That wouldn't be easy. His moods were obvious and Aunt Mary was too perceptive, but he would try. He wouldn't even go to church this Sunday. His aunt and uncle would worry, John would expect him there, and who knows, Laura might even be there. But that was just another reason to miss. He wasn't ready to face Laura again.

He wanted nothing to do with this land, but for now this land was his refuge. No one would interrupt his patterned ruts. He pulled the plow another notch deeper into the ground and the tractor's smoke turned black with the new strain of work. The plow turned little else than dust in fields that had not felt a drenching rain in three years. The sun shriveled the crops around him and the grasshoppers took more from the land that was already without life. In the midst of all this Erik was comforted by the solitude and the sense of His presence.

Chapter Fifteen

Laura had planned to arrive early for her interview, but not this early. Her timing was off because the landlord had been cleaning the carpets at the new apartment complex. She hadn't been able to sign the new rental agreement nor unload her pickup, and of greater concern, she wasn't able to clean herself up before the interview. She did the best possible at a service station bathroom, but she had hoped for a shower and an iron for her cotton dress.

When she pulled into the WinRight Grocery Store she was far too early. Her pickup didn't have air-conditioning so the heat would quickly destroy the curls she had just made at a Texaco gas station. The male station attendant had knocked on the door twice urging her to hurry.

"C'mon, lady. I saw you take your make-up in there. Read the sign. This is a private restroom for customers only and not some type of homeless shelter. I didn't pump any gas for you. There's a paying customer out here waiting, and that's more important than you trying to make yourself pretty."

The sweat caused her newly pressed cotton dress to cling to her side. She said a quick prayer to God for success. Neither success nor talking to God had happened much lately.

Soon her hair wasn't the only problem. The clinging cotton revealed more than she wanted and a circle of sweat started to form around her armpits. Before long she would look like one of the farmers who came into the Mint after work.

She had no choice but to go in much too early for the interview or be completely drenched and wind blown.

"Excuse me. I'm here for an interview. I didn't get an application yet. Do you know where I can get one?"Laura had chosen the one checker who didn't look busy at the time. She didn't want to bother the manager.

"Sure, I got one under my cash drawer. Have you talked with Ken yet?"

"I guess that was his name. He never did introduce himself and he didn't have a name tag. I'm suppose to meet with him at 1:30 so I'm way too early" Laura had a clear view of the wall clock that said 12:30 so she expected him to be at lunch.

"Sounds like him, forgetting his name tag. He's really a nice guy, but a scattered brain. He'll probably even forget he made the appointment. Just to let you know, don't let him try to say we don't need any help. We're really short of checkers no matter what he says There's no way I'm going to work another Sunday, so he better hire you."

"Thanks for letting me know. Where can I wait until he's free?"

"He will be free when you are. I'll make sure of that. He's

probably in the back eating his bologna sandwich with two Oreo cookies. The guy has the same lunch every day like his mom made it. How and why he can stand the same thing, I don't know. Here is a pen. Why don't you go over to the next aisle? As soon as you're done with the form, I'll make sure Ken will be free. By the way, my name is Barbara, good luck"

A customer had come to Barbara's aisle and she had begun ringing the items as she talked. "When you're ready, just go in the back through those double doors. You'll see him."

Laura filled out the application and then made her way through the swinging double doors that Barbara had indicated. The man she had spoke with yesterday was there.

"Excuse me. My name is Laura Randolph. I spoke with you yesterday, and you asked me to come back today."

Ken was unloading a box of lettuce and stacking them in neat rows. His quick dexterity showed a man who had performed the same job many times. "Sure, Laura, I'm glad you made it back. I'm sorry that I didn't have time to talk yesterday. Monday is our shipment day, and it takes all mine and everyone's attention to get it unloaded. I've been working people too much overtime as it is. Overtime pay is nice, but so is being home with the family."

Laura finally let herself breath. He seemed so nice.

"Got the application done?"

"It's all done except for my address and phone number. I just got a place at the Highline Apartments, but I forgot the address. I'll get it as soon as we're done and finish the form."

"That's no problem. I'm more concerned with the phone number. What's the deal there?"

I called from the apartment manager's office and the phone company said they could have one installed by Thursday afternoon, Friday morning at the latest. But I'll have to be there when it's being installed."

"Haven't even been hired and you're already asking for time off?"

Laura felt her face get red, but she could tell that Ken was only joking. He scanned the rest of her application indicating he didn't expect an answer.

"I see you've worked at the Mint Bar and the Glad Tidings Health Food Store. How much experience have you had with a cash drawer as a bar waitress?"

"I did most of the taking money, mopping the floors, hauling out the trash and when I had time I'd help the cook. It was a job when I needed one, but I can't say it was one that I enjoyed."

"I'm a little concerned about you working at the Mint. But I doubt any of your customers came from Fairfield. The ladies of Fairfield would love to gossip if they knew a barmaid was working at WinRight."

Laura had long ago left behind feeling bad about being a "barmaid" since that had been exactly what she was and she needed to make a living somehow, but she had never stopped to think of how others would perceive her.

"You have register experience but are you used to lines, and carts full to the brim with a farm family week's supply of groceries?"

"No, the bar was tables not lines, but it got awful busy, and the people at the health food store hardly ever had more than three or four items. But then again how many people in Fairfield have even that much experience?"

"Good answer, and quick thinking on your feet also. You said you didn't like the bar job, but you had to have a job. What would make me think that this job won't be the same and you'll be down the road in a couple months?"

"I have to admit I don't know about the future, but I do know if I got a good job and could work in a pleasant environment, I won't see any reason to leave. I talked to Barbara and she seems awful nice and you seemed very different than my old Mint boss. My first impression is I'd love to work here." Laura had felt more confident of that fact the more she talked. Now she didn't know why anyone would hire someone like her: no phone, no ties to the community, and no real experience.

"Let me be upfront with you, Laura," Ken began. Laura was ready to hear the bad news. "When I need a new employee, you would think it would be easy to find one in a small town with few jobs and a lot of farms not making it. You'd think it would be easy to find help with the wage we pay, but most women are tied to their families and guys don't want to put on an apron and get stuck inside all day.

"What I need is someone that is reliable and can pick up the job quickly. Mostly I need someone who is personable. The SaveCo store down the street is twice as big as us and they got lots of parking. What we have is people with a smile on their face. People in a place like Fairfield come to buy groceries, but they also come to visit with their friends from around the county that they might not see except for their trip to Win-Right. The same it true for them seeing a smiling, friendly face at the checkout stand. Some of the checkers are pretty new; some have been here for over 15 years. They know more about some of their customers than their own families.

"People here will put up with waiting in line for five minutes because a checker is slow, but they won't put up with a checker that doesn't care their new cat is sick or their joints hurt and the checker gets a weather forecast passed on that pain. That means something to most customers and it's the thing we rely on at my store.

"Do you think that you could handle a job like that?"

"I think I'd love a job like that."

"Well we'll soon find out. If you want the job, you start Monday. You were honest about your other jobs and honesty goes a long way with me. You can teach someone to work a register, but you can't teach honesty. I still have to call your references, but if they check out, you've got a job. When you get your phone, give me a call. I'll put you on the schedule for next week. One suggestion, the phone company isn't that busy, they just like to act like it. Bug them a little bit and they'll be out quicker."

Laura checked her excitement as she waved goodbye to Barbara who now was busy with a line of customers. The only thing she had to worry about was Ken checking her references. She could image that creep at the Mint giving her one last slap. Also she had wanted to leave Billings behind forever, and now her old friends would know her new location. But that was a risk she had to take. The WinRight just felt good. The whole move to Fairfield had seemed to come together in an almost miraculous way.

Not yet. Don't get too excited yet. Too much has happened to get too excited yet. The memories of last night still lingered in her thoughts.

Her thoughts had hardly passed through her mind when she turned the key to her pickup and there was no response. *Dead battery. Serves me right for thinking that everything was going to be okay. Nothing that easy for me.*

To her horror, Ken walked out as soon as she opened her hood.

"Well, I guess I don't have to worry about you going down the road for a better job."

Laura started to think about excuses, but Ken already had a pair of jumper cables in his hand.

"You aren't the first person this has happened to. They're a lot of "mature" cars in this county. I wind up starting three, four cars a week. Maybe I should use knowing how to use jumper cables as part of the interview. Do you know how to use these?"

"No"

"Well, I'll add that to the list of first day 'to do's'"

"My first day. I've got the job?"

"I just finished calling your references. Make sure you have clothes ready for work," Ken said with a smile.

Laura forgot to say thanks as her pickup started and left the lot, but somehow she didn't think it would matter.

Chapter Sixteen

Ken at WinRight was right. She gave the phone company another call and had a phone installed by Thursday. Ken scheduled Laura to begin her training on Friday and Saturday, take Sunday off and begin her regular shift on Monday.

Laura would train with Evelyn, the oldest and most experienced checker and who had seen everything from robbery to drunken cowboys to the rare local who thought they needed to be catered to. For the first hour Laura felt as the schoolgirl being lectured by the school matriarch. She dreaded facing two days of this. Then Barbara intervened.

'Evelyn, don't bore this girl to death with all your old stories and bad manners. We want her to stay around for a second year let alone a second day.Evelyn is from the old school, as in counting with her fingers and toes."

"Barbara, at least I can count. You're just jealous 'cause customers come to my register rather than yours. Laura here is sharp enough, she could probably take over your register and do twice your job"

"Now, Laura, before you believe her lies, know one thing, we all love each other," Barbara gave Evelyn a big hug.

"You can always tell when Barb's lost a fight, she'll come up and give you a big hug."

Evelyn's eyes sparkled as a mischievous child's. And the day went on.

There were customers who laughed at bad jokes, and customers who looked like they had never smiled. There was a small leak from the produce sprinkler that Barbara said had been there for years, and there were young stock boys who were absent when work needed to be done.

In other words, life was normal at the WinRight, and Laura felt stronger with every normal act. Here she didn't need to make excuses for the job. Here she didn't have to firmly discourage men from following her home.

Here the nightmares of the past faded and once again Laura could feel the hand of God's soft touch.

Evelyn and Barbara and Ann, the woman working the registers next to her, were as gracious as Gracie, and they were all quick to playfully joke with one another. Soon Laura found herself included.

"Laura, you better watch Matt, that stock boy who helps bag after school. He's been staring at you since the first time he saw you. He hasn't seen any one as pretty as you since the last movie he watched. Now, granted he's only a freshman in high school, but if you're willing to wait for eight years, he'll be a heck of a catch," and all the other checkers laughed as Matt was an awkward boy whose voice squeaked.

"Yeah, and in eight years I'll be old and grey and no one will want anything to do with me." Laura replied to deflect the compliment.

"Girl, you're so pretty you'll have men staring at you when you're 80 let alone eight years from now when you're, what, eighteen?" Evelyn showed in the wrinkles on her face the tough years of the plains in her advanced years, but she still carried a constant smile.

It had been a long time since Laura had felt beautiful. In those few days she began to feel it again. Things felt like they did before, and the nightmare of events didn't follow her like a shadow.

It was good, and at that point in her life, good was a giant step forward.

It was important for Laura to work that two days for the money. She would get a check, a small check, the next pay two weeks later, she would have enough money to get a few essential; Top Noodle soup, some panty hose that were required at WinRight and not at the Mint, and an extra white shirt. She could even splurge on some chocolate ice cream bars she would carefully ration for moments of pleasure.

And in all this she saw the soft hand of God.

***

She woke up earlier than she wanted on Sunday morning. She had already made the transition from graveyard to day shift, which was good unless she wanted to sleep in on her day off.She found herself making coffee at 7:30 that morning, unable to go back to sleep and with no plans for the day. She remember after her shower that she hadn't cleaned the cotton dress she wore to the interview. The only other dress she had was her barmaid dress from the Mint. She ran some water on the cotton dress to get it clean. It didn't work. Her only choice was the Mint Bar dress. She changed from jeans to dress to dress from jeans for thirty minutes. Finally she pulled on the Mint dress for good.

Well, am I going to go to church, or just sit around here all day? I could go and sit in the back unnoticed and just see how it feels. It's been a long time.

She never answered the question, but she finally chose the dress and started to curl her hair. Erik had talked to her about a church, so it would be easy to find.

The service started at 9:30 so she pulled into the gravel parking lot exactly at 9:30. Laura waited for several minutes until she saw the greeters leave the open front doors. She had been around churches enough to know the routine. If she had walked in earlier the greeters would have recognized her as a guest, and given her guest status. She wanted to be a face and that was all.

About fifty cars were parked in the lot; a small church, but still large enough for her to remain anonymous if she worked things right. She noticed the neatly groomed flowerbeds and a handmade wreath made from wheat on the front door.

The front doors had remained open to allow any breeze to make its way to the congregation, and Laura could hear singing long before she entered. Once in the main doors there was a short hallway to the left and she could see several people in the very back clapping their hands in worship as the first song started and all eyes shifted to the front. As she walking into the sanctuary, a greeter waiting for those latecomers handed her a bulletin with a softly whispered, "Welcome."

She quietly took a chair on the right aisle behind the last filled row. The sanctuary had no pews but folding chairs set in a half circle. It was so unlike the church in Billings she felt good at her first glance of it.

A curtained raised stage filled the front, but the organist and one guitarist didn't use the stage. A simple wooden podium acted as the pulpit. The most prominent feature of the church was a finely carved wooden banner shaped as a scroll that declared, "Jesus Christ, the same Yesterday, Today, and Forever." Other than that, the interior was as simple as the exterior.

Laura wasn't surprised to see Barbara from WinRight standing next to her husband and two sons. Barbara had mentioned the need to be off on Sunday so she could attend church.Laura would change the subject every time it came up.

Her thoughts went to Gracie, and she mouthed a short prayer. Laura was so tired she found it hard to focus on the service.

She thought of the WinRight and how fortunate she felt to happen on to such a good job with such good people.

"Please be seated and prepared for the offering," the worship leader directed. She was caught in mid-thought and left standing by herself. Fortunately, no one noticed her back row presence. The announcements started with the news of a Labor Day All-Church picnic.

The pastor wasn't the one leading the worship nor had he been standing in front. He had been sitting with his family with the rest of the congregation so Laura hadn't noticed him. Except for the sports jacket he looked like many of the men in Fairfield; mid-40's, shoulders slumping with too many hours of work, hair cut short but neatly combed

The microphone squealed as the pastor attached it to his lapel. The pastor didn't wear a tie in the summer heat, and with sweat on his brow, Laura wished he would lose the brown blazer as well. A microphone didn't seem necessary in that small of a room, but his soft voice made it a requirement.

Now as he rose and took his position and began his sermon, Laura felt as if she was sitting in a living room with a pastor casually chit-chatting. His tone was so soft she had problems staying awake as the usual announcements were made and her head began to drop then jerk up. At one point she was starting to realize what the pastor was talking about. Laura sat straight up with her hands on her barmaid dress.

"Today, I would like to talk about God's holiness. Holiness means purity, but purity needs to be viewed in its full context."

"Many times we think of holiness as not drinking or smoking or cursing, all those things that are observed by us. We see holiness as a state of "not doing" but holiness is really a state of "doing". Holiness is doing the right thing. The right thing goes well beyond the laws of the Old Testament. The right thing is to love your neighbor and yourself. The right thing is to trust in His love, and His peace and His forgiveness. God is holy because these things are a part of His very nature."

"God is holy because there is no variance in His life or nature. He doesn't love us one day and then disown us the next. He doesn't provide forgiveness one day and take it away the next. He never changes and His view of us never changes. There are no shadows of grey in His life. He is Light and there is no darkness. He is consistent.

"If you could see a perfectly pure white cloth with no marks or stains that covered as far as you could see, you would see the consistency of that pure white. That would represent the consistency of God's actions toward you. If there were any flaw in that white sheet it would be obvious since it would be so unlike the pure white. If you could see God's nature you would see the obvious pureness that carries no flaws, His pureness, and His holiness would be obvious because there is no inconsistency in the fiber of His being. Every thought and every action He has for you is consistently out of Love and Mercy.

"Then we look at our own lives. We aren't always loving and patient. We see our flaws and wonder how someone so flawed could be with Him who is so perfect."

Laura shifted in her seat wondering how she could have picked such a Sunday with such a topic to come to church. Her thoughts took her away from the pastor's words.

"We can easily come to the conclusion that He doesn't want anything to do with our stained lives. And what is His response to our flaws? He doesn't change. He still loves. He still is patient with us. He still desires our presence. As long as we don't walk away from Him, He won't walk away from us, and He sent His son who died for us so that our stains are washed away.

"When God looks at you all He sees is the love He has for you, and the desire to be your Father.

"By nature we have flaws and we do sin. We haven't arrived yet. In the midst of our inconsistency we must remember His consistency.

"Just imagine if every room and every square foot of your house was covered by a perfectly white carpet. You have just come home from the county fair and you forget to take off your shoes. Even if you had taken off your shoes, you feet would still be soiled with the dust and sweat of the day. Just imagine what would happen when you stepped on that perfectly white carpet. That carpet would no longer be perfectly white. It would carry the marks of your day at the fair."

"You could try as hard as possible to keep that carpet white, but as hard as you tried the soil of the day would dirty that rug. The carpet would no longer be pure white.

"Now I can see all the wives shuddering at the thoughts of a white carpet and what it would take to keep it white. You wives know it isn't possible for you to keep that carpet perfectly white. Sooner or later some accident of some idiot, excuse me men, would bring a stain to that rug, and wives you could spend your whole day trying to keep it pure and white. It still would drive you crazy after a while.

"The stain of sin will and has touched all of our lives. We need to know that is our nature, but it is the nature of our Saviour to love us and by His blood to wash the stains away. We need to know the consistency of God's holiness and Christ's sacrifice to consistently wash that sin pure white. We can't do it. His pure love for us, and forgiveness of us, and hope for us can."

At that point Laura's attention was drawn from the church to her memory of the room where she had lost her child. That room in her mind was now covered with a white carpet but it was covered red with the child's innocent blood. She looked down in disgust and could only see the dress that reminded her she was just a common barmaid. She still heard the pastor talking, but only a phrase here and there that she never fully understood.

His words continued, but unheard by Laura: "The Word states in Romans 10:19-23

"Therefore, brothers and sisters, since we have confidence to enter the Most Holy Place by the blood of Jesus, by a new and living way opened up for us through the curtain, that is his body, and since we have a great high priest over the house of God, let us draw near to God with a sincere heart with full assurance of faith, having our hearts sprinkled to cleanse us from a guilty conscience and having our bodies washed with pure water. Let us hold unswervingly to the hope we professed for he who promised is faithful."

"We don't have to stand back separated from Him because of our stains. We don't have to be followed by guilt because He is holy and His love and forgiveness is sufficient for all times. He has broken down the barriers. We're urged to draw close to him with a sincere heart, not to sit back in guilt. His sacrifice of blood for us gives us full assurance that His love will never end, for He is holy."

Laura's vision of that room swirled in her head until she felt herself physically sick. She turn her head as if to avoid the sight of her child.

That white carpet and her stain was all she could see.

It has to be my fault. I have stained my life and His love, and taken my child's life with my sin.

Pastor Hodgson continued to call the congregation to embrace His forgiveness, but Laura didn't hear.

No tears came to Laura's eyes. She did not cry. She held her head between her hands, hard.

Suddenly, a baby began to cry in the first row. The cry seemed to echo off the walls and Laura thought she heard the cry of her own child, and she became sick in her stomach at such a thought. Laura had to get out and quickly. She didn't recognize that at the same time the mother was carrying her child to the nursery. The mother and child and Laura bumped hard in the aisle as Laura sprang from her chair, and Laura reached out to prevent them from falling.

"I'm sorry" Laura said. "I wasn't looking. I should have been looking. It's all my fault." Laura saw the mother's expression move from shock to a look of forgiveness.

"That fine. I didn't see you either."

The baby quit crying with the change of events and looked directly at Laura. The baby girl had a bow tied to the small amount of hair on her head. She was held to her mother's side, but a smile quickly formed as she looked at the stranger. Her eyes were big and brown and beautiful. She wore a lace filled dress that appeared hand-made, and as Laura had reached to prevent a fall, the baby reached her arms back to her. Her hand touched Laura's bare arms, and Laura saw what her baby would have looked like.

The three walked to the foyer. Laura couldn't take her eyes off the baby. The mother shifted the child to her other hip and went right when Laura went left. She glanced back to make sure Laura wasn't following.

Laura recognized the look of fear in the mother's eyes. She had to get out of there. She fled out the front door and went to the back corner of the building and vomited.

Chapter Seventeen

In summer on the Northern Great Plains the sun raises so early it usually meets even the earliest riser. It's the best part of the day with fresh coolness making a person forget the coming heat, and quiet allowing thoughts to run without interruption. For the last few mornings that quiet met Erik as he left the bunkhouse before the sun arose with only the slight hint of color beginning to form on the horizon.

On the two previous days his early rising was rewarded with time to think. Later in the day his mind would be filled with the work of the day, and problems that needed to be fixed. For years the evening hours had been times of daydreaming. Now his mornings were the time to think clearly of the present.

This day he got up early to avoid going to church. He knew that Uncle Henry would come to the bunkhouse to get him. He'd have to have an excuse, so he would be busy with work that he'd claim couldn't be stopped. It was now one week since he had first met his Lord. It only made sense and was expected for him to go to church with his aunt and uncle, or at least go by himself to the New Life Chapel.

I'll go next week. I'm just afraid people will make too big a deal of me being saved. It is a big deal, but I don't want people telling me so.

Earlier in the week, Uncle Henry had come to the bunkhouse carrying a Remington 30/06 hunting rifle. "If you aren't too busy you might do me a favor and sight-in this rifle for me. I hear the mule deer have gathered in the few green ravines of the Sweet Grass Hills. I thought if you were so inclined we could both go up there and get some venison steaks and jerky. If they've been feeding off the grass of those ravines their meat'll taste more like beef than venison."

Erik appreciated the gesture. His uncle hadn't been hunting in years and the rifle would have to be carefully cleaned before it could be trusted to shoot. He knew neither he nor his uncle would ever have the time to go hunting, since the hunting season was in the midst of harvest, but Henry had come to give Erik something to do rather than lay in his room and that was appreciated.

" Your aunt and I will be leaving for church at eight on Sunday. Can we give you a ride?

"Thanks, but I need some time to think before I do anything."

"That's you choice. The offer stands any time you want it."

"And I will take that offer, just not yet." Erik immediately went back into the bunkhouse. Later he found some oil that worked to clear the muzzle and shine the stock, and then he put the rifle away until it was needed.

That Sunday the rifle was needed for a distraction to the day. Stopping by the shop he found an old, discarded and rusted baby moon hubcap from an old Chevy. It was an ideal target.

The ideal place to make a firing range was the coulee behind the farmhouse. He set the hubcap on the opposite ridge of the ravine, slightly below the level he would sit once he returned to his spot. In this manner he had created the distance and the position where he could most likely find a buck deer in the Sweetgrass Hills. He knew they would get busy and never go to the hills, but at least this day he could prepare as if they would.

Erik ran hard back to the spot he had chosen for his blind. He'd be breathing hard when he took a real shot so he needed to be winded now. If there really was a buck across the way, his heart would be pounding much faster than normal.

As he squeezed the trigger for the first shot it was obvious either his shooting skills or the sights of the rifle had become rusty. He fired off three other quick shots to see if a pattern was created for him to adjust the sights. The dirt flying from each bullet's impact were all high, but one was high right, one high left, and one high to the middle. He adjusted the front V of the sight a hair lower, and laughed at his own inaccuracy.

"Well, at least I can blame part of this on the old gun. The rest I can blame on the wind, which there is none, or not eating breakfast, or me being out of shape. It couldn't be that I'm just a lousy shot." Erik talked to himself a lot on the farm. There was no one else to talk to, so he talked to himself, and even laughed at his own jokes from time to time. The game of sighting in the rifle made his conversation with himself almost natural, as if someone else was there.

Erik put four more shells in the chamber. There was something about the simple pleasure of doing something different from the usual chores that allowed Erik to relax. After every shot he would make comments aloud to no one. The backfire of the light rifle was light to Erik's shoulder. The sensation was enough to make Erik feel he was at a hunt with others. He freely talked and laughed and joked to himself.

"I bet there isn't a hubcap in the county that isn't holding tight to the wheel not wanting to face Black Bart, formerly know as Erik Winter.

"On second thought, maybe the safest thing to be in the county is a hubcap. They're small enough I'll never hit them anyway. Everything else in a ten yard radius better worry though, cause that's about how close I'll be."

Erik was refreshed with the chance to forget everything and simply shoot the gun. *It would be nice to have someone to shoot with and enjoy my witty personality. If only they won't put in with asking all their questions.*

He only had one box of shells so he would shoot a few, readjust the sights, and rest in the renewed quiet of the morning before he reloaded. There was no reason to leave the coulee.

He had lingered longer than expected when he heard a voice behind him.

"Hey, did you shoot anything to bring home for dinner?"

Erik flinched with surprise. He was embarrassed that someone would know he was talking to himself, but he knew John's voice even before he turned to see him.

"If you want to eat sod, I've got a lot of it this morning." Erik said. "I've been trying to bag the rare, silver humped cap animal all morning, but it's too crafty for me. What are you doing here? Shouldn't you be in church?"

"Yes, I should, and I should be there with you. Pack up your ammo, and if we get moving we'll only be a few minutes late."

"Did my aunt and uncle rat on me again?" Erik's voice made it clear he wouldn't be mad if they had. "Can't anyone just live without everyone caring about them?"

"I know a lot of people who aren't cared for, but you aren't one of them. Now let's get going. I came out on my own accord to give you a ride and here I find you killing all those helpless blades of grass."

"They were dead before I got here. I wasn't planning on going to church today. I thought I'd spend some time in the Bible and have my own service in the temple of His coulee. Say that wouldn't be a bad name for my new church."

"Your church needs a few more parishioners. I was planning on taking you, and my plans over-ride your plans."

Erik gave up without a fight. He knew John wouldn't give up, and it might be good to be in church now that he knew whom he was worshipping. The rifle and shells were quickly gathered. Another few minutes in the bunkhouse and Erik came out dressed in slacks and a dress shirt. He headed for John's car where John waited for him.

"How does it feel being His child after one week?" John's blue Buick was freshly washed and the air conditioning made it feel like a luxury car to Erik. He had on his nicer cloths, but he was still afraid he might dirty the car by his very presence. The gravel roads had just received a fresh sheet of gravel and he would hate for John's car to get chip marks. If the car's interior was stained or the paint chipped it would be Erik' fault that John had to come to pick him up.

"I've spent a lot of time talking to Him the last week. If that's praying, it makes it a lot easier when you know someone is listening."

"Where did you go when you left Monday?"

"I went to the Park. There's a great hike to Chief Mountain that not many people know about. It gave me time to think...."

John interrupted Erik before he could get into a long, detailed story. "Great, but I'm not here to quiz you. I've done enough of that this week. I just want to make sure you're doing okay. I would like to get to be your friend, and it's hard to be friends if every time you get together you're involved in a heavy, deep discussion."

"I'm about as deep as the topsoil on that hilltop. I do appreciate the thought, however. I know Aunt Mary is going to sit me down pretty soon, but a whole lot has happened in a week and I do need to sort it out," Erik explained.

"Speaking about things happening, the strangest thing happened on the way back on Monday night. You know the waitress I tried to protect and got my jaw cracked for my effort? I saw her at the Point. Turns out she is a Christian, got fired because of the fight and is trying to move to Fairfield."

"Got fired? Didn't you say you went to the Mint to see her?

"Yeah, I did."

"Boy you know how to impress the ladies; getting her fired from a job is a new approach."

"She said it wasn't my fault. The boss wanted to fire her, and she wanted to get away from him and that place, anyway. But it was kind of a shock. I thought I'd never see her again, and it turns out she's a Christian. Sounds like she had an experience like mine several years ago."

"How's she doing now?"

"I don't really know. I asked her about her, you know, life with Christ. She got real defensive, said she'd walked away from Him. She sure has some problems with something."

Erik could tell by John's tone when he began speaking that a warning was coming. "People go through a lot of things in this world. Just because a person got saved several years ago doesn't always indicate where they're at today."

206 ~ Bart Tuma

"Well, she asked me where she could find a good church so maybe she's trying. Like I say it was just strange since my encounter with Christ started with going to see her."

"God had it all planned out before you were even born, Erik. Was there any significance that this girl started the process? Who knows? I do know IF He started the process through this girl that He uses all the tools He needs."

Erik was done talking about Laura. He had thought about her a lot in the last week, but he still hadn't decided what to think of the situation. The rules had changed now. Laura had become more than a daydream. Now she was real, and Christ was real, and everything was different. He hadn't known Christ for a long enough time to make sense out of all this. Besides he certainly wouldn't know what to do with a girl friend if he had one. He changed the subject. "How's the carpentry business? Doesn't seem like there would be enough work in a small town like Fairfield."

The ride to town went quickly and quietly.

When they arrived in front of the church, the lot was filled with cars. The doors remained wide open, but the greeters were no longer present at its entranceway, indicating that the services had already started. Erik said, "I want to make some things clear before we go in. I'm here to listen and not to talk.

"I don't want you to say anything to anyone about me.I want to sit and listen and see what it's like to be in a service without wondering how come it lasted so long. I do want to be here, but I don't want to be looked at as some type of new specimen that needs to be examined."

John nodded his head in agreement. "No problem. I have the ground rules, now you just relax and listen. We're already twenty minutes late so if there is a commotion you can blame it on yourself." He parked the car and they both got out and headed towards the church. Movement from the corner facing them caught Erik's attention. It was a girl moving to stand erect after having been obviously bent at the waist. She moved one shaky hand to the side of the church, supporting herself, while simultaneously releasing her hair from her other hand where she had cupped the long brown locks into a makeshift ponytail held back from her face. It was Laura. Not only did he recognize her by her height, her shape and the color of her long hair, but she wore the same dress she wore to the Mint.

Erik stopped in mid-stride. "John, I know her. It looks like she needs help."

"How do you know her?"

"It's Laura, the one I talked about"

"Oh, boy," were John's only words. He could only shake his head. *What has this boy gotten himself into?*

Erik didn't say anything until he was right next to Laura, who was again bent over.

"Laura, are you okay?"

Laura tried to spit her mouth clean and wiped herself with the back of her hand. She gave Erik a baleful look as she straightened. "I'm just great, can't you tell." She dug in her purse for a tissue. "Were did you come from? Did anyone else see me? I guess I must have...must have eaten something bad, but I'm fine now."

"No, just us. We came late to church and saw you here."

"Never seen a case of food poisoning that went away that fast," were John's first words to Laura.

Laura looked at the man who challenged her. She was used to men with smart mouths like this.

"Laura, this is John," Erik interceded as he saw the challenging look on both their faces.

"Nice to meet you, John," Laura said in a non-committal tone. "and, Erik, you might want to add this to the list of weird things that girl from Sweetgrass does. I knew I shouldn't have come today, so, my fault." Laura's attempt to straighten herself and make light of the situation made her forget the baby's face. "I just have to get somewhere to clean myself up."

"There's a kitchen in the back of the church. You can go in through that door and no one will see you" John's voice was still harder than Erik had ever heard.

Laura gave a curt nod of thanks. She made her way to the door John had indicated and Erik sensed that she would use the kitchen and leave post-haste. He couldn't blame her if that were her intention, not after the tone John had taken with her.

"What was that all about?" Erik asked as Laura disappeared into the kitchen. "You sounded like you wanted to bite her head off. She's my friend. I'd expect you to treat her with a little kindness."

"What do you mean?I was nice to her."

"You were nicer to a stranger in the restaurant last week. Your voice was sharper than I've ever heard it."

"Sorry, Erik, but it was a surprise to see the girl you've been talking about outside the church vomiting. Who knows what her story is?It looks to me like she could be hung over from a big drunk last night."

"You didn't talk to me that way when I'd just been in a bar fight! What, do you just not like women?"

"I've got nothing against women, but you've got to remember it was only a couple hours ago you were wondering if maybe God might be bringing you two together. You've got to be careful. Don't go running off like God's going to be pleased with everything you do or that you no longer have to use your head--"

Their conversation was cut short as Laura returned.

"Laura, I'm not sure want you meant by saying you should have never come today, but it's pretty obvious you're hurting more than a stomach ache. There's a rest area right at the west city limits. It's nice and overlooks the Fairfield River. Let go's there and talk," John suggested.

"I still have to unpack, so I think I'll pass."

"Laura, I think you're facing a losing argument. John'll keep hounding you until you say yes. It's a nice little spot with a couple of big oak trees and there will be other people there," Erik urged.

John interceded with a much softer voice. 'I'd really like to know what happened. This is my church, and I need to know if there was a misunderstanding or what happened.

Besides, it's pretty obvious something is wrong that needs to be talked out."

"Okay, I'll follow you, but I can't stay long. I still have unpacking to do, and this is my only day off." Laura surprised Erik by agreeing. Laura noticed the over eager look on Erik's face and quickly added, "It's just because I have the time. Nothing else."

"Good," John said. "We're going to stop and get some cold pop at the gas station. Can I get you something?"

"Sure I appreciate that. I'll take a bottle of 7-Up for my stomach."

Erik picked a park picnic table close to the ravine that carried the Fairfield River, which was more a small creek at this time of year. John handed Laura her pop and they all sat down, Laura on the bench opposite the two men across the table from her.

"Laura, Erik tells me I was sharp at the church, but I didn't mean to be. You just caught me off guard. Sorry about that.

"What do you mean, caught you off guard? Aren't you used to seeing girls getting sick at the corner of the church?"

Laura asked. "I'm the one who should be apologizing." She turned to Erik. "And as for you, Erik, I would have told John if he was rude. I'm a big girl. If I have a complaint, I'll tell you." Laura made it clear she didn't want pity or help.

"Laura, I know what you're talking about. That's what I've been telling him for years," John agreed.

"For years? I've only known you for a week."

"Well, it's seem like years having to put up with all your problems."

The playful sparring made everyone relaxed. Laura took the opportunity to start the conversation.

"If you're wondering if I had come to church to worship or to use the side of the building, I'd come to worship. It's just that some things that were said were unsettling. I hope I don't look like a charity case that needs help."

"I'd have to say we all need help from time to time," John interjected, but he knew Laura wasn't done.

"Something happened a while back. I've been trying to leave it behind. I thought I had and then today the sermon brought it all back. John, I'm a Christian and a bad one.Erik, I said I was no good the other night. I committed a sin against God, and I'd told myself and my friends and God it was something I would never do. I lied. I did it."

John said, "Hate to tell you, but we all are sinners, and we all have made mistakes we can never forget. Good thing for us we have a God who does forgive."

"I know that, John, but every time I convince myself that God does forgive me, has forgiven me, something happens that brings it all back, like the sermon today. The pastor talked about God's holiness being as a white sheet of pureness and all I could see was the stain of my mistake.I got sick to my stomach when I saw that sin, as if I had done it that second. Then when I was leaving, I bumped into a mother and her child. The child reached out to me as if she was my own. The baby touched me. The baby looked so vulnerable and I yet I felt more vulnerable than the child."

Erik wanted to say something, but couldn't.His silence pushed him further away from John and Laura.

John's said with a firm voice, "I know the pastor very well. If he talked about the holiness of God being pure, I know he had something else to say."

"He might of, but all I could think of is how much I'd failed. I know God forgives and all that, but I know what I did."

"So I guess that only leaves one question: what is more important, what you did or who God is? Seems to me you're looking at your problem, but you're no longer looking at God."

John continued, "We've got to be careful to not define God by our circumstances. If we are in a problem then we tend to see the problem first and how we perceive God changes with the problem. Suddenly He's forgotten us, or doesn't care or isn't close enough. But the reality is if there is a problem, that doesn't mean God changes. He's the same God. He doesn't change. He is always the same. He is consistent."

"I know that word. The pastor talked about consistency today, but I don't know what he was saying about it."

"You can't define God by circumstances. You define God by who He is," John said.

"Laura, you have to take your attention off what you did and remember what *He* did. He gave His life for you, and the Word said that His forgiveness and love doesn't end. He doesn't love you any less because you sinned. Don't let yourself believe anything else. He wants to embrace you like He did the first time you met Him."

John was finished talking. Laura fell into silence, thinking.

Erik sat involved in his own thoughts. He didn't know how to feel. When he dreamed of Laura in the bunkhouse this was never part of the picture. When he talked with her at the Point he had hoped she had been sent by God to be part of his life. Indeed, he thought as all three sat in silence, "*was she sent by God in all these strange circumstances to be part of my life for me, or for her to see God again?*"

A little poodle dog stopped next to the picnic table to bark at a nearby collie. The little dog alternated barking at the collie and darting behind Erik, using Erik as a shield. All three laughed of the absurdity of such a small dog trying to intimidate the bigger one.

"That reminds me of Erik trying to fight that big farmer. It wasn't a fair fight from the first punch," Laura teased.

"But, boy, that was a great first punch," Erik said, not minding her ribbing.

Chapter Eighteen

Laura knew exactly what John was talking about. She knew all the right words; *saved by grace and not by works, He makes all things new, if He saved us when we were yet sinners how much more does He love us now.* She went over those words in her mind time and time again the next week back at work.

She rehearsed those words at her first full week at Win-Right. When there was a pause as one customer finished and another emptied their carts, Laura remembered those words. She remember them when she went in the break room and pulled out her home made yogurt and fruit parfait. She looked around the cluttered break room and couldn't believe how her fortunes had changed, even when her break ended, and the morning quickly passed.

"Any chance your till might actually balance today?" Ken joked as he came to Laura's line and put a "Closed" sign at the head of the counter. Actually, Laura had done very well at the register, never being off more than a few pennies at the end of the shift. Considering she was new and had to key in thousands of items every shift, she had done amazingly well. At the same time Ken was in a good mood since it was Friday, and this Friday was the start of the county fair.

Friday was the day of running extra errands as he went to the bank to square things up for the weekend, making sure they didn't have excessive cash on hand, but enough cash to run the store until Monday morning. He counted out Laura's drawer in preparation for the early run when he deposited all the money up until noon, and he would pick up the coin. Later he would simply put the evening deposit in the bank's drop box.

There wasn't much money in Laura's till since Ken periodically took the larger bills. Laura was amazed at how fast he could count her money. She had already jokingly accused him of making her look bad by his quick counting while she was so slow. Years of doing the same task had allowed his chubby fingers to move instinctively.

Ken raised his voice in a mock game barker's chant that were in town that weekend for the Cascade County Fair. *"We have a winner here today, folks. Give the lady a teddy bear. She has actually finished five hours with no errors. If she can make it three more we'll give her a giant panda."*

At first Laura turned red, feeling the stares of the customers in the store, but then she responded in a much lower voice to Ken. "I'll shove that panda in your mouth if you don't keep it down. If you make a scene every time I balance, I'll make sure I never do it again. Maybe you should join the fair yourself." Laura had only been at the store for a week, but was already accustomed to the verbal jousting.

"Great idea! Everybody loves the fair, and my wife and I can live in a camper and hit the highway and become part of the carnival."

Every year in August the date of the county fair was marked in bold on calendars. The stores would be fuller than usual and almost every one in a three county area would come to Fairfield for the horse races, the cotton candy, or to exhibit their prize rabbits. Laura had never been to the fair since she had no one to go with, but the talk of everyone else at least made her feel that something different was around. Anything different was a good thing in Fairfield.

"But until then I'm going to the bank," Ken said. "Since you're closed, take your lunch and I'll be back before you're done."

"I can't wait, the store will probably fall apart while you're gone," she teased. Even in the short time she had been there Laura had appreciated working for Ken. He didn't take his job or himself too seriously and allowed other people to do the same.

When Laura got to the break room, she found Barbara and a box boy already there.

"You're on break or lunch?" Barbara asked.

"Ken sent me on lunch a little early since he closed me to count me. He's making a quick trip to the bank." Laura pulled a plastic container from the fridge and put its contents of beans and rice and chicken in a pot on the lone hotplate. She had gotten into the habit of making a large pot of the casserole and then eating it for the rest of the week.

Barbara said, "I guess I better get out there. I don't want Evelyn and Ann to get swamped, and I'm over my time anyway." But Barbara still stopped to talk. "How have you been? We've been so busy with the fair I haven't had a chance to talk. I saw you in church. Did you like it?"

Laura had the feeling that Barbara could keep talking and forget about getting back to work. Laura didn't want to talk anyway. She had said everything to Erik and John. She went to the hotplate and stirred her rice to look occupied and kept her answers short.

"I'm doing fine, just fine. Yes, I liked the church. I'll be back, but I don't want to keep you from going back to work with my boring life. We'll talk later."

The box boy left soon after Barbara. He felt uncomfortable eating with Laura as all the boys had talked about how pretty she was, and he was just a box boy. He left before his break was done.

The solitude felt good to Laura after the busy morning. She carefully picked out the chicken from the rice and slowly ate. Her back was to the door and she didn't notice who entered. Slowly it dawned on her that whoever it was was just standing there, staring at her back. Then she heard words in a voice that made her blood run cold.

"There's my lovely Laura. Damn, you look great!" She

knew that voice, had heard it a million times in her nightmares. She knew who it was before she turned to see him, but she still froze in disbelief when she finally forced herself to turn.

It was Marcus the man who had raped her. She said nothing, all her effort going to merely trying to draw a breath. He stood at the entrance to the break room and she immediately felt trapped.

"What are you doing here?" her words were very weak. "How did you find me here?"

I met you boss going out the door and he said I would find you in the back. What a nice guy. I think he liked me. I didn't have to look to find you in Fairfield. I'm working at Healthy Time, and when we got a call checking your references, I couldn't wait to see you."

"You're working at Healthy Time? What about Linda? Didn't Linda say anything?" Linda was the one person who was most upset about Laura getting pregnant and sinning against the Lord. She was the one who told Laura she could no longer work at Healthy Time, and yet she hired Marcus.

"Linda accepted the fact that I made a mistake and that I've repented. Actually, I've learned a lot from all of this and my walk is closer to Him than ever." Marcus had a laugh in his voice as he mentioned the Lord.

Laura cut him off before he could say anything more. She had heard all his lines before and this was typical Marcus talk.

"What happened to your great job in Denver that you had

to leave so fast to take?"

"Laura, I can sense a spirit of bitterness in your voice. I can understand that. I heard you lost the baby. I was as devastated as you were when I heard the news. I was coming back and I hoped to make the three of us a family. But, I guess the Lord just had other plans. His will be done. I lost that great job cause I wanted to build a family, and I found myself broke in Billings. So they gave me a job at the HealthRight store. It's great to see you again."

Laura couldn't even answer. *How could he even imply that he was as devastated as me? He didn't see that blood. He didn't feel the child alive, and then not. What a creep. If I could believe anything out of his mouth it would be one thing. It's the same ole Marcus. How dare he come to my world?*

"I'm told there's a nice little steakhouse in Valier. Your boss said your shift was over at 5:00. That'll give me time to check into a hotel and clean up and we can have a nice dinner and talk about the future."

Laura was still unable to respond. If she had, she would have screamed so the whole store would hear. Dinner, a hotel room, and talk about the future: he's not wasting any time. At least last time he told several weeks of his lies before he made his move. He's so pitiful, she'd laugh in his face if she weren't so sick even just seeing him.

"Sorry, I've got a busy life and I have to get back to work. Nice seeing you, but I don't want to see you again," was all

Laura could muster as she headed out of the break room. She tried to maneuver around him, skirting as far away from him as possible. He still didn't quit despite her abrupt ending of their meeting, but reached out for her as she tried to dart past. Her skin moved in revulsion as she felt him put his arm around her waist just below her belt line.

"Laura, I know you're hurt and bitter. I have it coming, but the Word says you need to forgive me in order for yourself to receive forgiveness. Let's start over from the beginning."

Laura evaded the man's hand and her pace didn't slow. She knew better than to respond at this point, and sought the refuge of her work and register. He followed even faster and once again put his hand on her hip. Laura could no longer hold back.

Chapter Nineteen

Erik's week could not have been better. He was thrilled at three encounters with Laura in one week's time, and he felt a kinship had been formed. Her life had faced many hardships, but so had Erik's. It was so perfect. It seemed so planned; first his bunkhouse dreams of her, the fight for her which ended in him finding the Lord, the "chance" meeting at the Point and the perfect timing at the church. No person could have orchestrated these events.

The workweek was also easy on the farm. The summer fallow had been plowed and it was two weeks before hay season and then harvest. The only chores were getting the machines ready for haying and harvest. This meant Erik and Henry could work in the shade of the shop and eat every meal at the dinner table rather than from a paper bag. Erik could finish the workday without a layer of dust on his body and he was in the bunkhouse early to study the Scriptures between his thoughts of Laura.

It was also the week of the Cascade County Fair that was an opportunity to get away from the farm and all the questions of the last few days. As long as he could remember the farm

224 - Bart Tuma

would shut down, and they would all go to the fair. Erik loved the taste of the fair's Pronto Pups. They weren't like the corn dogs he could find at the store or bought at a service station. These Pronto Pups were fat with dough and the covering had a taste that could not be duplicated. He'd spend more money than he would admit to win a stuffed animal at the games, and then watch the younger kids ride The Whirling Storm.

Friday was the best day to attend. Thursday was set up day, and the weekend was too crowded on the midway. Friday was perfect. When the family quit work at noon and he changed to his town clothes, he had his plans set. He hadn't told John or his aunt and uncle, he knew what their response would be, but he had planned all week to stop by the WinRight store and see if Laura wanted to go to the fair. He would pick up a few items as if that was the only reason he was there, and then he rehearsed what he would say to Laura.

"Laura, how has your week been? I got off early to go to the fair. It happened at the last minute so I'm just going alone, but I would be glad to show you around if you want to go." Erik had practiced the words for days in the bunkhouse. He chose the words carefully to make sure it didn't look like a date. He wanted to give her the opportunity to say no, and for him not to look like a fool if she did. It was a perfect plan, and one that held his thoughts for the past days.

He checked his hair in the rearview mirror when he pulled in front of the WinRight store, and brushed his pants of any last dust as he walked in the front door.

Erik hadn't seen Laura at the checkout stand so he checked the aisles to see if she was stocking shelves. As he came to the end of aisle Nine, he caught a glimpse of her to his right at the far side of the produce section. He saw her, but she didn't see him. When he came closer he saw a man with her. Erik first thought it was a boyfriend she hadn't bothered to mention.

He had never seen the man before. He knew he wasn't from Fairfield. He wore a leather coat on a hot August day, and no one from Fairfield would do that. Erik didn't know him, but Laura obviously did as the man arm was forcefully holding her waist. Erik stopped his approach. His first guess was wrong. Erik felt Laura's panic. This wasn't a friend. Laura pulled loose to escape. It was clear she was in trouble. Laura shook loose from the man's hand at her waist and turned to walk away. The man once again put his arm around Laura, and his grip seemed even more forceful. Laura spun in anger to face him.

Erik moved as quickly as he had at the Mint Bar. But this time his mind moved even quicker.

"Laura, there you are," Erik said loudly. "I was afraid you had already gone home to change. I know I said I'd pick you up at five, but I thought I'd see if we could go earlier." He then looked at the man with no hesitation in his voice as he continued.

"Laura and I are going to go to the fair. We talked about it all week." He then looked back to Laura. "I'm sorry I'm early,

I can come back at five if you prefer."

Laura's looked changed from "what?" to "I understand."

"No, actually right now is perfect. I just got done with my last break and I'm sure Ken will let me off early. We've been slow today. Marcus, I think you can find your way out of the store, and Highway 2 will take you to the Interstate back to Billings."

Marcus realized he had no alternative but to give a last insult. "I can find the way just fine. Nothing I care about here, anyway."

"You're right. There's nothing for you here, so I would expect never to see you here again."Erik was as surprised to hear the conviction in his voice as he had been when he punched the farmer.

"Have it your way. I got mine," Marcus shouted over his shoulder as he walked down the aisle.His own vanity made him look back so he could see the shocked look on their faces. Instead he saw Laura in a tight embrace with the other guy.

Laura had grabbed Erik to give a clear message to Marcus, but she held the hug longer and harder than planned. She finally slid away, but stayed much closer than normal. Neither spoke for a long minute.

"Well, I hope more strangers give you a hard time if I get a hug like that."

Laura blushed. "I'm sorry."

"Sorry for what?'

"For being in strange situations every time I see you, but thanks, Erik. Your timing couldn't have been better." Even after the long hug, Laura was visibly shaking,

"I guess you really are my knight in shining armor, but this time I hope I don't get fired." Laura looked around to see how many people had seen her push Marcus away. Only Barbara and the box boy seemed to have seen what happened. The box boy wouldn't say a word except maybe to his friends with a much-expanded story. Laura presumed Barbara wouldn't get her in trouble.

"Who was that guy? Some guy you seeing?"

"No, no way. I knew him for a short time and it's a long story that I don't want to go into. Ken called my old job in Billings for a reference and that guy found out I was working here. That guy is like a vulture. How dare he come close to me?" Laura's shaking had ceased as it was replaced with anger towards all of Billings.

She couldn't get too mad since Erik would want to know more, and Ken was just getting back from the bank. Barbara whispered something to Ken and he headed straight to Laura

"Laura what's going on? Are you okay?"

"That man you talked to is no friend of mine. Ken, if that man ever comes into this store again, please let me know first so I can leave out the back door. He is not my friend, and I'll call the police if he comes back here again."

"I'm sorry, I didn't know. He seemed like a nice guy and

he said the right things." Ken was more occupied by being ashamed of his mistake than any thought of reprimanding Laura "I won't do it again."

"It's not your fault. He can seem like an awful nice guy. I fell for that myself. I just don't want anything to do with him. I know we're busy, but if I can I'd like to take a couple more minutes break. I need to sit down."

"No, you can't take a break, but you can go home." At her devastated look, he quickly added, "No, you're not fired. I should be the one fired. It's company policy to ask you before I even let anyone know you work here. I can see you're shaken up, and it's probably better if you just go home. People are starting to go to the fair now, so we'll be slow for the rest of the day. Go home and rest up or go to the fair and have a good time. Don't worry, I'll clock you out at five so you won't lose any hours."

"Thank you," Laura reached over, touched Ken's arm. In the last ten minutes she had shown more thankfulness to a man than she had in the last nine months. "I'd take you to the fair if I had any money.'

"You're really trying to get me in trouble, aren't you, Laura. The others girls are going to see me letting you go home early and then hear you wanted to take me to the fair. They won't let me forget this one." Ken once again turned to humor to change the subject. "Why don't you take this guy to the fair? Even better, let him take you."

Chapter Twenty

For four days every August the dirt lots just east of Fairfield would be changed from a piece of useless land to a sea of sound and flashing lights of brilliantly colored rides. The caravan of trucks would pull into the fairgrounds on Wednesday after leaving Havre on their summer circuit.

There were a few other buildings on the grounds: a small grandstand in front of an oval track encircled by a faded white fence for horse-racing, three other buildings would be filled with 4-H and FFA projects, roosters, cows, sheep, goats, hogs, rabbits and other animals carrying the hopes of farm teenagers for ribbons, or crafts and pies with the wives hoping for the same, and slick vendors demonstrating food processors and always sharp knives.

For the majority of adults and all of the kids the focus of their attention would be the carnies as they hammered in the first stakes and raised the first ride. There was the "Zipper" and the "Whirling Saucers" and "Himalayan Express" with the calmer Ferris wheel and small kids' rides of miniature locomotives and the carved horses of the Merry Go Round.

To get to the rides they would have to walk through a

gauntlet of games with barkers telling the girls how pretty they were and challenging the boys to prove their manhood by knocking down the bowling pins or keeping the ball in the wicker basket. "It's easy; let me show you how to do it. Your honey, there, doesn't just need a teddy bear to carry home, she needs a giant bear. We have the biggest one on the midway."

For those days, the talk of drought and failed crops was changed to laughter with the eyes of the children filled with awe. It was a medicine that the town needed and Laura and Erik were no exception.

They walked together down through the maze of games once Erik had convinced Laura she really needed to come. He could tell by her calm hands that he was right. This wasn't the way he had planned things as he lay in the bunkhouse, but it seemed to be working out anyway. She was relaxing and he was walking with his dream girl.

"Do you need a big teddy bear for you new apartment?"

"Thanks for asking, but I really don't need one. Besides, you'll never win. The game's rigged and you know it. Go buy one for your aunt at the store if you want a bear."

"So you don't think I can do it. I accept the challenge." Erik pickup up three baseballs and handed the carnie three bucks. To no one's surprise none of the balls stayed in the wicker basket, so Erik laid more money on the rail.

"Hey you're leaning over the rail. Your hand can't go past this line. I told you that, the throw doesn't count," the carnie pulled out the ball that finally lay at the bottom of the basket.

"Your hand was over the rail when you showed me how to do it." Erik had just thrown nine balls that refused to stay in the leaning wooden basket, so the last one he leaned far over the ledge just to show he could win the game. He was joking with the carnie since he also knew he would never win, but part of the fun of the game was sparring with the carnie.

As Erik and Laura turned to leave, the carnie shouted, "Don't go. You're a nice guy and your girl is too pretty to go away without a bear. I'll give you a free ball if you buy two, and I'll show you how to win."

"You should have done that ten balls ago. Now, I'm broke."

The carnie knew Erik was done so he turned his attention to the next target. "Come on over. I need a winner so everyone can see how easy it is," was repeated time and time again.

"Let's get something to eat and sit down for a while. You've been standing all day."

Laura didn't object when Erik paid for the roasted chicken platter. She hadn't gotten a chance to finish her lunch and until payday she was broke.

"You're doing okay?" Erik asked.

"Yeah, I'm fine."

"Do you think this Marcus guy will give you any more trouble?"

"No, don't think so, or at least I hope not. Sounds like he's found greener pasture for a week or two and then he'll move on to the next."

"How did you get involved with a guy like that?"

"It's a long story. How's your pronto pup? Is it as good as you remembered?" Laura ended any mention of her past.

"Better. My aunt got a mix once and tried to make them for me on the farm. It just wasn't the same. It's probably the day old grease they put them in and a layer of dust that gives them the midway flavor."

"That's disgusting! Your best idea was sitting down. This shade feels good, and it is nice to get off my feet. The Win-Right has worn me down. I'm not used to standing at one place for so long."

"Once you're rested, where do want to go next? In the main pavilion they have a lot of barkers selling knives and mixers and all sorts of things."

"Sounds good, but let's just stay here a while longer. Don't want to have too much fun too fast."

"I envy you." Erik commented

"Me? What's there to envy in my life?"

"You're strong and independent. You aren't afraid to go to new places and do new things. So many people in Fairfield, including myself, seem to be stuck here. A lot of them will live in the same house their entire life. You aren't like that."

"I don't know how strong I am. I move because I have had to move. It hasn't always been by choice. I envy you. You have a place you can call home."

"What's made you move? Are your parents in Billings?" Her look told Erik he had once again brought up a forbidden subject.

"Yes, my patents are in Billings, but I haven't talked to them in years. They didn't like it when I found Christ. They thought I was rejecting them and I was way too fanatical. Little did they know how much that changed." Laura's voice tapered off as she talked about her parents.

"Sorry, I didn't know."

"Some things are better not known, so I haven't tried to contact them and tell them they were right. Let's drop my past. It isn't that interesting."

Silence visited them again as they pulled the last drops of fresh lemonade through their straws.

"There's another reason I envy you."

"Don't keep me guessing."

"You've been around Christ enough you can separate the good from the bad.I don't even know what to avoid. A lot of what I thought I knew before I almost have to unlearn. I never knew how much He loved me, but I don't always know what that means. There are things I wish would just go away, but they don't," Erik said.

"Don't worry about questions, 'cause sometimes there just aren't answers. Hold on to what you have. Don't envy me, and don't make the same mistake I did." Laura hadn't meant to get on the subject of God, but the more she talked the less guarded she became.

" I've been trying hard all week to be normal again, and then my past walks in the door. It's not as easy as it might seem.I'm like an old married wife. She loves her husband, but so many hurts have happened over the years that the husband becomes just the guy that takes out the garbage, not a love. Every time the wife tries to love again, she's reminded of how he's hurt her. Finally she sees the hurt as much as she sees the love."

"But you've seen and done so much, and know how God works. I don't know anything but this county and land that I've never liked."

A slight breeze cooled the couple as the afternoon started to meet the evening. The picnic area had filled and people were waiting for Erik and Laura to leave.

Laura said, "You're selling what you have too short. Just enjoy that life can be that simple."

"Laura, I just see how much you have going for yourself. You said you don't get along with your parents. I don't even have parents. My dad died when I was eleven and my mom left a long time ago. I only found out Sunday that she's also dead.

"You might not have talked to your folks in years, but you still can talk to them. You still can renew your walk with Christ. You might not have the ideal situation, but it's a situation you can repair. I can't repair what's already gone. Right after I got saved I thought I would go to my mom's and be a son to her. I can't. She's gone." Now Erik had no problem talking. "You're just so beautiful, and so nice. You've got everything I don't. I just feel lucky to be sitting next to you."

Laura didn't say a word. She stood up, picked up her plate and plastic cup, walked over to a nearby garbage can, threw them away and walked back "Looks like there's people who need the table. Where are the quilts you talked about earlier?" Laura's message was obvious.

They talked cordially, much like talking to a co-worker at the office, for the rest of the afternoon turned evening, but little else. Erik tried joking to make things better, but he wasn't good at small talk. The more the silence remained the harder it was for him to talk.

"One last thing before we go." Erik offered. If he couldn't talk he could take action.

"What do you want to do?"

"Let's take one ride."

"I told you, I don't like rides. I don't have the stomach for them."

"I'm just talking about the Ferris wheel. It's not even big, but tall enough to get a great view of the mountains, and if we hurry we'll even see the sunset."

"Okay, but only if you promise not to rock the carriage. I hate it when the carriage rocks."

"Deal. I'll get the tickets."

The wheel did carry a beautiful view of the Rockies just as Erik promised. Laura seemed to once again relax. They reached the pinnacle of the cycle just as the sunset had broken into deep scarlet. It was a breathtaking sight as the mountains amplified the tones.Erik looked at Laura and saw a smile formed on her lips and the sunset reflected in her eyes. Her beauty stunned him.

"Laura, you're so beautiful." He repeated what had been rejected before, but Erik spontaneously said what he was thinking. He regretted the words as soon as they escaped.

At the same moment the ride stopped to let off the first passengers.A new operator for the evening wanted more action so he stopped the ride hard. Erik and Laura's top carriage swung like a pendulum on a string. Laura stopped breathing and held tight to the safety bar. Her placid expression turned to one of fear.

"I don't like this. I really don't like this. Why did you make me do this?"

"Don't worry, it'll be fine. We are getting off now as soon as we get to the bottom." Erik tried to reassure her.

The wheel moved again, but only for a moment and once again the operator hit the brake hard and the carriage swung harder than when the last rider got off. The ride operator was enjoying himself. Laura was not.

"Get me off this thing."

Erik saw sheer panic rather than the sunset that had filled

Laura's eyes.

Erik didn't know what to do. He reached his arm around Laura shoulders in a hope to make her feel more secure. Instead her panic turned to anger.

"Get your arm off of me. I don't want to be touched. I've already been touched too much today. Who do you think you are, Marcus? This is all your fault, and I don't want to hear how beautiful I am. I don't know if you think we're a couple, but we aren't. I just want to get off this thing and be left alone."

Erik leaned as far away from Laura as he could. As soon as they reached the platform she pulled the pin and lifted the safety bar before the operator could help. She was gone before Erik had a chance to get out or react to her outburst. He could have tried to catch her, but he didn't.

"Well, so much for wishful thinking. Being told off three times in a week is enough. So much for Gods' will."

Chapter Twenty-One

Laura's sleep was shallow and without comfort that evening. Finally she got up and paced for a time. She had never smoked, but she had a strange sensation that she wished she did. She thought of her rudeness to Erik every time she had been around him. She thought of her fear and anger when she faced Marcus alone. She remembered the conversation with John and how much sense he made.

She remembered that evening six years ago as she had laid out her lunch and instead of eating had heard the Lord's invitation. She had come to the end of excuses six years ago, and she had nowhere to turn. The Lord turned to her and she responded.

She took inventory of the last few days; fired from her job, the memories of her stillborn child, the meeting with Marcus, and her constant pushing aside a guy who had done nothing but try to help. She was no longer able to control her anger and she knew it.

She was out of control. All the right sermons with all the right words from John or Gracie wouldn't help. Six years ago she had turned to Christ in a park for answers and forgiveness..

. Last night she turned to anger which had become her answer. Now, once again, she needed to be back at that beginning picnic table, asking for belief and forgiveness.

"Who am I kidding, Lord? I can try to find every excuse about my life being stained, but I can't avoid one fact... I've turned my back on You ever since that day my child was gone. I've prayed to the heavens, but I have not prayed to You. I felt distant from You because of my sin, but I have never tried to come to You.

"I know Your Word. I know Your presence, but I have looked at the hurt rather than Your love for me. I am that wife who only looks at her husband's faults. I have said the right things to others, but I haven't said the right things to You."

"My Lord, I want to be close to You again. But I know my heart is hard with all my scares and bitterness. I need Your help. Forgive me that my love has turned cold, and I have only known You from a distance."

For the first time in a long time she knew that she was praying from her heart to Him, and not saying words that sounded good.

But to know His forgiveness I better start by asking forgiveness from others. She had to find Erik and let him know that she wasn't crazy and that He was a great God. She needed to thank Erik for his patience rather than scold him. Then she needed to go back to Gracie and Billings and let her know that her starting over wasn't for the moment, but for a lifetime.

She needed to see Erik, and go to him rather than wait for Erik to come around. First she would go to work in the morning. Her Saturday shift ended at seven rather than five. She would go to the parking lot of the fairgrounds. She was certain he would be back at his beloved fair. Maybe she could borrow a few dollars from Barbara and buy Erik a pronto pup maybe two, and treat him like a king. She needed to apologize and she wanted to show she could be a normal person. First she needed to get some sleep. Then she needed to go to work.

Her shift went very slow that day. The WinRight was extremely busy with people stopping in either on their way to or from the fair. The fact that Laura's aisle was constantly full was the only thing that allowed her to maintain her composure. She knew what she had to do, and wanted to do it now.

Finally she pulled into the fair grounds without changing from her WinRight green smock. The main lot did not have Erik's Chevy pickup, nor did the side lot behind the racetrack or the small one next to the pavilion. He wasn't there yet.

She stood by the entrance and waited for him to show up. She shifted her feet as she stood guard to make sure he wasn't missed. The latecomers to the fair, mostly young people, eyed her and her green smock and wondered why this good-looking girl looked so lost.

The thought came to her that Erik might have come with someone else and was already in the gates. It would be almost impossible to find Erik in the maze of the rides and games and animal displays.She hurriedly went to every place they had stopped the day before. Several times she ran across the midway thinking she had found Erik only to find a stranger with little resemblance. Her eyes were playing tricks on her. She could wait for the next day and meet him at church, but what needed to be done, needed to be done today.

When it became clear Erik wasn't there she decided to go to him at his farm. She knew the farm was straight west of Sweetgrass which would make it straight north of Fairfield. That meant she knew the road, and Erik had described the farm house in such detail she knew she could find it. People would ask too many questions if she asked for directions and she didn't even know his aunt and uncle's name. It had already turned dark, so it was somewhat of a long shot that she would find the farm let alone find him there, but she needed to try. She needed to get things right.

Chapter Twenty-Two

The road north to the Cooper's farm was straight with no variance for twenty-five miles. The only exception was the first half-mile of paved road past the city limit. As the road left the city limits it curved to the right and then a sharp curve to the left. It then crossed over a deep ravine called Flat Rock. After this, the road had no turns.

Laura wasn't familiar with the road or its two curves. Her single focus was on Erik, wanting to make things right and trying to remember every detail he had conveyed to her about the farm so she wouldn't miss it. The road was empty with everyone at the fair, and the night was clear. Laura hardly noticed the first curve, but she was into the second faster than she expected. She held the steering wheel hard and heard the distinct sound of tires skidding on the pavement. She thought belatedly that she should have been concentrating on the road more and pushing on the gas less.

She still had the car under control when she heard a sound she didn't recognize. She turned the wheel to the left, but the car continued straight. The car left the road at the top of the ravine and went twenty yards in the air before it hit the bottom of Flat Rock ravine.

Chapter Twenty-Three

Erik was seated at the dinner table with his aunt and uncle eating the fried chicken that his aunt always made on Sunday's. He had attended services at the Fairfield Community Church rather than the New Life Center since he didn't want to see Laura. He had made up an excuse for Mary and Henry why he wanted to go with them without mentioning Laura. It made them feel good that he wanted to go with them. He had said nothing to anyone about taking Laura to the fair. He wanted to think that Laura was just a confused girl, but in the solitude of his bunkhouse he found that hard to do.

Aunt Mary was serving up dessert of warm peach cobbler when they all saw and heard John's Buick pull up to the back of the house.

"Wonder what he's doing? I told him I was going to go to church with you two so he shouldn't be wondering why I wasn't at New Life today. Maybe he just wants some of your chicken."

All three met him at the back door. John looked serious in a way Erik had never seen before. "Can I come in and sit down?'

"Of course, you can. I was just serving some peach cobbler.

I'll get you a plate." Mary immediately took her hospitable role.

"No, thanks. I have some news."

John didn't say anything else until they all sat down and Erik tried to guess what brought the worried look to John's face.

John waited longer than expected, as if he was searching for words. He cleared his throat, not for dramatic effect, but because tears were starting to form in the corners of his eyes. Erik wished he would just tell the news.

"I decided to come out and see you. I was hardly out of town when I saw police lights. I didn't see anything but the cars until I looked over the edge into the ravine. There were about ten people moving around an old oil rig thrown away years ago. I couldn't tell what was going on so I went out and checked."

Once again John became quiet and cleared his throat several times.

"Come on, what did you find?" Erik asked.

"Laura's been in a car accident, and it was fatal."

"Who else was in the car?" It must have been that guy.

"It was Laura, Erik. Laura's dead."

"What do mean, Laura's dead? I just talked to her on Friday. We went to the fair. Laura's not dead."

"Yes, she is. They don't know exactly what happened and the coroner thinks it happened some time last night, but they didn't find the car till late this morning. They think she was going too fast on that curve right before the ravine. She probably wasn't used to the road. The police could tell from the skid marks that she also blew out a tire right when she was in the curve. There are some new skid marks even before that. She left the road and went far enough to hit that old oil derrick. They expect she died instantly."

"Why didn't anyone see it last night"?

"It was dark. There's willow bushes and tall grass and then the oil derrick itself. You couldn't see it from the road. The road must have been empty when she crashed. A girl was riding her horse this morning when she noticed it. The coroner has a way to check to know for sure, but he says it's pretty definite it was last evening, probably just before dusk or maybe a little after. No one saw her go over...then, with the dark..."

Erik's head dropped and he remembered. He remembered what had been and thought of what could have been. He remembered the distinct smell of Laura' perfume or hand cream or whatever it was. That smell would follow him for years, unexpectedly appearing at random times. He remembered how the sunset reflected off Laura's eye as the Ferris wheel climbed. He remembered Laura bending close to him to take his order at the Mint Bar, and he would forever remember those times when Laura's voice sparkled as she spoke about the Lord.

Erik only knew Laura in person for a precious short time, but he couldn't remember a time without her. He knew her in the bunkhouse dreams even before he knew her name. He dreamt of her beauty, her courage, her heart and her wisdom. He hungered for her acceptance and in those dreams he hoped that someone so beautiful could ever love him. Now she was gone.

Tears welled in his eyes when he wondered what she missed in the future life she would never touch. He cried hoping her heart was open to Christ the moment she died. She was too beautiful, too strong, too caring to be snatched from this earth. People, not just himself, needed to know her and the joy she could have added to their lives.

He lifted his head, and immediately felt his aunt and uncle's stare. Their stare widened the gulf between them and him. *They don't understand. They didn't know Laura.* They didn't understand Erik, they hadn't felt the sting of death like Erik had.

And the reality of being left alone returned.

"John, what you're telling me is that we passed her car on the way to church and on the way back and we didn't even notice it? She might have been alive. We might have helped if I had only looked."

"No, Erik. She had a head injury. They think she died instantly."

"They can think what they want. We might have been able

to help! At least we didn't need to let her lay in her car in the hot sun. We could have done something. We should have seen her." Erik's voice was rising with disbelief and a morbid horror that he may have been in the position to help and been oblivious of needing to do so.

"Erik, no one saw her. There is nothing you could have done."

"Just like with dad and mom. There's nothing I could have done. If there's nothing I could have done, why does this keep happening to me? I just want to be loved by someone. I just want to be loved, and not left."

At that point Erik didn't say anything else. He would say little else for several weeks. John knew more about Laura than Henry or Mary, but none of them knew the place she held in Erik's life. He had dreamed about her for months. His going to The Mint had been used by God to find Him. He had prayed on Chief Mountain and then he met her again. Combined, Laura had been a deeper part of his life than anyone would know. Laura was an answer and the answer was now gone. She was dead.

Chapter Twenty-Four

Since Laura had still been a stranger to Fairfield there was little note of her death. There was talk about the accident, but it revolved around how it could have happened with little comment about Laura herself.

Erik called the Fairfield funeral home about the burial. It would be held in Billings on the next Thursday. He would be there. All three, Mary, Henry and John, insisted that they help Erik drive to Billings. "It's too long for you to make in one day by yourself." Erik insisted even harder and drove himself.

It had been fifteen years since he had been at a funeral, but they were all the same. To Erik, death was death no matter who lay in the coffin. This was a simple graveside ceremony for Laura while his dad had both a church and graveside, but that made little difference. Someone with unfinished hopes had died. He always wanted to prove himself to his dad, but he died too early. He wanted to share his thoughts and maybe even his life with Laura, and she was gone. Nothing changed in his life. The prairie winds blew each day, the drought would never leave, and those he loved were taken away.

Erik estimated there were about a dozen people at the funeral. He didn't care to count the exact number since it was too few for someone so special. He felt out of place as the others looked at him and wondered who he was. Fortunately there was a black lady who drew even more stares. No one cared to introduce him or herself, and Erik didn't want to meet them.

He didn't notice that the black lady had slipped away, and he jumped when she whispered behind him.

"You're that guy that got in the fight at the Mint." Gracie said.

'How did you know that was me."

"Cause you're the only one that looks like they care, and the way Laura described you, I knew right away."

"Yes, that was me. If I hadn't started that fight we wouldn't be here today. She would be still working at the Mint and none of this would have happened."

"Things happen as they do, and what you do or don't do won't change a plan," Gracie said. "Besides, one of the best things that happened to her was that fight and her losing that job. She told me so herself. If that fight hadn't happened, she still would be stuck in her misery and now she's sitting with the Lord. Sounds to me like you did her a favor."

"Standing in my shoes, it doesn't seem like much of a favor.She told me the same thing about the fight, but I don't know if I believe her."

"She told me you two talked about God when you were at the Point so you must know God."

"Yes, but only for a couple weeks. I accepted Him right after that fight."

"Well, then that fight was for good, and you ought to know better than to blame yourself."

"Sounds like you know the Lord, too."

"I've known about Him since I was a child but I don't know Him like Laura knew Him. I know about Him. Laura knew Him. That knowing is different. Are you different?"

"Yeah, I guess you would say I'm different."

"Then you're a lucky man and a lucky man for getting to know Laura. You're a lucky man for even being close to that lady. I rode a Greyhound bus for eight hours and used my last food money for the month to get here. I'd ride for forty hours and sell my last dress if I had to. There aren't many ladies like her. I knew that the first time I met her. I could only imagine what she was like before she got hurt. She was amazing, even after the hurt.

"She was a lady of class. She was a lady that had her problems, but never let that keep her from helping other people. It's a funny thing about class. There are people who have money and try to act classy, and there are people who are classy just the way they are. She had class and she made me feel like someone just being around her. Now that's class."

Erik looked down at the ground. "Yes, I'm a lucky man. I just hope my luck makes sense some day."

It was 11:30 at night by the time he got back from Billings. He had went the long way through Sweetgrass to drop off Gracie. When he got to the bunkhouse it wasn't long before John was at the door. Erik knew that John would be there, but he didn't expect it to happen so quickly. John must've waited for hours to catch Erik. John didn't say anything when he walked in. He waited to see if Erik wanted to talk.

"Does anyone know where Laura was going when she crashed?"

"Not that I'm aware of. I talked to the sheriff, but he didn't say much. He was investigating the car accident, but there wasn't much to investigate. They took all her things from the apartment to the funeral home. I don't know what happens then. I guess they sent them to her family."

"Do you think she was coming out to see me?" Erik had mulled that question on the way home.

"Like I said, I don't know, but if she was, it wasn't your fault. She had a blowout. It wasn't anyone's fault. It's an accident."

"I'm not talking about whose fault it was. I was wondering if she was coming out to see me, and what she wanted to say. I had a long time to think on the trip back. I was hoping that maybe she wanted to apologize. More than that, I was praying she had a chance to get things right with God before..." The thought of the crash quieted Erik.

"We went the county fair on Friday." Erik didn't bother to tell about the guy at the grocery store. He didn't want John to think Laura had a troubled background. Erik kept telling himself she didn't. "We had a nice time, but I talked her into going on the Ferris wheel and she panicked when it started to rock. Then I said too much and she got mad, again. I thought she might have been coming out to apologize. It's a crazy thought, but I thought it might be true."

"I couldn't tell you, but I guess it's a possibility. Whatever was the reason, God's eyes were on her. For whatever reason she was driving and the tire blew at that exact moment. God was still in control when she went into the ravine. I'm not saying God wanted her to get in a wreck, but I am saying He was still in control."

Erik shook his head, "There were so many things that happened in such a short time, I can't make sense out of any of it. She was the reason I went to the Mint, got in the fight and spent the night in the pickup. I just prayed that He would help me with my future in Fairfield and I come back to the Point and she's sitting there when I walked in the door. There were just too many things to cause me to wonder if He had a place for her in my life."

"He did have a place for her in your life," John confirmed. "There's no question. It's just there is no way to know what that meant. Sometimes we try to out guess God, but, again, all we can know is that He is in control and the best for us will happen.

"Remember one other thing, Erik. He used you to touch her life. It sounded to me like she needed to be close to Him again, and it sure seemed like with all that happened He used you to make that happen. Never try to out guess God, but never underestimate how He'll move mountains to have His plans fulfilled."

"But I don't understand why she had to die. I guess I don't understand a lot right now.

"I told you the first time we talked to keep things simple, and that hasn't changed. He came to you that night because He wanted to love and care for you. That will never change No matter what happens, put that in the front and the other questions will make a lot more sense."

"What I need to do right now is to sleep," Erik sat in total exhaustion. "I just need to sleep and get back to work. Maybe things will make sense later."

Erik pulled a single sheet over himself as he lay in the hot evening and tried to sleep. He should have fallen asleep out of sheer exhaustion, but it would be weeks until he slept soundly again.

Chapter Twenty-Five

This land was bone dry after years of drought. It would take more than one rainstorm to make this land look as the land should look. One rainstorm would turn the dust to lifeless mud for a short time. A few surface weeds with shallow roots would grow only to once again become victims of the sun. The moisture would quickly be zapped from the topsoil. Nothing would reach the hard dry ground beneath where only the longer roots would reach and the reserves of water usually waited.

After a few rain showers, a few buds and even leaves would come to the willow brush next to the Cooper's coulee. In false hope the bushes would be hoaxed into the fact that rains meant spring, and their roots would live by the lie for a time. But the other vegetation, without the benefit of the willow's roots and coulee runoff, would exhaust themselves with the sudden growth. They would not be able to sustain themselves once the cloud cover gave way to the sun.

Only a long rainfall measuring inches and days would bring a noticeable change to the land, and even that would be minimal. The rain in that type of storm would come in sheets. Its pellets would pierce the dust, driving splashes inches into the air. It would keep coming until the subsoil had had enough and then it would begin to make ravines in the topsoil.

The water would head to the coulee in whatever fashion it chose, being stopped only by boulders and occasion ditched roads. It would carry with it topsoil that was needed to grow the wheat, not to line the bottom of coulees. The contoured strips the farmer designed in his field were for protection from the winds that were always present, not the rain that was a stranger. However, any farmer would gladly exchange this loss of topsoil for relief from the drought. That rain would not mean a bumper crop. For that year it would mean there would be a harvest and a chance to sleep with the smell of growing freshness in the night air.

It was a shame to think that the hard thunderstorms almost brought more destruction to the land than help. Everyone would live on the euphoria that the rains had come, but such sudden, hard rains actually destroyed the land. Each such storm would take from topsoil already thin from the constant winds and make it more vulnerable to the next dry spell. Beneath the topsoil there was nothing to maintain growth but hardpan dirt. The farms that held the best farming land were those with few exposed hills. Their farms contained land that had gathered the deposits of the glaciers as they moved and dissolved in the plains. The glacier soil was rich with life.

The rains were the crucial element on the Great Plains, but without the topsoil the water did little good. The farmer would attempt to fertilize his crops to replenish the soils, but only native topsoil would guarantee a harvest. The fertilizers were expensive and could burn the crops if the sun came too quickly. So the rains were wanted and needed, but they came with a price if they struck the land and then quickly left.

This was the land that Henry Cooper had inherited from his father, and that Erik Winters worked. The Coopers believed the promise of restoring this land. Erik only worked the land. It's future wasn't his concern.

Erik couldn't leave his dreams of Laura. From time to time a certain smell or touch or a certain place brought her back. Laura was his future and his family and everything his life would ever need..He had only known Laura for a short time, but he had held dreams of her image for years. Laura was the face that made those dreams within grasp, and it felt like Erik had known Laura since the first time he had dreamt of someone needing him and wanting him and loving him. Then she, too, was gone.

No one else couldknow what Laura meant, or how important were those precious moments that Erik held. Many days his pain was so sharp he wished he had never met her.

His aunt and uncle did everything to make sure he wouldn't retreat to the bunkhouse after Laura died, but they failed.Christ was near in his thoughts and Christ would be his only companion.

Erik had tried to get involved with the New Life Center. At first people gave a warm reception for the new brother in their midst. After a time, Erik became just another parishioner and people's comments turned to questions of why he was such a loner if Christ had truly entered his life. It was almost being like the new kid in school that all the girls want to know on the first day, but forget by the first weekend.

A few people in the church started to question whether Erik really was any different or if his commitment to Christ was only on a surface level. A few parishioners gossiped that maybe Erik had made up the story merely to be accepted and be thought of as normal. They questioned how normal he could be after his parents had left him as they did, and him still living alone in that stale bunkhouse. They reasoned that if he had changed, he would have moved from that bunkhouse and joined the Coopers in their house. Not all the people carried these rumors. Still, there was enough talk by a few members who loved to create excitement to hide their boredom of Fairfield. Erik heard some of the comments. Some of the reports came from church members themselves who told Erik about the stories to protect him. He didn't know if they really did this to warn him or because they wanted to be part of the excitement and wanted to see how he would respond to the news. In this fashion, the cycle of gossip could be complete.

He knew he would never be on one of them. Years earlier, Erik accepted his place as an outcast and maybe even preferred it. He never wanted to be one of them. Now it gave him a sense that maybe things would never be different. He trusted God, but the people of Fairfield weren't so forgiving. John had told Erik earlier to keep it simple and simply love God and his neighbor. Now Erik began to realize how complex a task that would be.

During the two years after Laura's death, he also got involved with another girl.It was a natural progress if you were single and part of the church to date someone from the church. It was expected that a man in his mid-twenties would be looking to start a family. Of course Erik wanted a family, but with the people of Fairfield it was viewed as a task rather than a desire. Erik could sense it even with the ladies his age and it seemed to warp the whole idea of a family.

The girl he met was named Laurie. It was more than chance that he was attracted to someone with a name so close to Laura. Occasionally, he would even slip and call Laurie "Laura", but he would always cover it up as if he had merely mispronounced Laurie's name. Very few people remembered Laura so he was safe.

But Laurie would never be Laura. Laurie lacked something. She was very nice and very pleasant, but there was something missing. Excitement might be the word Erik would have used to explain the difference between the two girls. Maybe a better word would be adventure. There was no adventure with Laurie, only life in Fairfield.

Laurie had been part of the church and a Christian for as long as she could remember. She had never smoked, nor drank, and would never think of swearing. Erik didn't find this a fault, but Laurie had just never done anything. She had never done anything good or bad. She was just part of Fairfield, as plain as the plains themselves.

When a person looked north of Fairfield, he would see neat strips of fields uniformly cut into the earth. These fields were patterned without break or alteration. The same was true of Laurie. Her life was a perfect pattern. Her clothes were perfectly pressed, her manners, her conversation, even her fingernails that she polished every morning were made to be perfectly uniform. At times Erik almost hated to stand next to her in fear that his imperfections would be even more obvious. Certainly it wasn't a fault that Laurie had lived such a Christian life her whole life. Erik wished that he could have known and followed Christ and missed all the despair that had been his companion without Christ. It wasn't a fault in Laurie, but it was a difference from Erik.

In many ways they were an odd couple, but a couple by necessity. There were only a small number of unmarried Christian women in a town the size of Fairfield. Certainly Erik would be expected to date a Christian. For Laurie, there were even fewer Christian men, and she could not fathom being with an unbeliever. Erik knew that if he wanted to be involved with a girl, it would be Laurie.

Erik actually had few real "dates" with Laurie. He remembered once going to have dinner and meet her parents at Laurie's house. In the best of situations it was hard for anyone to feel examined by his girlfriend's parents and that seemed to be the purpose of the first dinner. To Erik, the ritual was unbearable.

As he pulled in front of the house he could already feel his throat tighten with nerves. As he walked up the steps he wondered if he could merely bow out by saying he was sick. That statement seemed more reality than excuse as he knocked on the door.

Laurie and her mother, Elizabeth, met Erik at the door. Of course, he had met the Simonsons before in church, but he had never really had a conversation with them. There had been the courtesy "hellos", but no long conversations. Now he visited in their home, but he felt more a stranger than a guest. As he looked around, his first thought was he didn't know there were houses like this in Fairfield. On the outside all the wood framed houses were very similar. As he entered the Simonson's home, the fine décor made him feel like he should be the delivery boy rather than Laurie's friend.

The dining room was an actual dining room and not just an extension of the kitchen, as in the Coopers' farm. A large China closet showed colors of fine polished wood and Erik hoped he did not need to eat off one of the fine plates it housed. He knew he would break it if he touched one. A chandelier

264 ~ Bart Tuma

drew Erik's eyes to the center of the room and its warm tones were accented with lit candles on the table. The room was perfect and beautiful. Erik knew he wasn't either.

The conversation started fine as Laurie's dad, Jake, asked Erik about the farm and his aunt and uncle. Erik's responses were short and only filled in the needed information. A witness at a trial is asked only to respond to the question and to not add any unnecessary facts. That evening Erik felt very much as one on the witness stand.

Because Erik's answers were so quick and to the point, the round of conversation was over in a short time. Erik searched his mind to add a comment to carry his end of the conversation. He made several attempts to ask Mr. Simonson about how his auto dealership was doing. Both men spoke a different language so the conversation was short. They both spoke English, but their lives were so dissimilar that a common interest could not be found

The attempts soon failed and the conversation switched to include only the family and Erik was certainly not a part of this family. It was as if the four people were playing double's tennis, but Erik never was given an opportunity to move his racket, let alone return the ball.

By the time Mrs. Simonson had removed the soup bowls and brought to the table a store bought ham, Erik knew he was doomed to silence. He realized there was no way he could add to the comments. By then Mr. Simonson had attempted to bring

Erik into the talk by asking him more questions. Erik stumbled on even a simple sentence and he resigned himself to looking busy with the food. He could almost literally feel himself pulling away from the table and the conversation.

The high point of the evening was the relief when it ended. The parents were genuinely warm and appreciative of Erik coming. Laurie walked Erik to the gate of their house, and thanked him for coming. Erik knew he would never be invited back and he did not regret that thought.

It wasn't that the Simonsons weren't fine, warm people. It wasn't that Laurie was some lifeless figure without care or emotion. She was very good towards Erik. At the same time she had little in common with Erik except for Christ and the need for companionship. This fact was very obvious whenever they were alone. They had little to talk about and the air would soon become thick with the tension of silence. Erik would attempt to come up with something to say, but usually what he had to offer came out as only silly babble. It was obvious he was trying too hard.

As with any man of his age, Erik wanted to be with someone. Laurie was someone, but her patterned life didn't allow for Erik. Erik finally found himself turning back to his dreams. They were not dreams of the barmaid, but of some girl that he had not yet met who could share his life with him. He dreamt of someone who would go fishing with him at the beaver dams as he had with his father and who would make conversation important and easy.

Soon he began to hold to these dreams more than to Laurie. Since there was so little to hold them together, they simply drifted apart. There were no arguments nor fights. They simply spent less and less time together until they never saw each other except at church services. They both knew after the dinner this would happen. Both continued on with their expected roles. It seemed Laurie was as willing to let the relationship go as Erik.

Erik wasn't sad to see the relationship end. He sensed he was cheating on Laura's memory when he dated Laurie. He knew it was silly to think such thoughts, and he knew if it continued he would never have a chance for a real relationship. His memories for Laura were strong enough that he didn't know what harm they might bring. Laura would never be replaced.

And the other people's gossip and whispers grew louder.

Erik spent less and less time with people until he finally began to avoid them as he had in the past. There was little room for an unmarried man in the social circles of the church in a town like Fairfield. That fact was obvious and Erik knew it by the stares. He didn't spend time with non-Christian acquaintances anymore since he had even less in common with them. It would have been easier if he had had friends before, but he hadn't. It left little place for Erik.

Erik didn't help this situation either. He still didn't feel at ease with people. He remembered all too well the abandonment he had received. He found himself talking to Christ in the solitude of his bunkhouse room, but no one else.

Erik, after these two years had passed, no longer doubted Christ's reality or love. His Bible studies and time alone had cemented that relationship to a level he had never thought possible. Those times alone with Christ were more precious than any daydream he had in the past. At the same time there was a gnawing reality. He had begun his Christian walk dedicated to healing his relationship with other people. That part of his life was still very much incomplete. He had the sense to know that his faith meant little unless it also meant being part of other people's lives. That had never been easy for Erik and it was no easier now.

There had been the rains of Christ's blessing, but Erik wondered if too if he had lost much of his heart to the past floods of despair.

There had been a time when he reached out, but then those whispers started and Laurie left, and he slowly felt himself slipping back to his solitude. It was almost a literal sense of slipping down a mountain some days as he fought his loneliness. It was like a man desperately thirsty in the desert coming to a pond. It only made sense to drink from that pond, but what if the water was bad? What if it was worse than the thirst itself? That man would have to decide if it was better to be thirsty or to take a chance on the water. Erik could not find the strength within himself after these years to trust people and to drink of their companionship. His fear of being abandoned again was too great.

Certainly, the Coopers had attempted to bring him into their family and show their love to Erik. At the same time they all knew, including Erik, that too much had happened in the past to simply come together as a real family. His aunt and uncle tried to have him move back to the house. They thought this would be a step to being a family and bring normalcy for Erik. Erik would not accept and always had some excuse to not insult them. It would be harder for Erik to allow the Coopers parenthood. He still wanted to be a Winters and he still wanted his solitude.

Erik knew they loved him. He had been forced on them. They didn't ask for him. He was left there by Children's Services. Accepting someone from Children's Services and loving them were two different things. No amount of words or explanation would change that fact. Erik was just different from them. *Maybe I'm different from everyone,* Erik thought, sometimes aloud.

Besides, he told himself that he wasn't like these people; not like any of them. They were Fairfield, and nothing good was ever in Fairfield. Even though Erik had left the mountains to return to the prairie, he knew he was not part of that town. He was going to leave Fairfield someday and become someone. Erik realized his inability to be part of other people's lives was a problem he needed to solve. He knew the fact, but he never acknowledged just how much it kept him from the healing the Lord had to offer.

It was an odd sound to hear at the beginning of July. Erik lay in his bed just before the alarm usually rang and he began to hear the distinct sound of raindrops hitting the metal roof. It began as a few faint taps that Erik didn't know if he heard or imagined. Then the taps came steady and pronounced. Finally a loud clap of thunder left no doubt that a summer rainstorm had visited the prairie land. It was an unusual sound because the taps were constant with a soothing rhythm. This was the sound of an April storm that was so welcomed by the farmers as it built a foundation for the coming year. This was July and it seldom rained in July, and when it did, it was violent and quick, not the gentle tapping he heard with this rain.

It was a pleasant sound to Erik. It had been a while since he had heard rain, and ever since he could remember that sound always brought laughter to the Cooper farm. He wanted to lie in bed as long as possible and just hear those drops tap the ceiling and bring life to the farm.

The long drought spell had broken last year and the crops were respectable. A farm that had kept the fields plowed and ready for rain had broke even, and the banks readily gave out loans for next years seed and diesel. This spring's rain was widespread with the fields starting strong. With this rain, there might even be hope for a bumper crop. Erik did not take pleas-

ure in this land, as did Uncle Henry. His whole life did not re-
volve around the success or failure of the wheat. At the same
time, there was no escaping the pleasant sound of life being
brought to the land and the harvest it would mean. Erik didn't
participate in this joy as completely as his aunt and uncle, but
the tap, tap, tap, tap sound of rain hitting the bunkhouse tin
roof still made him feel warm and secure as he heard it. It was
a pity he couldn't fully participate in the joy of the rain, but
still it brought warmth to his heart.

The Cooper farm was located just south of the Milk River
Ridge. Uncle Henry always said this ridge raised the clouds
and brought more rain. He said that if it rained an inch in Fairfield it rained an inch and a half at the Cooper farm. He constantly bragged how smart his dad was to pick such a great location. Other farmers had like stories of their preferential loca-
tions. No one ever knew if there was any fact to these claims,
but one thing was certain: no matter how good the farmer's
land he still had to carefully work the land to coax the largest
harvest from its soil. There had to be a constant vigilance to
bring in the harvest from the time of seeding to the time the
combine entered the field.

Erik found it difficult to give the same vigilance to his own
life. God's presence had allowed him to hope and feel joy as
never before, but the full harvest of God's life would not be
enjoyed until he could cultivate and join in the strength of other
people.

Only one person was able to break Erik's solitude. He allowed John O'Brian into his life. John was a lifeline to the outside world that Erik still held. He trusted John because it was John who had explained Christ to him that first day and never tried to sugar coat with an easy answer for Erik's problems. Erik was sure he would always get a straight answer from John.. If Erik needed to be straightened out, John wouldn't be shy to tell him.

At the same time, John was very aware of the hurt and distrust that had been a real part of Erik's past. He was always careful not to push too hard. Erik could trust John more than the Coopers. although the Coopers had never done anything wrong except to hide secrets they felt would hurt Erik. John volunteered to spend time with Erik as if he enjoyed it. Erik hadn't been thrust upon John like he had been with the Coopers. What he didn't realize was that John felt the Lord had brought Erik to his doorstep just as events had brought Erik to the Cooper's.

John held a Wednesday evening Bible study at his house each week. It was a loosely structured meeting of study, but even more importantly, caring for those that attended. It was a small group of five or six people. Sometimes the other people got so busy they couldn't made it. At times Erik was the only one who attended. It was those times of being alone with John that Erik appreciated the most. Those meetings allowed Erik to be free with his questions, and John to speak directly to Erik.

These studies were the highlight of Erik's week and in many ways his life. It was there that Erik could certify all his studies in the bunkhouse. These times alone were important times with Christ, but somehow they seemed hollow until they were shared with someone he trusted. It was as if people would go on a vacation by themselves and see the great monuments of the world. The trip would not be complete until they shared the pictures with those at home.

Erik didn't set out to be a loner, nor did he desire to be by himself. It was the course of his life and Erik seemed incapable to forge a change. Christ gave him an opportunity to talk to a Present God, but Erik also needed someone to sit with and eat with and be with. John did that, but John wasn't enough.

Chapter Twenty-Six

"Erik, come and get it. Dinner's ready!" In the open land you could hear Mary's shout and the clang of the dinner bell for miles, but it was all unnecessary. Erik was already out of his work clothes in the bunkhouse and even a whisper could have brought him to dinner.

"How much of the baling have you got done?" Henry quizzed as Erik sat down at the table looking like a starved animal.

"I got the three old pond bottoms done next to the Benders."

"Getting many bales off the bottoms?" Henry's first concern always was and always would be the yield of the farm. Now, however, he was old enough that he didn't participate in the direct labor on the farm except for crucial times like seeding and harvest.

"Yeah, I'd say about forty bales per bottom. That rain last spring must've left more water in those holes than I expected," Erik said as he shoveled the food into his mouth.

There had been several heavy rains that spring, but now the end of July had come, and after the one satisfying rain earlier in the month, there was no more rain. Most of the prairie was rapidly turning brown. Only the areas that somehow could hold onto the moisture were different.

"Good, that'll be enough to keep our steers fat until we can get them to auction. But I'm not surprised that there were that many bales. You always short-change what there is. You'd think you're the bearer of doom the way you talk sometimes," Henry said with a grin. He was joking with Erik. At the same time he was serious. He and Mary were trying as hard as they could to help Erik to change his outlook.

"Someone's got to be realistic around here," Erik replied. "The way you and Aunt Mary talk, I'd expect this to be paradise rather than a prairie." Erik also was half joking, half serious.

Henry was not to be outtalked. "I'll never forget the quote my teacher made me memorize in high school. The quote is, 'The mind is its own place; in itself it can make a heaven of hell, a hell of heaven'. That's from Milton's *Paradise Lost.*"

"In high school! Your mind has worked a major miracle to remember that far back, but I still don't know if anyone can make this place a heaven," Erik mused.

"I wish you'd try to make something out of it more than your complaining. Here, I've gone out to get something nice for you and all you do is complain." Henry's eyes now contained a hint of mischief.

"You got something nice for me? What, a one-way ticket to

Bermuda?" Erik was still joking, but he realized his remarks were beginning to be cutting and it was time to bring the joke to a close. Besides, he was curious what Henry had up his sleeve.

"Ha, ha, ha. No, I got you a one-way ticket to the Henry Cooper farm and a new place to live." Henry checked Erik's eyes to catch a reaction.

"A new place to live? What do you mean? I live in the bunkhouse."

"The bunkhouse is beginning to rub off on you. You're starting to smell like it even when you're away. The place has a pack of mice living in it, and it's only fit for them, not for my family. You are my family, Erik. I got a loan approved from next year's crop to buy a used mobile home. It'll be a place that you can make your own and not share with the hired hands during harvest. It can be your own place that other people can come to and you won't be ashamed to have them over. It will be here in a couple of weeks and we can park it next to the Quonset hut, put blocks under it, a skirt around it, and it'll be your real house."

"But Uncle, that's a lot of money, and who knows how good next year's crop will be," Erik protested. "Why don't we get those seeders that you need so badly instead? I've lived in the bunkhouse for this long. It won't hurt me to live there a little longer. Besides, I don't see a lot of visitors in my future anyway." He was grateful because he knew how hard it was for his uncle to spare the money, but it was a gesture he wished hadn't happened. Erik already had other plans. He meant to leave the farm, not have his uncle buy something that would tie him to this land even further.

"No, a little longer won't hurt you," his uncle conceded, "but you've lived in that place since high school as it is, and since there are so many more years to come, now is as good a time as any. There will always be things we can buy for the farm, but we don't get that many chances to buy you something. Those seeders can wait another season or two."

"But, Uncle, I don't know…"

"What don't you know? You'd think you had buried treasure under that bunkhouse the way you're attached to it. As long as you're living with us, you need someplace decent to live." Henry's voice was firm with conviction as if to bring the conversation to an end.

"The thing I don't know about is how much longer I'm going to be on this farm." Erik almost choked on the words as he blurted them out. It was not his intent to hurt his uncle, and this wasn't the time, especially if the mobile home had already been bought.

"What do you mean? Is something the matter? Is there something you haven't told us?" Henry was more concerned than hurt with Erik's unexpected revelation.

"No, nothing's wrong. I just have plans. I was hoping . . . I guess hoping for a change. I've thought before of signing up for the Havre Vo-Tech. They have a welding degree you can get in nine months. I hear there are a lot of openings on the West Coast for trained welders. I thought I might check it out." Erik didn't look Henry in the eyes as he talked.

Erik had started to talk and he couldn't stop now. "But I want to make sure the both of you know how much I appreciate each of you. I won't be leaving because of you. I just need my own life, not just my own house. I've got to get out of this wind blown country and if I don't leave soon, I never will."

Erik's voice raised.. He wanted to get his explanation out as quickly as possible, as if the words stung his throat as they were spoken. He felt bad that once again he was refusing to accept the kindness of the Coopers. It wasn't the first time he had turned his back on them, but others had done the same to him. Actually, he hadn't fully thought out the move to Havre. The offer for the trailer house had forced him to push up his plans. He couldn't allow them to get that trailer, and the move to Havre was the best explanation he knew. He had already thought about it, but thinking was all he had done.

If the Coopers bought the trailer they might as well put bars on its windows. There was no way he could leave once it was moved to the farm. Erik was twenty-four now. If he stayed on this farm much longer he knew he would never leave. In fact, he saw his uncle getting older and the childless Coopers proba- bly intended for Erik to completely take over the farm at some point. Certainly the Coopers would see this as a great honor to give the farm that they loved so much to Erik, but Erik would only see it as the end to any hope of any dreams being fulfilled.

Vo-Tech and a welding job were far from past dreams of Erik. Once, Erik dreamt of playing football at a four-year university that would lead to a city job with a brick house and a nice car and a boat. The dream had seemed reasonable to him. He had seen that house and car and boat many times in his dreams.

Now, he just wanted out.

A nine-month course at an inexpensive tech school was the quickest way to leave Fairfield.He had convinced himself that once out, he could do what he wanted.. Working for someone else wasn't a possibility. He didn't need another person telling him what to do. He thought that once he graduated he could buy a van with a portable welding unit and work for himself as a contractor. At some point he would start his own shop, and buy his own building. Being an owner of a welding shop was a dream worth dreaming.

All of these plans had been only dreams in the bunkhouse, and he didn't know if he even had the courage to leave. Now, with the offer of the trailer, those dreams needed to fast become reality. Erik didn't know if he was actually ready to move to Havre, but the current conversation was forcing him to make a choice.

Henry said, "You could have said something before I got the loan."

"You could have said something to me about getting the loan," Erik retorted. He sighed and went on, trying to explain. "It's just that I don't feel like I'm going anyplace in Fairfield. There is no future for me here that I can look forward to. I feel God would want me to do more." Erik wasn't sure what God wanted at that point, but the more he talked the more he was convinced this was God's plan. "You know, this land has never been my place. Too many things have happened here. Too many bad things happened here for me to forget. No matter how hard I try, it just isn't the place I want to spend my life."

Erik hated his timing, but now that the trailer was offered he had no choice. He looked at both his aunt and uncle, and both were looking away.He made some excuses about work that needed to be done and left the table. He knew that the matter wasn't finished and after their silence, he didn't look forward to that next conversation.

Chapter Twenty-Seven

It wasn't long before Erik received his acceptance letter from Havre Vo-Tech. He was amazed that he had received an answer only a week after he had sent in his application. He then realized that a place of this caliber, or lack of caliber, wasn't picky about who they accepted as long as the cash followed. Erik had mailed in the application the day after the talk in the hopes that the Coopers would think it had been done earlier. Actually, there had been little talk since that first conversation. Now the letter sealed the reality of Erik's departure. Mary and Henry seemed to be carrying out plans for Erik's leaving without discussion. There were questions about the farm and the harvest, but nothing about the decision itself. They rightfully concluded that Erik had made up his mind and there was nothing they could say to change it. It wasn't as if Erik was a person who was free with sharing what was on his mind anyway.

In a sense, this decision had been made the day his father died and sealed when his mother would never return. The associations with his past were too bitter for Erik, no matter what the land was like. Maybe that quote from *Paradise Lost* was right. Maybe he made this land into more of a hell in his mind, but all he knew was that he had to leave.

Uncle Henry and Aunt Mary had long discussions about Erik's move, but the discussions were always private.

"Honey, do you think Erik's running or does he really need to leave the farm?" Henry asked his wife.

"I'm not sure. I do know that a lot has happened in Erik's short life and I think he sees this place as a reminder of his dad and then being left alone. I'm afraid there are so many bad memories, maybe he does need to leave."

"I agree," Henry said as he stared vacantly at his already empty coffee cup. "I'm just afraid that if he leaves, he'll also be leaving John and the Bible studies that are so good for him, and us looking after him. I know he's a man, but I'm afraid in Havre he won't have anyone to pull him from his shell or depression or whatever it is that cuts him off to everyone else. He can't survive if he climbs into his own little world with no one to pull him out. I know he dearly loves God, but he needs people who can show him love here in this world also," Henry added.

"I know what you're talking about, dear. I so hoped that the Lord would open his heart and show him he could trust people. But I guess that would be forcing Erik to do something he isn't ready to do. He opened up for awhile and really tried, and I was so glad when he got involved with Laurie. I saw the same thing when his dad first met Maggie, but just like his dad, the ending of a relationship seemed to drive him further into himself. Then there were those silly gossip stories he heard in the church. In a way, I can't blame him. People have never really proven themselves to Erik. It's too easy for him to merely say, 'I tried', when people disappoint him again. I honestly don't know where that will leave him in a new town."

The Coopers didn't know how to approach Erik since it always seemed to backfire. They thought about going to John O'Brian to see if he could talk to Erik, but Erik beat them and went to John himself. *Maybe John'll understand, although sometimes he doesn't get me either,* he thought.

That day John was working in the hot July sun on a housing site on the south end of Fairfield. Carpentry is usually regarded a good, earthy type of work. John's face betrayed the fact that the labor was also very hard in the hot sun, and maybe not as noble as expected. Sweat dripped off his head and rolled down his barrel chest, completely saturating his body.

As a rule, John coped with the sun by working barechested, and this had made his skin rough with a deep copper tone. He looked much different from what Erik had first seen in the restaurant. At the restaurant his hair had been neatly combed and Erik hadn't noticed the strength of his shoulders. Now he looked more like a tavern brawler than a Christian saint.

However, Erik had also gotten to know John much better than that first impression. He knew John to have an earnest,

284 ~ Bart Tuma

soft personality that only highlighted his rough exterior. Although softness was present, John was also a confronting, honest person. That honesty gave him a transparent quality. Nothing was hidden in John, and he let other people know how he felt in any situation. It was a trait that Erik envied, but doubted he would ever possess.

Such openness would be considered offensive to Erik in any other person, but somehow it attracted him to John. He seemed to know how to speak honestly without hurting with his assessment. It was a rare ability, but one that Erik needed.

"Erik, looks like you've come just in time to do some work. I got a hammer over there for you."

"No, thanks, I already gave at the office. Besides, I have ten thumbs as it is, and I don't want to lose any of them whacking them with a hammer. Looks to me like you're having too much fun by yourself."

"Loads of fun, but that's fine," John joked in return. "You know us Christians, we love to share. But what brought you into town on a Wednesday? Did you get off for good behavior or are you AWOL?'

"Well, it's certainly not for good behavior," Erik said with a hint of seriousness in his voice. He quickly recounted the story of the trailer to John and then continued. "I know that I've hurt the Coopers and I know I have to leave. At least I feel like I have to leave. I don't want to hurt anyone, but I don't want me to hurt anymore, either. I need to start over. I know the Coopers are thinking that I'm not grateful, but they've never come out and really said anything. In a way, it's like right after my dad died and I was left at the farm. There's a feeling that something needs to be said, but it's not. Dad was dead and I was at their farm, but nothing was said."

"Have you tried saying anything? Maybe they think it's your turn to talk since you're making all the decisions," John said.

"I guess I haven't come right out and asked their opinion," Erik confessed, "but I need to go, and I need to know they know it's not because of them."

"Sounds like they could easily feel you're leaving is because of them. I mean, Erik, you're not the best for sharing gratitude, or anything else, for that matter."

"I know that, but it's something I have to do. I have to have my own life away from this place. I've felt that way for years and no matter how hard I try to make this place home, it's not. It's a place where I was left, not a place I chose. Can't you talk to them for me?" Erik pleaded.

"No, Erik, don't come and ask me to solve this. You've lived with the Coopers all your life, and they know you a lot better than me. They've got a lot more at stake in this relationship. I'm not going to be a guru when the only people who can answer you are with you every day. This is your decision. It's up to you, not me, to talk to them and then maybe even listen to them, not me."

"John, don't start lecturing me unless you realize what this means to me. It's my first real chance to leave Fairfield and make something out of my life."

"I'm not lecturing you, Erik, but you need to realize that what you do affects other people. Those people love you. Maybe it's hard to accept their love, but they love you, nonetheless. It seems like they have earned the right to at least know what you're thinking and for you to ask their advice. I know they aren't your parents by blood, but they have given their lives to you."

"You're right," Erik couldn't deny John's words. "I guess I have been wrapped up in myself . . . again. But it's not just the thought of leaving Fairfield," he added. "So far I really haven't done anything with my life. All I've done is work on a farm with a job that was given to me. All my life I've had dreams of what I could do and what I'd become, and so far those dreams have just kept slipping away. I thought I would go to college to play football, and that slipped away. I thought I'd get married, but who would want an old deadbeat like me? I thought I would find my mom but that was a dream too.

"I need to start making my life. I need to go someplace on my own, and have a try at the world myself away from the farm and Fairfield. It's a big world out there and all I've seen are dirt strips and a little farm town."

"I'll buy that, Erik, but don't expect to find something out there if you haven't found it here. Your surroundings might change, but you're still you. People are pretty much the same no matter where you go. Don't think that merely moving will answer all your problems. Problems also travel. It might be even harder because you're going to have to meet new people and establish new relationships. You have to admit that's not exactly one of your strengths," John added gently.

"I know the Coopers are worried that you'll leave yourself completely alone in Havre," he continued. "Frankly, I worry about the same thing. Even if you don't always know it, you have people here in Fairfield. It's not healthy for you, yourself, or your relationship with Christ to cut yourself off from people."

"I know that," Erik said in his defense. "It's just that in Havre it might be easier. People don't know my past. I can just be Erik, not Erik the orphan. It'll give me a chance to start over. You know as well as I do that Fairfield just doesn't let people change. Everybody knows everything and I've heard what they have to say about me."

"That's true. I know about Fairfield, but I also know about Erik. You're too used to being in your own little world. Do you think you can make new friends and be part of a church or Bible study like you have here? That's going to be crucial if you want to follow Christ. The example He gave by His life was not to become a monk on a mountain who separated Himself from the people. He walked with the people and He told us to be with the people to tell them about Him. I know you have a great one-on-one relationship with Christ, but you also know that isn't all we're called to do."

"I know that, and it's not like I haven't tried and haven't prayed about it. I remember coming back from Chief Mountain. I told you about that day. I was convinced that I would try and that Christ would heal me so I could be part of Fairfield. It just didn't happen. Oh, for a while it was fine, but after awhile it seemed like that conviction was as far away as that mountain. You know there was Laura...," he trailed off, his eyes taking on a distant look for a brief second. Then he continued, "Then I tried with Laurie. She's a great girl, but it just didn't work out, and it hurt when it didn't. And then people talked. I know they did. Then it was just easier to stay on the farm. I thought God would change all that and make it easier, but it just wasn't. I wish He would've made it easier, but it just wasn't," Erik repeated. He hesitated adding anything further.

"You know Christ has changed you," John saw that hesitation. "He has softened your heart and allowed you new life. At the same time God is not in the business of taking a paintbrush and repainting your life so everything has white picket fences and beautiful smiles. He gives you the brush and the strength and the paint of a new life. Then you have to take what ability He gave you and you make the difference. Before Him, you had no option but to live in your own little world, but with Him, you can make things different. He gives the strength and the paint of His life, and you apply it to your world."

"You make everything sound so simple."

"As you said, Erik, you and I both know it's not that easy, but it is that simple. You have to decide if you want to carry it out in your life. That's the hard part because for years you haven't lived that way and it's easy to fall back into old habits. But you can make that decision, just as you made the decision to follow Christ. It really doesn't come down to if you're a shy person or if you like being around people or not. It's how you view your life with Christ. Has He made you new? Does He protect you so you don't have to protect yourself from what people might say or do? Is He a big enough God that He can make things worth living even here in Fairfield? Again if He can't here, I really doubt He can in Havre, and you're only going to be disappointed again thinking your dreams have been dashed."

"Of course, you're right," Erik sighed. "But what else is new. It seems as if you're always right, John. But there is one thing I don't think you realize. I feel that this move is more than my decision. You knew me when I first became a Christian. I wanted nothing more than to get out of this place, but there was no way I could. Sure I could have packed my car and left, but I just was too scared to leave. I think God has given me the strength, and now has opened a door to leave. At first I thought the trailer house was an excuse to leave, but now I think it was a way God used to wake me up. I think He knows it's time for me to go. I've never felt so good about anything in my life.

"This means a whole new life for me. I'll have possibilities I don't even know of yet. You might think that I'm just a loner and don't like people, but that's really not me. Hey, I'm twenty-four and I'm single. I can't spend the rest of my life just living on a farm staring at walls every night. The walls of a trailer house aren't much different from the walls of a bunkhouse. I want a family, and kids to father like I was never fathered. I want a house with a big lawn and maybe a dog and a boat. I don't think God would want to deny me that, and I think He wants to start that part of my life."

"Fantastic, Erik. If you feel God is the author of this move, I certainly won't disagree. You know what the Bible says. Wisdom from above is first pure, peaceful and full of reason. If you are at peace with this, and if it makes sense, I'm all for it. But still use your mind and don't think God will just do it all. Check out the school to see if there will be jobs after you finish school. Check out if you have enough money to get by, or if it would be better to get a longer degree. This has to be more than a pipe dream that you give up on if it gets hard. If it's of God, you need to be willing to stick it out.

"At the same time do something for me. Don't cut the Coopers out of this move. Tell them what you're telling me. Ask for their advice and let them help. They've helped you when your were smart enough to ask for help. Don't cut them off now. Let them know that you still need them, and that you always will. You owe that to them. That can be a start for you if you decide to let Christ help paint a new life for you. You've cut them out of your life too much. It's nonsense to be able to tell me so much, and not be able to confide with those closest to you. It's maybe natural, but it's still nonsense."

"Yeah, I'll talk with them," Erik's tone was not negative because he was reluctant, but because he knew he was guilty for waiting this long to do it. Still, he was too excited about what the future held to not tell the Coopers. John was right. He owed them that. Finally all those things he had dreamed about for years now had the possibility of actually happening. This was not just a dream. It was a plan with a purpose and, hopefully, a happy ending.

"Yes, the Lord is faithful and He is good, and has done so much for me. He gave me strength when I didn't even know it, and now it is time to put it into practice." Erik's hand slapped the side of his jeans to brush off the dirt. The jeans had been dirty all day, but he only noticed the dirt as he rose to leave.

Chapter Twenty-Eight

Erik picked the Friday evening meal to have his talk with the Coopers. That meal was the most relaxed of the week, but at this point no one was relaxed.. His plans had progressed to a point that he could taste the reality of the move. His excitement overshadowed any nerves. Besides, he had made the decision to view things differently. He had decided to attempt to at least try something new and openly talk about his feelings. If he could talk to John he owed it to the Cooper's to be upfront with them. The Coopers certainly weren't scary or judgmental people.

"What do you think about me going to school in Havre?" Erik knew of no other way to start the conversation than to get to the point.

"I thought it was kind of a past topic," Mary answered. "What is there to think since you've already made up your mind?"

Erik was surprised, but prepared for the question. He had thought many times of the answer. "I didn't mean to make that decision without you and Uncle Henry," he said as his fork paused in mid-air. "It's just that I'm not totally used to talking things out. But what do you think?" And he took a bite and waited expectantly.

"Well, it could be a very good idea," Henry allowed. "It depends on why you're going."

"I'm going to learn a trade to move to the West Coast eventually."

"What do you want to find on the coast?" Henry asked.

Erik let his fork rest on his plate. "I want to find my own job and maybe start a shop someday. Get a house and start making something of myself. Who knows? Maybe I'll find someone to get married to. I just want to go someplace where the odds aren't against me and there's a chance to do something of my own. I want to go someplace that gives me a chance." With a little nod, Erik picked up his fork again. He hoped his words, and his voice, had conveyed his firmness. He had thought through this decision.

"You haven't been anyone here, in Fairfield, and you don't have a chance?" It was Mary's turn to question.

"Sure, I'm someone, but I'm just here. Nothing changes here. I haven't had a chance to do any of those things I've always wanted. I've never had a chance to make my dreams come true."

"I'm sure you've had a lot of dreams." a smile crept over Henry's lips as he said those words. "You know if it was twenty five years ago I would swear that it was your dad talking. He also had a lot of dreams, Erik; only he never had the ability to stick to those dreams. He talked a lot about them, much more than you've ever talked. But he was never able to follow though. I'm not sure what you think of your dad, but in many ways you're just like him. It's amazing how little you were around him, but how much you're like him.

"Erik, the only way you're going to make your dreams come true is if you stick to the Lord and allow Him to work through you. It's not enough to just have dreams, or plans for that matter. You need His strength to back you up. If not, Erik, that world out there that is so exciting to you—will eat you up."

This was the first time that Henry had even mentioned Erik's dad to him. The talk, however, seemed completely natural in its timing. It was as if Erik had come of age. Even if he was now twenty-four, it had never been time before. Before this he was still too young. It was as if Erik was receiving his first recognition as an equal. Erik somehow sensed the significance of the fact, and said nothing to stop the conversation.

Henry shifted his weight so he was looking straight at Erik. "If you can allow the Lord access to your plans, I don't see a thing wrong about going to Havre and wherever after that. But if you're going just because of some fantasy about the big world out there, it'll be about three days before you're back here on the farm. Your dad never had a chance to teach you about growing up. Maybe 'cause he never did. But I can tell you one thing. The Lord is great in fulfilling promises. However, there can be a lot of difference between a dream and a promise. You've got to have His promise to make your dreams come true."

Mary listened quietly and observed. As she looked at Erik she remembered his dad, Jimmie, and their walks to school. She thought of his nightmares and later his excitement as Maggie came into his life and they became married. Jimmie was full of dreams then. Then Maggie left him, and his heart never seemed to feel again. She feared the same thing would happen to Erik if this dream in Havre was an illusion.

At the same time, she realized this was personal to her and Henry. As she looked around the kitchen, the normal gathering place for countless conversations, she saw consistency. Those were the same kitchen cabinets that were in the house since it was built. The phone that carried calls from friends and doom-sayers, with words of joy and sadness and even boredom, was attached on the wall close enough to the table that its long cord could be extended to anyone without their getting up from their place. The table itself was oversized to accommodate farm hands and family, but it never seemed too big to huddle at one end to share their hopes and fears or the comfort of simply talking about nothing important. So much had happened in this kitchen, but every spoon and dish and kitchen utensil was at the exact same spot each day. Now there was going to be change. Erik was no longer going to be part of their home.

Erik had been part of their lives for the past eleven years.

Erik was right that nothing ever changed on the farm. To Erik that was a curse. To Mary that was her comfort. It was hard to even imagine their lives without Erik at the breakfast table. He was their child. It would not be easy to lose that part of their lives and disturb their comfortable nest. She knew that she was being selfish, but she was only being honest. She loved her life and her home. Somehow she now felt a hint of failure that she had never been able to make Erik feel the same.

"One other thing," Henry was saying, "you're going to have to rely on the Lord to make it. You're also going to have to start relying on other people. To look to the Lord for help is to also look to other people. We all know you aren't very good at that, but it's about time to start. You don't have a choice anymore. When you leave, there'll be no old bunkhouse to crawl into.

"When you get into a jam, and you will, don't just crawl into a hole and hope that the Lord will get you out of it. Pray like everything that the Lord will help, and then reach out to people for help. If you're going to take on the world, you're going to need all the ammo you can get. People will disappoint you, but you have no choice. None of us are perfect, but God will send people your way to help you, so don't push them aside. Hey, if you expect to be able to have a family, you'll have to first start trusting people."

Erik waited for a second before he could answer. Uncle Henry and Aunt Mary being so honest didn't hurt him. He knew they were right and were really just saying what John had said and what Erik already knew. Since it was time for him to respond, he wanted to make sure he expressed his exact feelings.

"See, I think the only way some of my dreams can come true is by leaving. Then I will be in a place to see things happen. I just don't think I have that chance here. I work five and a half days a week and I know exactly what will happen each day. Nothing changes. I come home and you give me dinner that I know will always be on the table when I get there. Then I go out to the bunkhouse, talk to the Lord, read the Bible and wait for the next day. I don't have to worry about where the next meal is going to come from, or if I'll come up with the rent. In a way it's safe, but it's just existing. There's no chance to make something of myself.

"Uncle Henry, you talked about making His promises your dream. The more I think about it the more I know it is His promise. I believe it is in His plans for me to go to Havre.

"It's not like I'm just leaving this place. This farm will always be a part of me whether I like it or not. I realize that now, but at the same time you've got to realize that this land can't be my whole life like it is yours. Maybe it would be different if I was your son, but I'm not. I'm a Winters, and maybe I am like my dad. I don't know. But when school starts two months from now, I think I need to be there. It's my first chance to do something to see my dreams come true. I want to see if those things

I read in the Bible about His watching over me will work out there outside of my safe nest. You say it's a big world. I need to see how big my God is." Erik's shoulders slumped down as if to rest after his oration.

"That's all we wanted to hear, Erik." Henry put his hand on the back of Erik's head. "We just wanted to hear that you're doing this because you want to better yourself out of trust of the Lord, not out of running from your past. We want to know that you're excited about something, and that you'll do it no matter what gets in your way. Sure, we'll miss you and worry about you. We wouldn't love you if we didn't. You are our son no matter what last name you have. We'll do everything possible to help you in your dreams. Just don't forget us back here. We won't expect you to write. We know you better than that, but making a collect call every once in a while would be nice.

"Thank you, Uncle Henry and you, Aunt Mary. I really am sorry I didn't come to you before. I know you love me. I've been too excited about Havre. I know I said I wanted to have a home of my own. I will always know my home is also here." Erik knew that all that needed to be said had passed. Now it was time to look to the future. It was an unknown future, but one he felt prepared to conquer. As he thought these thoughts he had little idea of how high the obstacles would be. If he knew the future, he might have thought again and retreated back to the bunkhouse.

Chapter Twenty-Nine

It happened about a month later, the latter part of August. Erik wouldn't be able to remember the exact date, but it was sometime right before harvest. He had quit work early on a Saturday. The machines were all ready for harvest so there wasn't much else to do until the wheat was golden and ready. Erik had taken a short nap to catch up on the sleep he had lost during the long week of work. When he awoke, his vision was blurred in his left eye.

He wasn't alarmed at first. He merely thought something had gotten into his eye. His vision was like looking through a thin fog, and floating in that fog were tiny particles, almost like hairs on the lens of a home movie projector.

His lack of concern kept him from mentioning it to the Coopers. Harvest was close, and they had enough worries as it was. Since he never trusted doctors, he didn't even consider going to one.

Instead of clearing, however, the eye gradually became enveloped in a thicker fog. By then harvest had begun, and Erik was too busy to do anything about it. His right eye was perfectly fine so he relied on it.

It was only after the harvest and the work had slowed that he began to get more concerned about his eye. School would start in three weeks, and he noticed that his lack of depth perception hindered his work. Because of his worsening vision he volunteered one Wednesday to go into Fairfield and pick up some needed parts. This was usually Henry's job, but Erik insisted without telling the Coopers why. His plan was to stop by Dr. Irvin's office for a quick check-up. He wouldn't mention it to the Coopers. At first, Henry insisted that the errand was his job, but Erik insisted even harder. Henry had no idea what the problem was, and decided against pushing the issue.

The doctor said very little to Erik when he finally arrived at the clinic. This worried Erik even more. Fairfield had no specialist, just two general practitioners like Dr. Irvin who now poked at Erik's eyelids. The doctor was an older, gruff man who was not qualified to say anything except that it was obvious there was some type of fluid in Erik's eye. He told Erik he needed to see an eye doctor immediately.

It was the doctor's unwillingness to talk that worried Erik the most. It was obvious that the problem was more than a scratch. Dr. Irvin arranged an appointed with a doctor in Great Falls for the next day. He didn't give Erik an option about whether he wanted to go or not.

The appointment was set for 11 am so the Coopers would have enough time to drive the two hours to Great Falls. The doctor said Erik shouldn't be driving and the Coopers would have to take him. The specialist would be more qualified to tell him more. He didn't want to say anything else and make a false evaluation. That refusal, combined with Dr. Irvin's side-glances and whispers to his nurse, made Erik's thoughts run wild in speculation. Erik didn't dream in the bunkhouse. Neither did he sleep.

When Erik got back to the Coopers', it was decided that Henry would take Erik to Great Falls. Dr. Irvin had personally called the Coopers to make sure Erik didn't make the drive himself or simply stay home. The Coopers knew as much information as Erik when he pulled into the driveway leading to the farmhouse.

Mary would stay home to make meals for the one hired hand that was left after the harvest. They also felt that it was making too big of a deal of the matter if they both went. They knew it was serious, but until they knew exactly what was happening they didn't want to scare Erik even more. Besides, if Mary had insisted on going, she knew she would talk constantly on the way to Great Falls because of her nerves. Neither man needed that.

The two had to leave the farm by 8:30 to make sure they had time to make the trip and find the office. Great Falls was still only a medium-sized town of 100,000 to most, but a large city to anyone from Fairfield.

As Mary turned the last batch of bacon, it was clear that

neither had slept. The silence also made it clear that neither man was looking forward to the trip today. Usually the trip to Great Falls carried a certain excitement. The trip meant going to the "big city" and stores that Fairfield didn't have. Not that day. Erik had never been to any doctor except Dr. Irvin and he envisioned a specialist's office as a sterile combination of machines and sick people. Henry stole looks in Erik's direction as often as possible. He was afraid of Erik's reaction as much as he was Erik's eyes. Each time his uncle looked, the car went over the center line.

"You might want to pay more attention to the road than looking at me or we'll both be seeing a doctor, but not a eye doctor," Erik said, his stare remaining straight ahead.

As they passed through Shelby and headed south to Great Falls, Henry tried but wasn't at all successful in getting Erik to talk. Erik would only engage in trivial matters about the farm and soon grew flippant in his remarks. Every time Henry would ask about Erik's eyes, Erik would get even more sarcastic. It was an old habit that Henry hated to see. It was obvious that there was nothing Henry could do. Under his breath he prayed, knowing that Erik had retreated into his own world. He had been through so much with Erik that it was impossible to imagine what might happen now.

Erik's mood changed quickly as they pulled up to the brick building that housed the eye clinic. There was something about the reality of those bricks that could not be overlooked or flippantly put aside. As they walked into the office with its brightly colored partitions and magazine shelves, both men were silent.

A receptionist was arguing with a patient about a bill that needed to be paid before the visit. The Hispanic-looking man had problems speaking English, and this only increased the fervor of her pleas. Erik wished the argument could be solved so that he could check in and be seated. He wanted to lose himself in the waiting room like he had in his own bunkhouse. As he looked around many of the patients had large patches or thick lens glasses. Still, he told himself that none of them had a problem as great as his. Somehow seeing those other patients finally made him acknowledge he had a problem. He couldn't yet define the magnitude of the problem, but he knew the consequences would be great. In a strange way he now wanted his problem to be greater than the others.

It was a full hour before Erik was taken back to a room, and another half hour before the doctor came in. Erik told Henry to go get something to eat from the diner they saw next door. Of course, Henry refused and even insisted on going back to the examining room with Erik. Many thoughts passed through Erik's mind as he waited for the doctor. None of them were positive. The only positive presence was Uncle Henry. Erik felt like a little kid whose mommy had brought him to the doctor, but that was a feeling he cherished as he sat there looking at a bad picture hung on the wall.

When the doctor finally arrived, it was obvious he was a busy man who was already behind in his schedule. He stuck out his hand as a hollow gesture of greeting, and stated that his name was Dr. Adler. Adler didn't wait for Erik's response. He was focused on his job, not the person. He turned down the lights and put a banded light on his head that reminded Erik of a miner going to work. Uncle Henry was not acknowledged as he sat in his corner of the room. He leaned forward to hear the doctor but still far enough away to not get in the way.

Dr. Adler quickly asked Erik a series of question as if reading from a cue card. "Have you seen strobe light flashing lights? When did you first notice the sight loss? Do you see better in the morning or evening?"

Many of the questions Erik couldn't answer. If something seemed different it was just a bad day and not an eye problem. It was just an eye, and nothing would happen to his eyes.

Then the doctor asked even stranger questions of Erik. "Are you constantly thirsty? Have you lost weight recently? Are you constantly urinating? Are you having problems with depression? The nurse will be putting drops in your eyes so I can see them better."

The doctor left without saying when he'd be back. The nurse put the drops in his eyes and said he'd have to wait twenty minutes and she was gone. Erik and Uncle Henry were left in the semi-dark room alone.

Neither Erik nor Henry talked for the forty-five minutes before the doctor returned.. Every minute or two, Erik would look at his watch to see how long they had been waiting. He didn't know if it was the drops or the darkness or a worsening of his good eye, but his watch was both a marker of time and his worsening sight. The quiet room carried thoughts of the worst scenarios.

When the doctor returned, the exam did not take long. Dr. Adler directed a light that was bright enough to hurt. The doctor firmly held Erik's eyelids open, and gave a series of directions.

"Look up towards the ceiling. More, as far up as you can. Now look to the right. To the upper right. Now to the lower right." He barked the orders like a drill sergeant. He was as a man who had done this so many times before that it had long ago lost its significance. He had Erik turn both eyes in every possible direction. Although the doctor's grasp was firm, the pain wasn't that bad, but Erik still grew sick in his stomach. He tried to hide his emotions, but then that didn't matter. The doctor's exam was too close and too thorough for there not to be a problem. The doctor placed the light on the table, and reached to flip the room light switch to on.

"Erik, do you have any history of diabetes in your family?" the doctor quizzed.

"I...I don't know. My parents are dead."

"None that we know of," Henry contributed from the back of the room.

"Well, for one reason or another, you've had a growth of blood vessels on the retina of both eyes. Usually that's attributed to diabetes. We think the eye does not receive enough oxygen because of the diabetes, and the eye tries to compensate for this deficiency by growing additional blood vessels. Unfortunately, those vessels are weak and randomly scattered like weeds in a garden."

"You may have been a diabetic for years and never known it because you didn't have the common symptoms. Type II diabetes, which you might have, still produces some insulin in the body. You're young and active so you might not have noticed it. At the same time, it could have attacked your body. But I can only guess at that. You'll have to go to an endricologist, a diabetic specialist, to find that out. What I know is that these vessels have grown. The vessels are extremely delicate and grow in no set pattern. They can become like clothes lines from one side of your eye to the other. That has happened in your left eye and is in the process in your right eye. In your left eye the vessels have burst and filled your eye with blood. That fog you mentioned is your own blood.

"The other eye obviously hasn't hemorrhaged yet, and we'll start treatment right away to minimize that possibility. We have developed a new laser treatment by which we shoot the retina of the eye with a laser beam. It actually kills the spot we hit and tends to make the vessels recede. We've had success with this treatment if we do it early enough. I wish you would have come in earlier. I'm not sure how far the process has spread or if we can stop it at this point.

"Your bad eye is in a different category. When you first saw specks in your left eye, we could have helped it with laser. It's too late for that now. We'll have to look at other surgery for that. I don't do that surgery. You'll have to go to Seattle if you want to try it."

"But what made it bleed? I was sleeping when it happened. There's no way I could've strained it." Erik had developed a frightened edge to his voice as he heard words that made no sense to him.

"The hemorrhages can happen at any time. You could have hibernated for the winter and they still would've burst. It's not a function of exertion. It's a function of the disease process. Small vessels have developed. The traction caused by those vessels are tugging at other vessels and pulling them loose, causing the bleeding. The bad news is that if that condition remains it will pull your whole retina apart and there will be no chance for your eye."

"What's the chance for it now?"

"I've got to be honest with you, Mr. Winters. We don't exactly know. The specialist in Seattle will be able to tell you more, but they have only been doing the surgery for two years now and it's still somewhat experimental. The results are sometimes not satisfactory. Just be glad because two years ago you wouldn't even have had this option."

"What is the surgery/"?

"They will place two tubes in your eye. One tube will remove the blood and vitreous fluid, and with a micro-drill they cut away the clothes line vessels. The other tube will replace the lost fluid to keep your eye at a constant pressure. It's called a vitrectomy."

"What happens if I decide not to do it?"

"Your eye will continue to have the traction placed on it, and at some point the retina will be torn loose. At that point there is no treatment for your eye. You'll be totally blind, not just legally blind."

"When would I need this vit…whatever?"

"As soon as possible. I'll contact Seattle, but you should start making arrangements. The longer the traction exists, the worse it will get. You have already waited a long time by not coming in. Actually, because of the strain on your bad eye, we'll have to put off laser treatment on the other eye until we have your eye stabilized after surgery. Your good eye is in an advanced stage, and it could hemorrhage at any time, but we will wait because of how bad the other eye has become. It would have been different if you had come in earlier, but there is now no time to wait. The sooner we can get both eyes done, the more hope there is that you don't have a total loss of vision."

"Why do I have to go to Seattle? Why can't you do it here? You said it was just putting in two tubes."

"Those tubes constitute probably one of the most delicate surgeries around, and, as I said, it's still experimental. Seattle and San Francisco are the only two places west of Minnesota that do the surgery. You'll be in the hospital for about a week, and it'll take a month to recover at home."

Erik didn't want to hear any more. Previously, his stomach had felt nauseous with the bright light. Now he was sick at the thought of what lay ahead. He just wanted to get out of that room with its smell and its darkness. They were wrong. The whole crummy place with its bad pictures and crowded lobby was wrong. He just wanted to get out. As soon as the doctor moved his equipment to the side, Erik was gone. He didn't exactly run, but his feet were quick to move towards the door. Henry tried to stop him, saying there were arrangements that needed to be made, but Erik told him he could make the arrangements. No one could keep him in that office any longer.

Once outside the building, Erik walked. He didn't walk in a specific direction, or with any destination in mind. He walked with long, quick strides that took him past the city buildings. This was not a metropolitan area, but Erik saw the pavement and stuffiness a city brings. He saw objects that he normally would have overlooked; a sign marking a pedestrian crossing, the sculptured face work of the older buildings, and people of every description walking without seeing each other.

Finally a small park allowed Erik to stop as he sat down on one of the benches. There he could sense a light breeze and a fresh smell of trees through the city's staleness. A giant oak stood in the middle of the park, the leaves glistening with sunlight as the breeze turned them as crystals to the afternoon sun. The grass had a path worn through the middle by people finding a shortcut from street to street. A small softball field stood empty after a summer's work, its children already back at school. People were scurrying to meet their lunch deadlines, and Erik saw all that his eyes would show him, but it was not enough.

He cried. Not since that morning of his salvation in the old pickup had he cried so openly and so freely. He was aware that people would notice him on that bench, but he neither cared nor was there little he could do to stop. There was little he could do to hope. He couldn't help but think that the end had come. Not the end of his life. Blindness wouldn't kill him. It was the end of his hope. There would be no school in Havre, and there was no need for blind welders. He had wanted to go to the coast, but not for this. This trip would not be to become somebody. It would be a trip to try to keep his life together, and that too was uncertain.

The things he had hoped for so long and so hard were gone. He had dreamt all his life, but only one other time had he felt so helpless. That was the night of the fight at the Mint Bar when he realized he was only a dreamer who had no future. But that night with Christ had changed all that, and once again he had hoped. He had hoped even bigger dreams and made the plans because he felt God had promised him those dreams. Now there was nothing. There was only a broken man crying alone in the unkempt park amid the dirt of a crowded downtown.

He felt utterly alone. It was one thing to be abandoned by his mom. This was worse. The mere possibility of being abandoned by God left Erik chilled in his solitude. For the past two years, God had been his constant companion. Whenever he needed to talk, he talked to God. Now, although he didn't even feel like trying, no words would leave his lips, and he was sure there would be no response if he did speak. If God had abandoned him, it must mean he was worthless to everyone.

This wasn't supposed to happen. He was supposed to be getting ready to start his life. God had promised him. Erik was supposed to be protected by God, not eaten inside by some disease he didn't even know existed. Yes, bad things sometimes happen to Christians, but not now, not to him. He felt the next moment, the next year, and the rest of his life had no significance. Erik, in his despair, mused that his life never had any significance, so why would he think that would ever change? Time no longer held a future. Time now was only a commodity measured by clocks, not time to carry out one's dreams.

There must be a mistake. There had to be a mistake. However, as Erik held his hand over his good eye, he knew there was no mistake. Erik couldn't even see the giant oak tree through his bad eye. All he could see was a semi-green outline that to his senses wasn't a tree, although he knew it was. His life seemed the same as the outline of that tree; not precise or defined, only vague in its existence.

"No, it can't be. It isn't. God, you can't let this happen. It's not supposed to happen this way," Erik said aloud when he finally could speak. He didn't care who might hear or what they might think. "Where is your healing? What about Your promise of my new life? Why did You let this happen in the first place? Was my life so bad that You decided to end any hope by taking my eyes? God, You've got to do something. What am I suppose to do now?"

Erik's fear in the pit of his stomach reminded him of the meetings at Hay Lake Hall in the sixties. Mary had remembered the hall for its dances and Henry. Erik remembered the hall in his nightmares. It was the Cold War and Russia was on everyone's mind. The Civil Defense System would call monthly meetings to prepare the people for nuclear war. Fairfield was within a hundred mile circle of a battery of Minutemen missile silos, all supposedly pointed at Russia. The northern Montana missiles would be a primary Russian nuclear target, and Fairfield would lie in ashes.

The meeting at Hay Lake Hall would start with a gentleman in an odd looking uniform coming forward. It wasn't military issue and his shirt sleeves were so long it made it awkward to use the pointer he loved to wave. He seemed to relish the attention from the rows of terrified folks as he came to the front of the room.

"Thank you for all coming this evening. As you all know, Cascade County lies in dangerous country when the Russians decide to attack. It is only with great preparation that we can hope to survive a nuclear blast, so I hope you all watch the next film carefully because the danger is real. Your life depends on your response that we will direct."

The man didn't say, 'if the Russians decide to act'. He said, 'when they attack' with great certainty. Erik, even at a young age, had gotten into a habit of watching the Huntley-Brinkley news report on NBC. The man in the front was so certain the Russian were coming. How come Chet Huntley hadn't said that on the news that evening? Was it a secret that only this man knew and it was being hid from the rest of the country so they wouldn't panic? Or was that little man just trying to act like he knew something? Either way, Erik had watched the film, para-lyzed in his seat as the large plume of an H-bomb enveloped the screen before him.

Once home, Erik would sleep on the floor. The film said the lowest ground was the safest. But then he began to think. What if the Russians didn't attack with the bomb? Maybe they would send troops over the Pole and through Canada to take out the Minutemen with sheer force. That's what he would do. He would save his bombs for the cities and send troops for the missiles before anyone knew better. No one would know the troops were coming, but they would show up at their farmhouse first since they lived on the unguarded border. Low ground wouldn't be good enough. He would have to find a place in the culverts or the coulee brush where the troops would overlook a small boy.

As he finally drifted off to sleep, he would see wave after wave of soldiers crossing the fields, and Erik, undecided and unable, would never find a place to hide. The Russians would take him. It was only a matter of time. He knew it was inevitable, but he could do nothing to avoid it.

The fear he felt now felt the same as after the Hay Lake Hall movies. He knew the inevitable was coming and there was nothing he could do to hide from its consequences. He didn't know how or when the attack would be complete, but his fear bore witness that it was close and final.

His fear was mixed with thoughts racing through his mind. He thought of what could have been, and what needed to be. He most feared that he would never be able to see his child from a wife he didn't even know yet. What woman would want to marry a man who could neither see her nor provide for her? More than any other sight, he wanted to see that child. He wanted to witness the baby holding its arms out, reaching and calling for daddy, and then for him to be able to pick up the child and comfort it, and show that it was loved and needed. Erik wanted to do for a child what no one had ever done for him. That scene might not be possible now, and that reality made him sick to his stomach. He wanted his son to know his father as a complete man, not a cripple like Erik's father had been with booze and that Erik was now.

As he looked around, he strained to pick out details that he might have missed before, and that he might not have the chance to see again. He abhorred the thought that he could lose his sight. He had seen nothing so far in his life, at least nothing worthwhile. Nothing but the dirt covered land, and yet that would be all he would have to hold in his memory. He had not seen the color of waves breaking on the shores of the Pacific. He had never witnessed a fine play at a theater, or the magnificence of a skyscraper. He hated the land he now abhorred not seeing again more than ever. He had told God before he would go back to that land to make things right. Now God seemed to no longer exist. There was no reason to return. There was no reason for anything.

Chapter Thirty

The trip home had never been longer. Erik tried to notice everything that might make this ride different from the others. He wanted to see something that he had missed before so he could hold it in his memory when his eyes would no longer carrying the image.

He noticed a yellow farmhouse that, unlike most, wasn't white but had bright yellow paint covering its three floors with a large patch of trees to its left. Out front there was an old horse plow where the mailbox hung and a sign that read "The Halverson's" There was a small ravine into which the road dipped and a stream laced its bottom. Alongside, a few birch trees lived, fed by the stream's flow.

By the highway there was a notice warning of crossing deer, but Erik had never seen deer there. He believed that sign was only put there to generate false hope, as were the pictures of the "Farmer's Journal" wheat fields.

On that trip there wasn't enough to keep Erik from going back into his thoughts. He had always lived in those thoughts more than his surroundings and this day made it even easier. Henry continually tried to capture Erik's attention with conversation, and several times succeeded, but only briefly.

"Erik, you didn't wait to hear all the doctor had to say. He thinks there might be a chance they'll have good success with your eyes. If the surgery goes well you might be able to see forms out of your bad eye."

"Forms? What good will forms do me?"

"He said that it would help in your depth perception. That way you wouldn't reach for something and find it wasn't there."

"Yeah, I know what depth perception is. I've lived without it for the past few weeks. But it seems to be the story of my life. I reach for something and it simply isn't there. How many times can you do that until you realize its better not to even reach?" The realities of Erik's remarks were too sharp for there to be a response and they simply traveled once again in silence.

"Erik, are you going to have the surgery?" Henry finally tried again.

"Do I have a choice?"

"Of course you have a choice, but I think only one smart choice. Dr. Adler said you would have complete blindness in that eye if you just let it go, and your other eye could progress, so you need to keep everything you can."

Erik's voice was wistful, as if he were a small boy. "Couldn't we put off the surgery for a couple of months, until next year or something? Let me get some of the school done?"

"You heard what the doctor said. It's a crucial time right

now, especially to keep the other eye from doing the same thing. Besides, you're going to be limited in what you can do for a while. The doctor said you shouldn't be driving, and I don't know if it would be smart to head off to school right now. Erik, what do you think? Erik?"

Once again Erik's eyes were transfixed out the front window. Tears began to swell in his eyes so he turned farther away until he was looking straight into the side window glass. The window had a slight layer of dust, and the sun was growing dim on the horizon. With the dust backing, the window acted as a faint mirror.Erik saw himself as inlaid on the passing country side.

His reflection froze on the glass as a ghostly image impressed on the window. The landscape rose and fell with the rolling plains, only his face remained entombed on the makeshift mirror. He had always known he was part of this land, but the image showed him as the land itself.

He looked at his eyes--the eyes carried his strength; those eyes guided the tractor and witnessed the sunset. It was his eyes that always portrayed the softness in Erik, and now they were dying.

He tried to see if the damage to the eyes could be seen. The left eye seemed lifeless. He didn't know if that came from the sickness within the eye or the sickness within his heart. In the best of times, Erik's eyes danced with life and light. Now they were merely stone encased within his face against the picture of the passing land.

The passing land contained harvested fields and strips waiting for next year's crops. What Erik saw wasn't any specific feature of the land, but the rising and falling landscape against his face. It was as if his life was passing by in that window, but he was encased and unable to move. He wanted to move or to shout or to cry, but the land merely passed by and his image in the dust-covered mirror reflected no hope of change.

"Erik. Erik."

"Yeah?"

"I think it would be good if Sunday you'd let the elders anoint you with oil and let the people pray for you."

"Sure, I'll do that. I'll let them do that," Erik responded without conviction.

"Don't give up on God, Erik."

"I don't know right now, Uncle Henry. I don't know anything. It's like I'm just in another dream, but this time it's a bad dream. I don't know what to do or what to think. Where do I go from here?"

"You can only take one step at a time," Henry reminded him. "It's too early to know how your vision will turn out so don't turn your back on Him. No matter how your eyes turn out, you can't shut Him out. Don't start thinking about the future. Think about what is going to happen this week."

"I don't even know what's going to happen this week. Sure, I'll let them cut into my eyes, but what will that accomplish?

See, I was just about to take the first real step that meant something new in my life, and you say take one step. How can you take a step if you aren't going anywhere?"

"Erik, I'm not good like John at explaining things, but I do know the Word of God, and I do know Him. I know that He has been true to your aunt and me all our lives. There've been times when I just couldn't figure things out, but He has always been true.

"I don't know if you even remember, but there was a time in my life when I thought all my dreams for the farm had ended. You were only thirteen so maybe you didn't even know what had happened.

"Your aunt and I had just put a third mortgage on the farm to buy the 200 acres from the Hylands. I had to plead with the bank to get the money, but I knew that land was good and our farm was just too small at the time to survive. I felt I needed to trust the Lord to keep the farm. By the end of the first year I thought I was a genius and it was clear to me that the Lord had been with the purchase. That year the crops were great.

"They were more than great. They were the best I ever saw; at least seventy-five bushels per acre. I had taken the chance and planted barley and the samples showed it would be malting barley rather than feed barley, so the price for that grain would be five times normal. I thanked God every day as I walked through those fields and saw the harvest become ready. The barley was so heavy it lodged over on itself; the heads were so full of kernels that the stems couldn't hold them straight."

"I couldn't believe that the Lord had opened up buying that land just in time for the best harvest ever. It was great. I knew He was great." Henry paused, remembering.

"Then came the first day of harvest. I'll never forget that day. I had just pulled the combine into the first field, the forty acres straight east of the house. It was a great feeling to see the reel of the combine pulling in that barley. I could almost see myself handing the check to the banker and telling him how great my God was."

"Late the same afternoon I glanced towards the west. Some clouds were starting to build. They weren't the normal clouds. They were tall and they were topped with white. I had seen those clouds before. They were hail clouds. The weatherman hadn't said anything about a storm, but I could see the clouds getting bigger and bigger and closer and closer.

"My first instinct was to stop the combine and cry and then to pray. But there was no time to stop. I needed that harvest. So I prayed out loud while the combine worked. I tried to make the combine go faster, but the machine could only handle the thick grain so fast. I could only go at a crawl while the storm looked like it was on a locomotive. I prayed that the Lord would steer the storm north or south or anywhere but here. As the clouds came dead on towards me, I prayed that the Lord would change the hailstones to drops of rain.

"But those clouds didn't stop. They seemed only to build in

size and speed. Within an hour they hit the field I was working. It sounded like machine gun fire was hitting that combine when the storm hit with its hailstones. The fields right in front of me that stood so tall with grain was flat to the ground in minutes. The hail stones were so big they left pit marks on the sides of the red combine. Until I sold that combine I was reminded of that storm.

"Those stones left nothing of the crops. The heads were so full they were knocked free of all their kernels. And it wasn't just the forty acres I was working on. It wiped out all the fields on the main farm. The only crops the storm missed were the two hundred acres of the Hyland's farm that was separated from ours. "

"I guess I should have thanked the Lord that He gave me the one piece of land that was spared, but I wasn't in the mood for thanks. It seemed to be that land and its mortgage might cost me the whole farm. Those two hundred acres wouldn't pay the mortgage or seeds for next year or even hardly enough to put food on the table.

"In two hours time I had gone from the excitement of the harvest to despair that the harvest now lay useless on the ground. I thought my life had ended 'cause I thought I had lost the farm. I thought the land I worked for years would be taken over by the banks with that third mortgage. I had trusted the Lord and it seemed like the Lord hadn't answered my prayers.

"I thought I was going to die, but a funny thing happened. I didn't. I didn't lose the farm, and my life didn't come to an end. Things were tight for a long time, but the Lord took us through it and He protected our lives. He was true. The hail destroyed the harvest, but it couldn't destroy our lives unless we let it.

"I remember going to talk to Pastor Griffith. I'm not sure if you remember him, but he was a great man. I told him about my problems and asked him to pray for me that the Lord would miraculously provide me with money. He said he would be glad to, but then he asked me a strange question. He asked me where I would be a thousand years from then. Of course, I said "with my Lord in heaven." He told me not to forget that. He wanted to remind me that today is important, but we also need to remember that the conclusion of today is not the conclusion of our life. He reminded me that Scripture said of Jesus that He knew where He came from and He knew where He was going. It was because of Him knowing His final destiny that He could live through the crisis of the day."

It was unusual for Henry to give such a long story, but today was an unusual day. Erik did remember that time for a different reason. Usually, when they would all go to town, the Coopers would give Erik $2.00 to spend on candy and then they would go to the Point Drive-In for lunch. After that storm there would be no $2.00 and there wasn't enough money to even buy a Coke from the Point. Times were tough. Erik just didn't realize why at the time.

Erik could have felt insulted that a simple destroyed crop could be compared to his destroyed life. Erik knew better. He knew Uncle Henry's farm was his life, and to lose it would mean the end to his dreams, just as sight was the end to Erik's. But too much had happened the last two days for a nice story to make a difference. It was like listening to the old men talk about the old revivals. They were great stories, but they just didn't change today. Besides, his uncle had his wife to help support him while Erik had no one. Erik didn't know if he had the grit of Uncle Henry.

Someday that story of the hailstorm would be important for Erik to remember, but today's sorrow closed his heart and ears.

"Anyway, Erik, you're talking like you'll never have a chance again. If you want to show you can do something, show you've got the guts to still make those dreams come true. You don't know how your eyes will come out. Neither do I. He does. Your life is far from over with or without your eyes if you don't hide from Him. You need to see His hand in your life."

"It just doesn't make sense to me," Erik replied when it was obvious Henry had finished. "God shouldn't let this happen. You picked a funny choice of words when you said that I needed to "see" God's hand. That's the problem. I don't know if I will be able to see and what I see of Him seems so different. This isn't the God I've read about in the Bible or that I've seen in my life. He doesn't take people's eyes and make them go blind. Why did He let this happen?" Erik asked for the fifth time that day without an answer.

"I don't know, Erik. I've asked that myself, not only about your eyes, but at other times when things like that storm happened. I don't have an answer."

"Neither do I. Neither do I," Erik almost mourned as he turned again to his image imprisoned in the windowed scene.

Chapter Thirty-One

"Bless the Lord, O my soul
And all that is within me. Bless His
Holy name.
Bless the Lord, O my soul
And forget none of His benefits.
Who pardons all your iniquities?
Who heals all your diseases;
Who redeems your life from the pit;
Who crowns you with loving kindness
And compassion
So that your youth is renewed like the eagles."

Erik kept reading those words of Psalm 103. How foreign they sounded. At the same time, how much he needed them to be true. He knew the truth of the Bible, but now he didn't know how it all worked out in the world he lived.

"The Lord ...heals, redeems, satisfies your years, and renews your youth." Those words hung with him, not as a comfort, but as a presence that neither healed him nor allowed him to forget. If he was to believe the Bible, indeed believe God, he needed to deal with those words.

He had gone to church that Sunday. He had been prayed over and anointed with oil, but there was no change in his eyesight. Now he had to deal with the reality of surgery, a reality he neither wanted nor trusted. He wanted someone to shake his shoulders and tell him that he didn't need to do it. He wanted them to say a medicine was found, or that the Lord would still be a healer, but no one would. Not even John had any simple answers. They all advised him to have the surgery. They said God could work through surgery. To Erik, this seemed like a cop-out.

The thought of even needing a surgery was too much for him to comprehend. *Why when everything is ahead of me would of God let this happen?* There would also be tests to see if he was a diabetic and that, if positive, could mean other complications. Somehow, God had not dealt with what was before Erik, and it left Erik feeling as if he had to deal with it alone.

Erik wasn't being a coward. It wasn't the knife of surgery that bothered him. It was the fact that he once again seemed alone. There is no such thing as a coward or a hero. The only difference between the two is the hero is able to look beyond what is before him. Erik had dreamt too much in his life to look beyond this. He had seen too many dreams vanish and now the outcome seemed too final. He had decided to go ahead with the surgery, but it was a decision from unwillingness to fight rather than from bravery.

"Erik, can I talk to you?"

Erik jumped; as he was unaware anyone was in the bunk-house. John came in without knocking.

"Sure, come on in."

"I heard you decided to have the surgery Friday."

"Yeah, they didn't give me much of a choice. Crazy situation, isn't it? Don't know what to do now."

"I wish I could give you some good suggestions, but I don't have any," John admitted.

"I sure wish you did. I wish someone did. Before you told me my parents found themselves in their hopelessness because they never turned their lives over to Christ. Well, here I am, a full-fledged child of God, flat on my back."

"Doesn't make sense, I know, Erik."

"You're telling me. You're the man with all the answers. What are they?"

"I don't have any answers. I know what's happened doesn't make any sense at all. Unfortunately I also know that things like this will happen again. What are your answers, Erik?"

"My answer, huh. I'm the one asking, not answering."

"But you're the only one who can answer, Erik. You're the one it's happening to, and you're the one living with the consequences. You know God well enough. What is your answer?"

"I think I've got to question. It looks like a lot of those

things in the Bible don't work out in real life."

"Like what?"

"Like, how does Christ touch our physical lives with healing? Sure, I've been healed before with things like headaches and colds and sniffles, but the biggies... Why can't I be healed now? Is God too uninterested or too weak to do the big ones? Or is there something wrong with me? There are other people in church in wheelchairs. Why aren't they healed?"

"I don't know, Erik. I do know it has nothing to do with God's bigness or His lack of love for you. I probably won't understand until I get to heaven and then I have a lot of questions. But then somehow I think those questions won't be that important. Those people will be too busy dancing and shouting for joy without wheelchairs. But you know that's not the real question. He could heal every wheel chaired person and your eyes, and that wouldn't be the real question or answer. The only question is if He loves you today. Does He love you enough that He cries with your pain and at the same time is He big enough to still make a future for you, healed or unhealed? If God can't touch your life today, healing is the least of your concerns. What do you think? Does He still care? Have you given up on Him?"

"No, I sometimes wish that it would be that easy--to just get mad at Him and give up, like canceling a subscription to a magazine or something. Just tell Him I don't want to be part of His club any longer, but God has been too good to me to just say He doesn't matter anymore. There was a time I had to decide if I wanted to keep following Him, but that was a time back. There's no turning back now. It just seems all vague out there. No answer from God. No hope for tomorrow. I'm just breathing, that's all. I'd put all my hopes and dreams in going to Havre.

"Do you think that maybe one of the problems was putting your hopes in an event rather than in Him?"

"You're playing word games with me. I was putting my hope in Him, thinking that He wanted me to go to Havre. Now it seems like maybe He couldn't pull it off."

"Or maybe He had different plans. I have no idea, Erik. I'm not about to say what God's plan for you might be. But if I were you I wouldn't be too quick to say His plans still can't be worked out. The only way His plans will ever be fulfilled is if you don't abandon them by abandoning Him. You've told me before that you felt your mom abandoned you and your dad because she wanted more than you both had to offer. Well, don't abandon God because He hasn't acted like you expected Him to act. If you abandon God when He doesn't act like you hoped, all you're saying is you don't like what He offers that day," John concluded.

"You're right, again," Erik conceded. "This is just so unexpected. I had everything so figured out, but I never figured this could have happened. I know God. You know that I do, but I never expected this."

"Erik, before I asked you if you felt you were strong enough to make it by yourself in Havre. Now you need to ask yourself if you're strong enough to stay here and still believe He can work here."

"I was strong enough when you asked me, but now it's all different. Now there's no chance to leave. I have to face surgery and who knows what after that. I'm stuck. About the only strength I have is to wake up tomorrow."

"That's a start. What if God wanted you to stay here in Fairfield and work on the farm and make a life here? What if He had dreams for you here?"

"You mean God took my eyesight to make me stay?"

"No, God didn't do this. Don't even entertain that thought. This happened because it did. People get sick in this world. It happens to everyone, Christian or not. What I mean is that God is big enough that He still has dreams for you and those dreams are even better than you could imagine. Could you cooperate in that plan by still giving Him a place here or do you think He can't reach you in Fairfield?"

"Something good here?" Erik asked, skeptical.

"Yeah, to have things you were so excited about come true here on the farm. You dreamt to make a mark, to find a wife, to have a child and build your own home. That can happen here. Your tomorrow didn't end just because the trip to Havre didn't come off. Who knows what the future holds? You didn't expect this to happen. Give room for unexpected good things to happen."

"But, I can't even work the farm if I'm blind."

"If you're blind. No one said that it's certain. You're only thinking the worst. There's going to be surgery Friday. Let God still work through that surgery, and remember the doctor said there was a chance your other eye would stay good."

"A chance. My chances haven't gone very well lately."

"Erik, hold onto that chance. You're a dreamer, now dream. Don't let this be an end because you can no longer dream. Now you have the Lord of the universe to give legs to those dreams."

"But it seems so hopeless."

"If my whole life hinged on the outcome of one last bet, I'd sure bet on my Lord and His dreams for me. He's the surest thing around, even when you can't see His working."

"I guess I don't really have a choice, do I? I'd run or go someplace else if I had a choice, but there's no place to go, and no one who would take me if I got there. I'll hope in Him, but that's all I can do. I'll hope, but I can't say I believe yet."

Erik wasn't over-confident. He had heard things before and had determined things in his mind before. Later those decisions were tested. Now the test was stronger and he didn't know if he was strong enough. He was the one who had lost his sight, and he was the one whose life would hinge on that bet. Was God big enough and still caring for Erik's life? Now he could only wait to see the outcome.

Chapter Thirty-Two

Two months passed since Erik first learned of his eye problems. He had the surgery and his good eye developed bleeders soon after and it too required the same surgery. The time had come and gone for him to go to school and he hadn't. The doctors were supposed to know what the outcome of the surgery was by now, but they didn't. Erik was supposed to be able to see out of his bad eye, but he couldn't.

His eyes were still filled with the remnants of the hemorrhage. Some of the weaker vessels had been removed so there was the chance the blood would naturally drain from the eye over time. However, there was the question of whether the blood would drain or new blood would leak from new bleeders. There was also the question on how much damage the center of the retina had sustained. If the damage was too severe, even if no blood was present, there might be no sight.

As the doctor had stated, the procedure was new and no guess could be made as to its outcome. The one emotion that was constantly with Erik was uncertainty. He knew only of that day. He knew that the time for school to start had passed, and that there was no sight in his eyes. As for tomorrow, it was hidden along with his vision.

It had been a shock at first when the second eye became as the first. It seemed as if his fears were realized and his hopes dimmed along with his sight. Then he rationalized that the second eye shouldn't have been a surprise. He knew the possibility of blindness all too well, and it might well have been his own fault for not having the eye cared for earlier. The doctor had talked of his prospects in terms that sounded much like the odds of horse racing. Erik didn't listen to the doctors any longer. He only relied on what he could or could not see. He could not see tomorrow so he did not trust it.

Days had passed since the first news of his eyes, and so had many of the emotions. He no longer was held in shock by the news. It was impossible to come to grips with the future since the future was so unknown. He tried to think of a plan or possibilities for the rest of his life, but there were no avenues to be found. He knew that he simply could not feel sorry for himself the rest of his life. At the same time, he did not know what the rest of his life would look like if his vision was completely lost.

He had begun to spend a considerable amount of time by the large oak tree that stood next to the coulee. He spent time with people also; he talked with the Coopers and John about what would happen now. Even the people of Fairfield and former classmates would make the drive to the Coopers farm to wish Erik well and give him cards that said the same. Laurie looked somewhat guilty when she came by, as if she should have given Erik more of a chance. Erik quickly ended that conversation since he didn't want anyone to feel sorry for him. He felt sorry enough for himself, he didn't need anyone to add to it.

Erik had no reason to feel alone in what he was going through since there were many people coming to him. Yet, at the same time, he was aware that he must go through this time absolutely alone. The word "loneliness" could not be used to describe his present condition. The stark reality of living in a world without sight was beyond an over-used abstraction. He was simply alone. The prayers and help of the people were necessary, but the reality was only his. Only he could experience waking up in the morning and not being able to focus on the walls.

The Coopers had given him a cassette player and Scripture tapes that covered most of the Bible. This gift might have seemed premature since he still had vision in his one eye, but that vision was fading and the small print Bible that he had worn out for the past two years quickly tired his eye. He played those tapes for hours, and had begun to memorize portions of their content. However, there came a time when he even had to turn the cassettes off.

The Scripture had been a source of strength and hope and understanding, but even those words could not make answers for him. Only his belief in those words, not just their printing, would bring reality to Erik. He knew the reality of losing his sight. Now he had to accept the reality of what he could see, not only with his eyes, but with his heart. He needed belief if those words were to mean anything.

He remembered Laura many times. He knew her problem. He knew that she had shut out God because of her feelings of guilt. Now for Erik it was hard to not feel isolated with his blindness. He remembered John's words of warming that Laura risked losing her joy of His presence if she didn't lay aside blaming herself for what had happened, and feeling guilty for turning her back on God. Now Erik had to lay aside the disappointment of an unfulfilled future.

As he sat once again by the big oak at an hour approaching evening, Erik thought over his life. There were no highlights that would make his life notable. There were those football games in high school, but those were for a little school in a small town. Besides that, there was nothing other people could see. Everything that had been impressive in his life had happened inside, in his spirit. No one else could see how God had touched him in that pickup. No one would have noticed God with him on Chief Mountain and the depth of Erik's convictions. No one even knew of his thoughts and feelings for Laura. Everything that made a difference could not be seen with eyes, but only felt with the Spirit.

He thought over the times when he rode the tractor, lay on his bed, or walked the meadows of the coulee. At those times he had added color and vitality to this bland, colorless land.

Those times had nothing to do with what he saw, but what he believed God had created. God had created within him an imagination to dream. He remembered driving the tractor through clouds of dust as he had sat at the wheel shouting as a pastor addressing the assembled congregation. There were the times when he had gone to the alkali lake and skipped rocks over the lifeless water. At that moment, it wasn't lifeless water; it was the sea with waves breaking to the beaches. There were times when he would go to the highest point on the farm and look for miles over the wheat-filled strips and barbed wired fences, but to his inner eyes they were not filled with dust. He was on his mountain amidst the mountain meadows. Somehow Erik had built a kingdom out of the dreams of God's promised fulfillment, and he did not see the desolation, but desolation brought to beauty and life.

As he reflected, his first thoughts were of how foolish he had been. They were only dreams and they had taken him nowhere. He had spent years visiting those dreams. Yet, somehow, they encircled him that day.

He reasoned they were fantasies and nothing else. He knew they would be erased as soon as the next gust of wind brought dust to his face. They were mirages that were common in the summer sun, but empty to the touch. He thought more and he prayed.

"Christ I've held my dreams as if they were real and I know they weren't. It's strange because as I look at those fantasies it

makes me realize how real You are. I know the fantasies and I know Your presence and they share nothing in common. I guess because I can see the façade I can easy identify the un-movable. My home in You is real. My hope in You will never be erased with the next gust of problems. Your beauty goes before this land. This land is almost not fit to be inhabited, but my life is not this land. It is Your hope. I saw Laura wrestle with that hope as if it had been left behind, but I also saw that hope never leave her life. I can no longer see the details of this farm, but I will always see the beauty of Your life. You have transformed my life. I will always look to Your land. I will see the Kingdom You have established within my heart."

He remembered that *Paradise Lost* quote that his uncle had used: 'The mind is its own place; in itself it can make a heaven of hell, a hell of heaven'.

"The poet's wrong," Erik thought. "The difference isn't how a person's mind perceives the world. The mind can make you think things you don't believe. The difference is seeing the Ruler of the land. The difference is Who rules my world. My life can be either the reality of this empty land, or the paradise of my Father's Kingdom. I can't make this land a paradise. His life within me can."

Erik thought of his uncle's hope in the farm. The farmer couldn't leave the land because of a few years of drought. The farmer gave so much of himself to the land that there never was a thought that the land would not return its harvest. His hope was for the rains of next season

"Lord I can't leave You because my eyes can't see. You have given me life, and I will wait and work and see Your rains in my life."

As he thought these thoughts, the sun once again touched the horizon. His sight did not need to be sharp to picture the scene. The image that had been painted years ago, the evening before that trip to Sweet Grass, was once again before him. Once again the sunset started with a slight tint of pink, and grew as a spill until it totally engulfed the whole land with its scarlet. A stray cloud caught fire on its border, and then burst to flames engulfed by the sun. The alkali lake that before was stale and dead suddenly become a pool of gold with the foxtail torches of tar. The willow bushes near the coulee seemed to be touched by a spell to become the King's silver arrows.

This was the Kingdom Land as Erik allowed the King's reign. One could reason that the land was only painted that way by a chance setting of the sun. To Erik it was more. To Erik, he saw the hand of God reaching to him in His love. The dimness of his sight did not take away from the sharpness of his vision. This was no illusion. This was the hope of Christ, which Erik saw within himself more real than ever.

He would stay in this land. He would stay with Christ for eternity.

Erik knew he had never been and never would be alone in

this land.

Chapter Thirty-Three

"What am I supposed to do now? It's useless." Erik was not referring to his life but the laces of his work boots as they broke in his hands. Erik had just begun to lace the boots for another day of work. As he pulled them taut they had burst in his hands. They hadn't broken at the end; that would have been easy. He could have tied a quick knot and again pulled the laces tight and be to work. Instead, they had broken in the middle, by the third eye, where the laces had worn thin with wear. Here a knot would be blocked by the eye and be unable to tighten. He would make the mend, but it meant working all day with one boot loose and irritation with every step.

He was not talking about his life, but he might as well have been. Really, it was silly to be putting on work boots anyway. There would be no work today. There was little Erik could do to work. He could get around fine; his vision was fogged, not allowing him to see any details, but not completely gone. The doctors called it "legally blind," but he hated doctors for their technical language that seemed to forget they were talking to real people. Work on a farm with its large machinery was not an option. He could do the chores he did as a six year old with his dad; gather the eggs, by feel, in the places he knew the hens would lay, fill the water tank and hold the light for his uncle.

These are things a six year old did, and at times he felt as useless as those boot laces, with the constant irritation of feeling rather than seeing details.

He knew that God was with him. There was a renewed joy in Erik's heart that Christ was his Savior and God was his Father, and the change in his heart had been dramatic. He knew that God could make a life of beauty on this farm. He just didn't know how it would be possible. His spirit had been renewed, but he still lived in a land without purpose.

He thought of the hailstorm that his uncle had spoken about. He knew that the Coopers hadn't lost the farm and God had been faithful to protect their lives even as the crops were destroyed. What Erik didn't know was the exact "hows" of how it all worked out. Certainly, his uncle had said there were tough times. Just how tough was the wait to find the answer and how long did they have to wait to see the answer?

Erik could have asked his uncle those questions, but the answer to the hailstorm was not the answer Erik sought. Erik wanted to know from God how long he would feel as useless as those boot laces before he could fully strap on his life and get on with a purpose to his life.

Every morning his first thought was to look. He would look at the room around him and see if he could pick out new details. Was the edge of the bureau more apparent and defined today than yesterday? Had the operation begun to clear his eyes? Had the Lord begun the healing process or even miraculously restored his sight?

His first thought each morning was to look, but the answer was a constant, "what am I suppose to do now? It's useless."

He had known the call of God and knew the beauty he had seen in his belief. "But what now?"

He mended the laces as best as he could and went out into the farmyard. He didn't have a destination or a task. He merely wanted to be doing something, even if that meant walking aimlessly around. There weren't any chores that needed to be done, but he needed to be close to where work should be done.

It wasn't long before he tired. The walk didn't tire him. The boredom of doing nothing did. As he walked around the barns and sheds of the farm, he shuffled his feet in case there was some undetected object that could trip him, and his hands were extended in front in a defensive stance whenever he came close to an obstacle. The frustration of his sight was the lack of definition to anything. It was as if he could not see it, but could only see a form. There was always a question of what lay outside his small range of vision. The feeling it gave him was that of being in the culvert as a kid with the round sides his world. As a kid, he had sought refuge by the closeness of that place. As a blind adult the borders of his sight were his prison.

He returned to the bunkhouse and once again flopped on the bed. As usual, he picked up the Bible that lay close by and he also reached for help. He had been given a device by the Foundation that had two magnifying glasses stacked on each other with an adapter for a flashlight to illuminate through the thick lenses. If he placed the device flat on the page and used it as a microscope. He could read the enlarged print. It would have been easier to flip on the Bible cassette, but he needed to see the words to prove he could.

He first turned to a page marked by repeated use, Ephesians 6:10: *Finally, my brethren, be strong in the Lord and in the power of His might. Put on the whole armor of God that you may be able to stand against the wiles of the devil. For we do not wrestle against flesh and blood, but against principalities, against powers, against the rulers of the darkness of this age, against spiritual hosts of wickedness in the heavenly places. Therefore, take up the whole armor of God, that you may be able to withstand in the evil days, and having done all, to stand.*

Some parts of those verses and their implications were not clear to Erik, but one item he had repeated to himself many times over the past month: . . .*and having done all, to stand.* He had done everything he knew to do. He had prayed. He had believed. He had seen the Lord touch his life. Now all he could do was stand, but stand he must.

His thoughts were then carried to another verse, and example, that was not as common to him. At first he wasn't sure why he thought of this verse, but somehow that day he had felt as helpless as David in front of Goliath, so he turned to 1 Samuel 17:45, and he read.

Then David said to the Philistine, ' You come to me with a sword and with a spear and with a javelin. But I come to you in the name of the Lord of hosts, the God of the armies of Israel, whom you have defied. This day the Lord will deliver you into my hand, and I will strike you and take your head from you. And this day I will give the carcasses of the camp of the Philistines to the birds of the air and wild beasts of the earth, that all the earth may know that there is a God in Israel. Then all this assembly shall know that the Lord does not save with sword and spear: for the battle is the Lord's and He will give you into our hands. '

Erik thought back to those times that he had so boldly exclaimed the greatness of his Lord. He remembered sitting by the meadow on Chief Mountain and his determination to make something of this land. He remembered his proclamation that his greatest dreams and victories would not come from what he could see, but from what vision the Lord had for his life. He remembered those times of announcing the greatness of God, and he continued the verse.

"So it was, when the Philistine arose and came and drew near to meet David. . . "

Erik thought somehow it would have seemed nice or right, after David had stood so strongly with the Lord that the giant would merely turn and run. Maybe the giant could die from fear or get hit by a bolt of lightning. God needed to do something miraculous. Instead, the giant didn't stop. He still stood before David and the giant moved even closer.

Erik had done all the right things, but his blindness still stood before him.

And Erik continued reading,

"So David put his hand in his bag and took out a stone, and he slung it and struck the Philistine in the forehead, and he fell on his face to the earth."

Erik thought how he had been paralyzed by the fear of blindness the last few months. Certainly, David had every right to respond in the same fashion, but David did not forget his proclamation that the Lord would finish the fight. David took his small strength in that which he knew and let the Lord provide the power of victory.

The thoughts made Erik stop and then pace the room as he pondered the implications to his life. The boot with the mended lace still rubbed sore against his heal. The mend had not worked. He could tell a blister had begun to form.

It was one thing for David to take a stone and allow God to use it. David had hunted with stones before. What did Erik have that God could use? His quick inventory showed nothing. There was nothing on the farm that a man with very limited sight could do. There was nothing in Fairfield or Cascade County that a limited sighted or blind man could do. He had no stone to sling. He had nothing God could use.

All he had done all his life was dream in the bunkhouse.

His mind had created pictures of great beauty, but they were only in his mind. His faith had pictures of His love, but his faith could not drive tractors. He was a dreamer, a believer, not a farmer. Even if he had his full sight he didn't know if he could really farm, but certainly not now. Erik knew that it really wasn't the farm he hated. He hated the thought of living without aspirations. He hated the thought of working the rest of his life at something he could only do half-heartedly. Now without his eyes that fact was clear.

What did he have to give to God that God could use to bring down the darkness before him and fulfill his dreams? Then he realized he only had to offer what God had already given to him: the dreams themselves. In the last few minutes, he, no Him, had provided the answer. It was his dreams that were so sharp and so real and changed everything he saw. The answer to his dreams had always been in his grasp.

Just as he had realized by the oak tree that God had stood next to him all along, he now realized that God had long ago deposited a gift in his life. He had a stone the Lord had formed years earlier and he would give it to Him for His use.

Those pictures in his mind, his faith that drew God's hand in this land, they were his stones.

He went into the dormitory room. In one corner were boxes that contained items that had no value. He found one that he had packed years ago after high school. Below stacks of old homework was a Smith-Corona typewriter. It was old, but a quick check showed it still worked.He put the typewriter on a makeshift desk made by a wooded crate. He pulled off the work boots to allow the healing to begin as he straddled the crate. An old term paper whose sheets had begun to yellow with age was reversed and fed into the machine. He put his fingers on the home keys by touch as his high school teacher had instructed, and he thought.

Soon the keys clicked out a rhythm. It seemed a rhythm of dreams fulfilled as his mind quickly transferred dreams to pages. In his heart he could hear a giant fall to the ground face first in worship. And Erik wrote.

THE KINGDOM LAND

One

The last black of diesel smoke hadn't cleared the stack before I swung open the cab door and slid down the steps of the 9020 John Deere tractor. It was time to leave the thoughts of the field behind. My day was done and on a Saturday afternoon I wasn't about to spend an extra moment in the fields.

Without stopping I stripped myself of my dust-covered shirt and snapped it in the air in a vain attempt to rid myself of any association with the land. With long strides I reached the old '54 Chevy pickup, and took the last drink from the water

KINGDOM LAND ~ 353

jug that lay on the seat. The water was too stale and hot to swallow, but it served well to rinse the dust from my mouth. When I spat the water to the ground it was absorbed without leaving a hint of mud behind. The soil was even thirstier than me after three years of drought . . .

And Erik's dreams became his quest.

Made in the USA
Charleston, SC
20 September 2013